conversations
with
sanji

on learning how to relax

a novel
by
louis joseph mattia
and
david byron keener

PublishAmerica
Baltimore

First printing

ISBN: 1-4137-5727-8
PUBLISHED BY PUBLISHAMERICA, LLLP
www.publishamerica.com
Baltimore

Printed in the United States of America

To my wife, Joan, a true friend and companion on this journey and
whose ideas inspired this story.
And to my daughter, Jessica, brother, Bill, and sister, Mary Jane,
all of whom walked with me with love and dedication.
And to God, that mighty and wonderful author of life.

—Lou

Ruth Ann, my wonderful wife of 42 years, whose patience and love
made most of this story possible.
My three children: David Jr., Lisa and Colleen, their families and
my grandchildren, Dave III, Lee Ann, Derek, Kathleen, Bobby, Joey,
Brianne, Danielle, Jessica and Christian.
Also to Patricia, my dear sister.
All are the joys of my life.

—David

"The Life of every man is a diary in which he means to write one story, and writes another; and his humblest hour is when he compares the volume as it is with what he hoped to make it."

—Sir James Matthew Barrie

1

first light

*"A single event can awaken within us
a stranger totally unknown to us.
To live is to be slowly born."*
—Antoine de Saint-Exupery

Congressman Hanson's fist came thundering down on his desk and a pile of papers careened off the side onto the floor. His steely blue eyes didn't leave me for an instant as he glared right into my face. His aide, a tall, lanky young man in a white shirt closed the door to the office.

"You're killing me, Louis, just killing me!" he screamed. "I was happy as hell when your firm got this job, and I smoothed it through the system, didn't I, and for the last three years it's been one damn problem after another. My constituents want blood, do you understand, blood?"

I tried to explain but it was no use. Hanson ranted and raved like a madman for ten minutes. For a while he looked rabidly around on his desk as if he was trying to find something to use as a hammer, his fists gliding up and down in the air. When no hammer was found, he fumbled on the desktop for something to throw but the best he could find was a large magnifying glass, which he picked up and waved threateningly through the air. My partner Bill and I sat in stony silence as Hanson's ferocious soliloquy continued. I caught the brunt of it since

I had been the principle manager on the project and I thought for a minute that if it continued much longer I would be forced into some kind of out-of-body experience.

But the tirade was over as abruptly as it had begun. Hanson gave us six months to finish the project or we would be terminated. He would see to that.

Bill and I rode back through Washington, D.C. to our offices in Alexandria, Virginia, just across the Potomac River. For eight years, we had built a thriving engineering business, but this project, widening just four miles of the Capital Beltway to eight lanes, was going to be our downfall. I glanced down at the large brown official envelop in my lap, addressed to me, Louis Walker, Project Manager, Walker & Webb, Consultants, and pondered the immensity of the situation. The problem was I didn't know if I cared anymore. I had been going at a reckless pace for so long I'd lost sight of the finish line. What was it all for?

Bill Webb and I owned a very demanding engineering company. It absorbed me totally, six days a week, twelve hours a day and it has from the start. But I used to work for other people, which in my mind was like slopping the hogs every day and then watching through the dining room window as someone else ate the bacon. So now I had the bacon and the heartburn to go along with it.

"Louis," Bill said, "why don't you take a break, get out of town for a few weeks. Let me try to put things back on track."

Bill had always been a better businessman than me; in fact, he was better at most everything. Maybe he could do something to get the project finished. I was at the end of a very frayed rope and just about no good to anyone.

"Where the hell would I go, Bill?" I said sarcastically. "I haven't been on a good vacation in years. Besides, whenever we did go away, I always took some work with me, hardly noticed a thing."

With a sideways glance and a grin Bill just nodded his head.

"That's the problem; you really need to get away. And as a matter of fact I do know just the place," he replied without hesitation as he turned onto the 14th Street Bridge.

The traffic wasn't heavy this time of day and I looked pathetically at the flowing water of the river below us as we cruised along.

Washington, D.C. was the best and worst of places. Complex and, arguably, the most important city in the world, it contained a volatile intermixture of money, politics, and diplomatic immunity. This was my home. I was born here and even though I had escaped for a few years, the magnetic field of power and success had lured me back into its gravitational hold. Yet, in its success and vibrancy, the urban panorama was leaving people isolated, lonely and bewildered. I was one of them all right, but there were many like me. The post-modern lifestyle was exciting enough to be sure, but there was a void inside the heart, an emptiness of soul, which late night TV, shopping malls or portfolios could not fill. I had returned to Washington to seek some degree of material comfort and had come to find that what I lacked was more than what I had gained. I was a mess.

"Right," I said, after this pause of reflection, "where's this place you think I need to go?"

"It's a little beach at the southern tip of North Carolina. It's quiet. Last summer the family and I were there for two weeks. Best thing I ever did."

Excitedly he reached into a file folder next to him and pulled out a brochure with a colored map on the back.

It was a little resort island called Sunset Beach, far away from any of the big tourist spots and almost hidden in the southernmost part of the North Carolina coastline.

"It's a real place alright," Bill offered as I studied the map, "an authentic piece of paradise undiscovered, so to speak. It's the kind of place where life is real and people live by the land and fish the sea. No suits, Louis; imagine living in a place where everything is simple and down to earth. The closest town is Shallotte; it's about ten miles inland. I'll tell you the honest to God truth, Louis, if ever there existed a perfect getaway, this sure is it, a great place to escape from the city for a few weeks."

I knew what he was really thinking; it would be a great place for me to hide out for a while and enjoy the onset of a mid-life crisis.

"You'll love it, Louis. Book yourself in at the Continental Motel just off the bridge over the Inter-coastal. Take care of yourself for a few weeks, eat some seafood, drink a few beers."

Bill was making me an offer I couldn't refuse. He had always been more than a business partner, he was a good friend, I knew that, but now I could sense powerfully his deep concern for me. I took a long look at the map and the white sand beaches in glossy color. It looked very tempting.

"I'll think about it, Bill, it looks great of course, but what would I do?"

"For God's sake, Louis, don't do anything. Just unwind and relax. You deserve that much, don't you?"

"Sure, sure, maybe you're right. Maybe that's exactly what I need to do."

"And don't worry about things up here," he said, "I'll take care of that."

"Yeah, okay," I said. I wasn't really sure at all but I didn't have much fight left in me. I knew Bill was right.

"Tell you what," I said, "drop me off at the office and I'll clear up a few things on my desk and then I'll head straight home and start packing."

"Now you're talking," he said approvingly.

As we pulled into the parking garage on King Street in downtown Alexandria, I had already begun constructing my conversation with Marie. She and I had been married for twenty-one years. They had been good years with a fully-grown blonde-haired daughter and lots of great memories. Marie had seen me lately deteriorating under the pressures of the job and she had even encouraged me to take some time off alone, "to develop yourself," she would say. After I explained what had happened this morning she wouldn't need any convincing if I went off alone—she would probably applaud. Marie was French, brunette, and beautiful. But her real strength lied in her strong will and convictions. She despised weakness and vacillation and, as was common to the French temperament, she was not easily able to hide her opinions. Her thoughts were open to all and she would spread them out like a thick Brie cheese all over any problem that reeled its head. She had often told me to go somewhere these past few years. The beach was one of the nicer destinations she had mentioned.

Marie was still at work when I arrived home. It was a three-story townhouse further up King Street in Alexandria. It had been built about five years ago along with a hundred other just like it in what had been an abandoned warehouse site. The theme was upscale, catering to rising baby-boomer executives. It was brick, plush, and plastic. The thing was, even though it had all the amenities—fireplace, granite kitchen counter tops, and 3.5 bathrooms—the deck off the second floor sported a direct close-up view of the townhouses 20 feet away in the next row, no more, no less. I had given up trying to barbecue in peace and quiet because it seemed all the neighbors wanted to barbecue at the same time, thus cluttering my fine view with the wails of humanity. Each Sunday afternoon, providing the weather was not too inclement, the men would don their chef's aprons, sharpen their knives and barbecue forks and light up the fires in some kind of primordial rite of weekly sacrifice. Not that I didn't like the people, I just wanted to have the place to myself once in a while.

Marie and I have a large, all white, male cat named Mr. White. The name was inspired by the fact that Mr. White was the easiest to remember, and was more befitting such a regal creature than the other name I had given him earlier on in life, Mr. Poop. I guess I had been inspired by my duties: a cleaner of the cat litter pan. Marie preferred Mr. White.

By the time Marie arrived home, I was half-heartedly starting to pack my bags. When she came in, I explained what had happened today and what Bill had suggested and how uncertain I was about the whole idea. She didn't hesitate.

"Do it," she said emphatically. "Absolutely. You really need to get away. Don't worry about me, I've got plenty to keep me busy up here."

"Are you sure?" I asked.

"Never so sure in my whole life. You and I can go away somewhere later in the year. This one's for you."

With that said she helped me finish packing. I zippered shut the suitcase and with a farewell kiss I was out the door, mahogany mind you, with a wonderful stain glass oval in the center. All the houses had one just like it.

So with all the trepidation of a kid going to his first circus, excited but scared to death and afraid of the clowns, I hit the road. And now here I am, late on Monday night, held over at the Blue Lagoon Bar somewhere outside of Wilmington, North Carolina, still about an hour from Sunset Beach. The rain and the late start had conspired to make me find shelter for the night. It was around 9:00 P.M. when I was fortunate enough to find a Motel 8 with this little dive of a bar just next door. I must have looked lonely and beleaguered indeed, alone, sitting on a barstool mopping up a beer, someplace on the way to somewhere else.

The Blue Lagoon is a classic local watering hole, I knew that before I even went in, but it had atmosphere, you know, the typical laminated brown tables, vinyl chairs, dark maroon carpet, and shabby everything else, all accented by a flashing neon Budweiser sign in the window. But it did boast one attraction—a talking parrot named Bob. I suppose a lot of people come to talk to Bob except, this being Monday night, it was just me, Bob and the bartender, an ex-Marine out of Camp Lejune named Teddy. As it so happened Teddy poured the coldest beer around, or so he said. But I doubt that people ever argued with Teddy—with arms like jackhammers, it seemed reasonable to me to praise the coldness down to the last drop.

Bob the parrot and I became fast friends. He wasn't exactly the best talker but he was a captive listener, contained as he was in his bamboo cage set up at the end of the bar. Every now and then he would show his attentiveness by a well-spoken, empathetic comment like, "well shiver me timbers" or now and again, "have another beer?" I'm sure Teddy taught him that in order to up the business but it was Bob's timing that really impressed me. Just as my beer was a quarter of the way from the bottom, he'd pipe off with his question, "have another beer?"—but only after politely letting me finish my sentence.

"You should have seen Hanson this morning," I told him. "His face was so red I thought he would burst. What a fickle asshole—when things are good he's on your side, but when things are bad he's your worst enemy. How was I supposed to have torn up four miles of Beltway with a hundred thousand cars a day and keep traffic moving along at full clip? Half of Hanson's constituency in Northern Virginia called him every day about the delays. Just keeping traffic moving at all was, in my mind anyway, a major achievement."

"Want another beer?" Bob asked.

"Hell yes, I'll have another, thank you very much." This was now my fourth.

"Now show us some leg," Bob blurted out from nowhere.

"What?" I gulped. "You're starting to amaze me with your vocabulary, little fellow."

Ted yelled over, "Yeah, he's a big hit with the ladies. Every once in a while I have to put him away for bad behavior."

"Never a dull moment around here," I blurted back to Ted.

Every time Bob spoke he'd raise his wings up and flap them once, showing me the bright yellow plumage under each wing. Bob was colorful, all green on top except at the face where above his eyes a wonderful bright red outlined his head. His intelligent yellow eyes glowed iridescently in the soft light.

"Damn shame they got you locked up here, Bob, bet you were hell on wheels out where you came from. Yeah I can see it now, tropical forests, warm breezes, fresh fruit—bet you had it all."

Bob just looked at me and then turned sideways on his perch. I could swear he knew exactly what I was saying.

As if to appease him I said, "You and I are pretty much in the same boat, old fella. Yep, pretty much the same—you got your cage and I got mine. It's just that mine has the illusion of freedom but underneath we're both caught."

Teddy the bartender glanced over now and then but was captivated by a big time wrestling event on the television over at the other end of the bar.

"Well, Bob," I continued, "I'm heading to the beach. That's right, me, myself, and I."

"Well show us some leg," he said, rejoining the conversation.

"Not right now if it's okay with you." I knew I was beginning to feel sorry for myself but why I didn't know for sure. I glanced down to see I was still wearing my silk Brooks Brothers suit, my gold Pulsar watch was still ticking away on my wrist and I had money in my pocket. Hell, it couldn't be all that bad. But then I realized I didn't have a clue what to do next and sure as hell didn't know what I wanted. In a lot of ways I had been a success, well an average success anyway, but inside I knew I didn't know much about myself or what made me tick or even what made me happy. I considered myself smart but not brilliant, and in social situations pretty much an introvert. When it came to people I usually relied on finding a way to start talking about numbers, plans, or business matters—emotions were taboo.

I wished I could say that I had set out on a great quest, like a modern Don Quixote, but at this point it seemed more like I had been ejected from the game. Whether I wanted it or not, my journey had begun after a lifetime of avoidance. Now I would face myself after all these years and protestations.

I swallowed my last bit of beer and knew it was getting late.

"Well, gotta go, Bob. I'm rooting for you, buddy. One day you'll be free again, don't give up now you hear?"

"Want another beer?" Bob said sorrowfully.

"No thanks, Bob, I'm quite done for the night. How about some other time, my friend?"

2

hooch

"Living is not so much in the breathing, but in the seeing."
—Anonymous

It was late Tuesday morning and, after a couple of Advil to stifle my morning hangover, I made the final one-hour drive to Sunset Beach. I was now far away from Washington, D.C. and it was summer, early June. Ready or not, there was no turning back. Before checking in, I pulled off at the first beach parking lot I saw to pay my respects to the mighty Atlantic.

The sun was hot in a crystal blue sky and clouds, pure white fleece, floated effortlessly in the infinite space above me. Sunlight sparkled across the tops of the waves as they rolled into shore, crashing in a glistening and foamy elegance. Salty air and sea spray caressed my skin, softening the sharp rays of the sun, mellowing the heat like a fine whisky. The smell of life was everywhere, clean and fresh. Before me lay a carpet of fine sand, multiple shades of browns, thousands upon thousands of grains, sloping gently toward the sea, disappearing gradually into the vast ocean. Formed over eons of geologic history, the edge of land and the beginning of the sea, this boundary of life stretched into the distance for as far as the eye could see, bounded only by the undulating dune grasses, the sky and the sea itself.

As I walked along the edge of the water, I felt my tension beginning to ease. My eyes took in everything. Like a starving man just released from prison, I was savoring each sight of creation as if it were sustenance itself. Before me the children danced back and forth between wave and shore, barely noticing me as I plodded my way between them. My feet set their own cadence, slowly and deliberately along the beach, and I watched the exquisite grandeur of everything around me. A long walk on the beach is good for the soul. I knew that in theory, but now I was there, and my heart was beginning to anticipate the days ahead. My mind raced over dozens of events stalking my life this past year. Traffic jams, hectic meetings, business deals, and unanswered e-mails invaded my head as I mentally and physically began my escape from the urban jungle.

What a fool I'd been to work so damn hard, and for what? I needed this break badly. I deserved it. My job was running me into the ground and the doctor told me to get some exercise. The booze wasn't helping either but it did lower the background noise. Of one thing I was now certain, forced into it or not, I was going to make this escape count for something. If nothing else, I would learn how to take it easy!

I've read somewhere that every ten years or so in a person's life the human psyche goes through a change, passing through a transforming matrix. Call it stages of life or whatever, reality changes as people grow and mature. Or perhaps it is only people who change, and what seemed good at one time no longer seems good enough or right enough. Ten years of storming the gates of life seems to be time enough to complete one cycle, a predetermined number written into our biological code, part of some eternal pattern. We try things, we work hard for a long stretch, and then we either sense success or failure. We find happiness or perplexity or maybe both, then we pass through.

But I didn't believe much in all those theories or psychologists. Every couple of years all the theories change anyway. So what if I was almost forty-seven. That's a great age, not too young and not too old. And I certainly wasn't having a mid-life crisis! All I needed was some time on the beach to think, maybe read a couple of good books, but I was thinking about reading novels this time, not a single self-help book. There was no way in this creation that I was going to resort to those self-help gurus. It seemed to me they were little more than self-proclaimed prophets of the good life—10 steps, 13 ways, 15 principles—the hell with all that. What a scam. If all those people really knew about happiness they probably wouldn't have time to be writing books. They'd be living it. Besides, it had to be obvious to anyone of reasonable intelligence that the books all radically contradicted each other. I had picked up a number of books over the years at airports and hotel shops—I had even read a couple of them. I would neatly categorize them on two shelves at home, one for "motivational books" and the other for books on "tranquility or inner peace." At night I could swear they waged battle against each other. The motivational books declare their secret is found in grabbing hold of life for all it's worth. Being assertive, even aggressive, and controlling were what they demanded. On the other hand, the inner peace books purported that the secret to a happy life was in the letting go and in coming into a sublime synchronization with the flow of life, the very opposite of control. No, none of that nonsense, thank you. All I needed was right here, the beach, just a simple, wild, and stunning piece of real estate on the edge of the continent. It was a view to die for. This was an appropriate setting, providing all of its own inspiration and wisdom, all that was required for any kind of serious thinking.

Of course I was no fool. If I was going to do any serious reflection, it would take something more than the physical environment alone. I supposed that what I really wanted was some practical down to earth advice. A mentor would be great, someone who could just edge me in the right direction. If there was only someone who had passed through all the trials and trivialities of life and had acquired a perspective that lifted one above the mundane realities of everyday living. Maybe what I wanted was just a few tips on loosening up. Maybe what I wanted was impossible to find. I didn't know.

I once had a high school science teacher who taught our class how to breathe deeply. It really helped. She wasn't all that bad looking either, as I remember. Then, there was Transcendental Meditation in college. I suppose I would have gotten more out of it if I hadn't been simultaneously stoned. Of course, I wasn't interested in finding inner peace in college; it was adventure I wanted. But now I was almost middle-aged and I had had just about as much adventure as I could stand. What I needed now was to settle down a little, take the edge off, and iron out the wrinkles. That was a tall order, I knew. Too much had happened recently.

My foot kicked up a clamshell from beneath the warm sand and I looked down from my thoughts. Seashells in an infinite array lie neatly in a long line at the edge of the wet sand. All was still and quiet. As I gazed down the long strip of shoreline I was struck by the beautiful houses tucked neatly behind the sand dunes. Like a row of regimental soldiers, multi-colored flags waving in the stiff breeze, they stood bravely on the berm, fixed stoutly against any charging storms. I envied those who lived in those houses. It must be like owning a piece of heaven itself to have a place right on the beach. Each house was a fortress against the world, a secret hideaway perched at the edge of rapturous nature. Looking at the beautifully-architectured porches, I visualized myself sitting on those weathered wooden decks overlooking the ocean with a cold beverage in my hand. That would be the life, yep, that sure would.

As I scanned the beach, children frolicked in the surf. They looked like they didn't have a care in the world. Their days were filled with the joy of discovery and reckless abandon. I wondered how long it had been since I had known such freedom. I couldn't remember playing with such simple and focused joy for a long time.

When I was a kid the family would go to the beach every summer for a week or two, depending on how much cash had been earned or borrowed for the time off. We'd mostly go to Jersey. Ocean City was our favorite spot. Memories of boardwalk pizza and sticky buns and riding the waves all day on a rented inflatable were ingrained in my psyche like rings on an old tree. The beach was freedom from everything that chained a person to the affairs of the city.

Well, that was then and this is now. Alone I stood on the beach. Maybe I'd be lucky; maybe this summer would change my life.

The walk in the sand and wind was rejuvenating. I must have walked for two miles and was on my way back down the beach. Stopping now and then, I would breathe in all the beauty of the day while my eyes scanned the whole scene of sun and sand, birds and clouds, people and waves. Somewhere, I would find the answer.

At one place I stopped to see a small pool of cool water, which had formed from the incoming waves. Just on the edge of the pool someone had built a wonderfully ornate sandcastle. I admired its design. With a mote all around, high impenetrable walls, and towers protruding skyward from every corner, it was a picture of gothic splendor. How lovely, I thought to myself, what creative energy and vision. Yet, in a few hours all would be washed away by the ever constant return of the ocean. Such was the fate so often of even the greatest achievements of life. I stopped myself at this thought, realizing I didn't want to get too fatalistic. Or was I just being realistic?

As I gazed at the castle, absorbed and saddened by visions of its eventual demise, a lone figure caught my eye up toward the sand dune. He was sitting motionless on a small beach chair, gazing intently at the surf and sky, a look of implacable serenity. For a moment or two I meditated on the lone stranger. There was something unique about him but I couldn't quite put my finger on it. He seemed so relaxed, legs stretched out, toes dug deep into the sand. He sat motionless, arms draped over the side of his sand chair, locked in a frozen gaze out to sea.

Suddenly, in the middle of my meditation, a frisbee came rocketing out of nowhere, striking the solitary figure squarely on the side of the head. *WHAP!* His baseball cap went sailing backward and his head jerked to one side, but his arms never moved. A young boy ran up, apologetically grabbed the assaulting disc and ran off. As the boy turned to run, however, his foot kicked up a large cloud of sand that completely blanketed the man's face and chest.

My eyes were now glued on the scene. I was amazed. The look of complete and utter serenity never faltered and not a word was uttered. He didn't seem bothered in the least by the incident. He simply patted the sand off his cheeks and lips, smiled broadly, put his hat neatly back on his head and then resumed his pose. Now this was truly remarkable, so unlike most people I knew. My own reaction would have been a little more demonstrative. I am sure I would have made quite a scene—I had lost what little self-control I once possessed. But here, in front of my eyes, something very unique had occurred, something of another order.

To say the least I was intrigued. Even more than intrigued I was mesmerized. Whoever this guy was, there was something refreshing about his peaceful presence. I began talking to myself. I really should find a way to meet this guy, perhaps, just perhaps, I might have something to learn here. In this brief instant I knew that this man had a quality that I didn't have, and I aimed to find out what it was.

Now I don't make a habit of approaching strangers on the beach or anywhere else for that matter, but there was something different here and for all I knew a chance to broaden out a bit. "Why not?" I mumbled to myself.

Hitching up my shorts with both hands, I rallied forth. Approaching the man rather slowly and timidly, I cleared my throat. Not knowing exactly what to say, the words came out before I could think.

"Pardon me, could I bother you for a minute?"

No answer. He just looked at me, smiling through his sunglasses, which had remained somewhat askew after the frisbee incident. His face was tanned and rugged, yet inviting. Dark, slightly graying hair wisped out from under his baseball cap and he somehow resembled an aging James Dean character; smug and assured, almost cocky with half a grin turned up on one side of his face.

"I don't mean to be a nuisance, but could I ask you something?"

This time his lips parted and he motioned with one hand to sit down next to him. It was an offer I couldn't refuse. I sat down in the warm sand.

After a brief silence while I adjusted myself to the contours of the sand, he said, "I like strangers, especially people from the city."

"How'd you know I was from the city?"

"Black socks and tennis shoes for starters. Then the milky white legs tell me you are a big time white collar guy, and the Calvin Klein dress shorts aren't exactly beach apparel."

I gazed down slowly at my socks and shorts. Embarrassed that I looked so out of place, I was, for a moment, at a loss for words.

"Well, errr, I just arrived about an hour ago from Washington and I didn't have much of a chance to change yet." It was a bit lame but my first reaction was always a good defense.

"Sure, sure, that's fine, just be careful you don't burn on your first day in the sun." His manner was matter-of-fact but friendly enough.

"Say," I said, "I don't usually just walk up to people I don't know but I couldn't help noticing how you handled that situation with the frisbee. What I mean is that you didn't seem to get upset."

He smiled and took in a slow, deep breath and looked back out to the sea.

During the pause I found my eyes surveying the figure in front of me. He was quite ordinary in many respects, in his mid-fifties with a stocky, somewhat muscular build. The top of his swimsuit was hidden by a slight paunch but otherwise he was in good shape, even muscular. Whatever he did for a living, it wasn't white-collar work. His skin was too weathered and he looked too comfortable in the outdoors. I couldn't see his eyes behind the sunglasses but he had a neatly trimmed moustache and a strong chin. I stared unwittingly for a moment and then caught myself. Curiosity about his relaxed manner, and an inner urgency to find some answers to my issues drove me on.

The silence seemed a little awkward for me so I pushed a more direct question out toward him, "How do you remain so calm after those young hooligans slapped you on the side of the head with their frisbee and then nearly buried you in sand?"

He looked at me carefully, sizing me up and down once.

"You sound like you're wound up awfully tight, my friend," he said.

"Well I probably am a little tense. Living in the city will wind anyone up." I wasn't going to say any more.

A brief pause was marked only by the sound of sea gulls fluttering overhead.

Now the man spoke, "So you've come down here to relax a little, unwind, and find some answers about why you're so miserable—more or less?"

Now it was my turn to pause. How in the hell did he know I was miserable? And how did he figure I needed any answers. For a moment

I was offended and ruffled. But my honesty prevailed.

"Yes, you got that right. How did you know, do I look that bad then?" I asked.

"It's not just you," he replied. "It's the whole world, everyone's under too much stress. Almost everyone I know is looking for some kind of answers. Some way to happiness and peace."

"You look like the calmest person I ever saw. What in the world do you do to stay so relaxed?"

He didn't immediately answer. I had hoped that I hadn't been stupid to ask such a question of someone I didn't even know. He spent a moment reflecting, gazing out to sea. Then his hand moved toward the green insulated cooler bag beside his chair. "That's a long story," he said.

Slowly, he slid the black zipper open on the bag and gently slipped his hand inside. Out came a clear one-quart Mason jar. The yellow liquid shimmered iridescently in the sunlight. Cool drops of condensation dripped between his fingers. Ice tinkled like delicate wind chimes from inside the jar.

Offering the jar to me, he said, "Have some hooch!"

I just stared.

"Go on, have a swig," he insisted with a twinkle in his eye.

I was a bit suspicious; things without labels worry me. "What's in it?"

Smiling deeply now, he whispered, "It's my secret recipe, certain special ingredients."

"But what is it?" I insisted, feeling very reluctant but burning with curiosity at the same time.

"It's hooch," he said, "the nectar of the gods."

"Hooch?" I echoed.

"That's right, hooch. You might say it's a little thirst quencher for a hot summer day. But don't be misled by its simple appearance, it's deliciously good and especially if it's made just the right way."

Cautiously, I took the jar from his hand and swallowed a mouthful.

"That's fantastic," I blurted out. The sweet, cool liquid had exploded across my palate, brightening every sensation and leaving my mouth tingling.

"But how do you make it?" I wanted to know.

He scanned the horizon slowly as if pondering some deep, long hidden secret, took a deep breath and turned toward me.

"It's IGA pineapple juice and vodka. I only use the sweetened juice, though, can't stand the unsweetened. I've tried all the other store brands of pineapple juice, but they aren't the same. I don't know what I'll do if IGA goes out of business. Makes the best hooch."

I stared in amazement. I had been thinking of some exotic ingredients, some special mix, and it was only pineapple juice and vodka, so profoundly simple, and so disappointing at the same time. The hooch was good enough alright but I had expected a more sublime answer to my question about how to relax, maybe even something spiritual. Maybe I wanted to hear something along the lines of yoga, exercise, ginseng tea, anything but booze.

"Is that your only secret to being so relaxed? Hooch? Is that how you stay calm?" I was noticeably alarmed.

He laughed in a deep rolling tone. "You know," he said, "you gotta learn how to relax. Of course that's not all I have. I've got a lot more than this going for me. It's just that this one tastes the best on a nice hot day." He handed me the jar again.

The second swig was better than the first and I felt like talking.

"I just arrived from D.C. today, a horrendous rat race. Dog eat dog, you know. Everyone's trying to make money, and everyone wants a pound of flesh—I've had enough."

Without saying a word, he capped the jar. "Been there, done that."

"What do you mean?" I asked.

"Oh, I lived up in the city for many years, grew up there in fact. Then I owned a little business a few years back, an auto repair garage. From dawn to dusk I'd fix cars, all kind of cars, but especially Volkswagens. I was a regular auto mechanic, big time wrench turner; the only good thing was I had my own shop. But one day I just got tired of it all, year after year the same thing. I got tired of people complaining all the time. If it wasn't arguing over the bill, it was something else breaking and them blaming it on me. It never failed, they'd come in telling me,

'Yesterday you repaired my radiator and today my tire's flat.' After 35 years of turning wrenches, I'd had enough. I just got all wrenched out and on top of that I got all rat-raced out! It was the last year that really got to me. I lost my desire to keep going. Every day was a struggle. But I've always been a positive-thinking person and I've always been focused. I knew I could make it if I could just focus so I made up a little saying. And to tell you the truth, I would say that little saying out loud to myself 15 to 20 times on the way through traffic.

I'm going to always think positive, be happy,
and don't worry about nothin'.

"That's what helped me make it my last year. I've helped a lot of people the last several years with that saying. I've even written it down for them so they can remember it and say it over and over to themselves.

After that year the wife and I came down here and I just never went home. I decided this is where I wanted to spend the rest of my life, relaxing in the sun and surf. I even quit smoking after 30 years."

"So, you've really found peace here then?"

He just laughed with a deep roll. "Have some more hooch!"

Taking the now familiar jar, I downed another slug of the sweet liquid, enjoying the coolness as it slid down my throat. I was beginning to feel the effects of its magic nectar.

"Look," I said, "I don't want to bother you, it's just that I was interested in talking to someone who seemed to have life all figured out. You seem to be content sitting here. You don't look like you have a worry in the world."

I stopped there to see what kind of response he might give.

Just as I was pondering the possibilities, he reached out his hand and said, "I'm D.B.—D.B. Kennedy—but most people here just call me Sanji."

"Sanji?" I stuttered.

What kind of name is that, I thought to myself. It sounded like it was from India. This was getting a bit more mysterious all the time.

"How do you spell that?" I asked, trying to figure out something to say.

"It's spelled S-A-N-J-I, but it's pronounced, SAUN-JEE. You see the 'i' sounds like a long 'e.'"

Surprised and now tongue-tied, I nodded my head.

"Well," he said, "so what's your name?"

"I'm, ah, Louis—yes, Louis, just plain Louis," I said slowly.

A moment passed by as I stared at Sanji. He didn't look like an Indian, or even mixed race in any way. He was white, about 55, pure bred Americana. Gazing at his face I asked, "Sanji, isn't that some kind of Indian name? And if you don't mind my asking, you don't look Indian."

Looking again out to sea, as if watching for some sign from the wind or clouds, he snickered a little, pulled down his sunglasses to the end of his nose, revealing piercing blue eyes, and peered right into me. "Guess some people think of me as special. I don't say much about things unless someone asks. Whenever they do ask, I usually have a piece of wisdom for them, mostly a little saying. So after a while, well, someone gave me this little nickname and now all locals use it."

We talked for a few more minutes and I was impressed with the man. I told him I was staying up at the Continental Motel. He said he knew it well.

The whole time I kept thinking that this guy is just an auto mechanic, isn't he? How could he be so wise and cool-headed? Does this happen? I had never heard of such a thing before. My mind flooded with questions. Does just a regular average American guy, a car mechanic to boot, have certain secrets to a happy life? Why would the locals give him this name? Could I have accidentally met someone so fast just walking along the beach—someone who really did have it all together?

All I did know was that I had been led here to Sunset Beach by a sudden series of events. Perhaps only time would tell if I would get the answers I needed. Yes, only time would tell.

3

ᏜISCOVEᎡᎽ

"The journey begins with the first step."

Our good-byes had been brief but I was sure I would see Sanji again, though I didn't know when or how. For now I contented myself with knowing I had two weeks to enjoy the seashore without any distractions. No cell phones, beepers, or e-mails to ensnare me.

The Continental Motel is a two-story block and cement affair from the 1960s just across the road from the beach. How it got the name *Continental*, I don't know. But whatever inspiration gave it the name, the structure was typical of those old mom-and-pop motels that run all up and down the southeastern seaboard from Florida to the Carolinas. The cinder block is painted in a cream color and the rooms empty out onto a narrow, covered walkway. There are no trees or shrubs to speak of and a small rectangular pool sits in the middle of the asphalt parking lot. Slate blue wood panels enclose the lower portion of the walkway and from the second floor you can see the ocean. Outside each room is an old wooden bench, weathered but freshly painted for the season. Screen doors add authentic charm to each room allowing the sea breeze to freshen the small living quarters. It is well kept, neat, and beachy. Nate, a widower from up north, owns the place and pretty much runs the front office by himself. From my room, I had a great view of the fishing pier, rows of stores and beach houses, but it didn't feel cluttered. A feeling of quaintness governed the scene. The Island Market just across the street was perfect for picking up all those little items one needs at the beach and it was great for ice cream and snacks.

As I passed by the front desk for my key, I casually glanced at the bulletin board. Something small caught my eye. It was an index card with a sentence in broad magic marker. It read, *Try to learn one new thing every day,* signed *Sanji.*

The letters were neatly written in broad block letters and the card was prominent even against a background littered with business cards, sightseeing brochures and notices.

Turning quickly to Nate I asked, "Do you know the guy who wrote this card?"

"Well," he said nonchalantly, "I guess I know him about as well as anyone else does."

"What do you mean by that?" I queried. "The guy is a remarkable man," he said, "and he's helped a lot of people with little sayings like that, but I can't say anyone really knows him that well. He kinda keeps to himself. But he's a smart guy, that's for sure. If you look, you'll find his sayings all over town."

"You're kidding," I said really surprised now. 'This guy has his sayings all over town?"

"Sure does, and why not, it's really good stuff, real positive, gets you through a tough day," he replied, shuffling sheets of paper on the counter.

"But where does he get the sayings?" I pressed.

"Makes them up as far as we know, all out of his head," he said, looking up from the pile in front of him.

Moving up closer to the counter I asked, "Do you have any other sayings around?"

"Sure do," he said, reaching under the counter. "Here's one he gave me about a year ago when business was down after a hurricane."

He pulled a small slip of paper from under the counter and handed it to me. It was printed on the back of a restaurant receipt and in pencil, scribed in the same neat block letters, it read, *Tomorrow ain't just another day, you could go fishing.*

"That one little sentence has really helped this year, put a lot of things in perspective for me," he said proudly.

"That's very nice," I said, not really being so impressed. "So you don't know the guy very well?'

"No, not really," he shook his head, "moved down here about six years ago I think, built a real nice house up on the river. He likes to eat out. That's about it."

'Thanks, I appreciate the help."

"Say, are you looking for this guy or something?"

"Oh, no, not really," I said hesitantly, "but I think I found him."

That evening I was back at my room, alone and deep in thought. Room 8 was small but neatly furnished. Double bed, dresser and small desk, all modern vintage, just perfect for the task I had obligated myself to—writing down anything I would learn in the following weeks.

I had been stunned by the suddenness of my chance encounter that afternoon. Little did I know then that this meeting would change my life. At the moment I was simply intrigued by the man I had met and I couldn't wait to see what unfolded. Even though it was a rather quick meeting, this guy called Sanji had already peaked my curiosity. Each hour I spent in my room, the mystery of who he was ate deeper at me.

As I puttered around the small room sipping on a glass of ten-year-old scotch, I pondered the name "Sanji." What did it mean? Why did the locals give it to him? There had to be a story here, if only I could get to it. I decided to do a little research. In my mind it seemed that the name Sanji was not just some haphazard nickname. There had to be some rhyme or reason to it. Then I remembered who could help.

My wife Marie and I had several friends from India whom we had met at an embassy party in Washington, D.C. one night. Once in a while we'd see them for dinner. They would know what the name meant for sure. About 8:00 P.M. I called Marie.

"Hey, sweetie, this is Louis."

"So good to hear your voice," she said, "I miss you already."

"I know, I miss you, too," I said, and I really did miss her. This was my first trip to a beach or, for that matter, anywhere on vacation without her. I felt like something was missing.

"Just wanted to let you know I got in safe," I said reassuringly.

"Good, you never know with the roads these days," she replied. "By the way, the Washington Post called today, something about a big problem on the I-495 job."

This sent shivers up and down my spine and my heart shrunk at the prospect of being suddenly drawn back in.

"Tell them to call Bill," I said, "he'll be able to take care of anything that comes up." I continued, not wanting to think at all about work, "Say, could you do a little research for me?"

"I guess I can, what do you need?" She was always ready to help.

"I wonder if you could call our friends, the Rajiis, and ask them about a name? I need to know what the word 'Sanji' means."

"San what?"

"That's S-A-N-J-I —Sanji."

"Okay, got it," she replied. "But what in the world do you need to know this for?" She was inquisitive and I knew I'd have to tell her before long but I didn't want to tell her anything yet. She would worry for sure that I had met some kind of kook or crackpot. No, I had to stall.

"Oh, just a name in a book I'm reading, that's all. But I really would like to know what it means. Okay?"

"Sure, I'll call the Rajiis tomorrow."

"Great, I'll give you a call back tomorrow night. Love you."

"Love you, too," she said. "Are you sure you're okay? I worry about you these days, you know."

"I'm really fine," I replied, "in fact, doing better than I thought I would.

"Okay then," she said, "talk to you tomorrow."

Hanging up the phone, I was positive that this little research would unwrap part of the mystery.

The next morning I woke early. The sunlight was just beginning to stream in through the slits in the blinds, crisscrossing the room with bands of light, and for me, hope. And this morning I did have hope.

Something new and exciting was happening. Instinctively I had known for years that I simply had to find a way to relax, a way to get peace. Now I felt as if there really were some answers out there and I had come to the right place to find them. If it was a coincidence or miracle I didn't know but I surely had to press this experience like fine grapes until I drained all the good juice out of it.

At breakfast in a little restaurant across the street, the Beachside Diner, I saw another saying on the cash register. This time it was written on back of a napkin and neatly taped to the front of the machine. It read, *Change your oil every 3000 miles, it's the secret to long engine life.*

I looked at the waitress as she pressed the keys of the register, "Another saying by Sanji?" I asked.

"Yep, sure is," she said brightly, "a lot of customers see it and remember to have their oil changed; we think it's a good reminder to everyone."

"So," I said, "this guy Sanji seems like he really can hit the nail on the head."

"He's a good man," she said, looking me straight in the eyes. "I suppose he's just trying to do what he can to help people. He comes in quite a bit and usually leaves a little saying on a napkin. Sometimes it's for the waitress and sometimes for someone he met. Good tipper, too."

"Thanks," I said, stuffing my change in her hand (I had forgotten to leave a tip). Opening the front door, the morning sun broke onto my face reminding of something.

"Oh," I said, "could you tell me where the nearest bookshop is?"

"Just over the bridge there's a real nice one, honey."

"Thanks again, see you later," and I walked out the door.

"You come back again now!" she said as the door closed behind me.

Since it was still early, the bookstore was just opening. *Beach Books and More* was the name painted on a broad piece of grayish driftwood nailed across the lintel of the front door. As I entered a middled-aged woman, rather plump but nicely dressed in a blue cotton dress, was tidying up behind the counter.

"Good morning," I offered.

"Yes, it is isn't it? Good morning right back at you," she said cheerfully.

"Just going to browse a bit if you don't mind," I said almost apologetically.

"Help yourself, that's what we're here for."

"Thanks," I replied as I made my way inside.

As bookshops go, it wasn't big. Cozy might be the best word to describe it. Pine boards, unfinished and crudely nailed, served as bookshelves towering over the walls and aisles. They were filled with paperbacks, magazines, comic books, and tourist stuff. I had set my mind to find a serious novel to read, and my first impression was that I might not be so lucky in here. One of Dostoevsky's books would be great. He was a Russian existentialist who I had remembered from college. I didn't like him that much then and didn't know if I would fare any better this time but I knew that there's no one who can get you thinking like he does. A bit somber and pessimistic I suppose but good poignant and interior stuff. To my great surprise I extricated one copy of the *Notes From Underground,* which was sandwiched between two dime store romances. "Great," I muttered, "just what I wanted."

Having found my quarry, I ambled up to the counter.

"Found what you want?" the woman behind the counter asked.

"I think so, but we'll see. It's pretty heavy stuff you know, but I'm going to try and plod through it."

"Oh my, Dostoevsky, that is heavy stuff indeed, serious, too. Want something a little more perky?" she asked, her blue eyes glistening behind her glasses.

"Maybe, what do you have?" I replied, staring down at my book with it's rather sinister looking and dark cover.

"It's just a small little book really, not so thick, but it's by a local guy who wrote down a bunch of his sayings. People tend to like it, even send copies to friends."

"That wouldn't be Sanji, would it?" I asked almost perturbed.

"Why yes it is, how did you know?" she asked surprised.

"Just a hunch," I said matter-of-factly. "Sure, I'll take it."

"Do you know him?" she asked as she picked up the thin hard cover from a small rack on the counter.

I thought about my reply for a minute and then consented, "I met him on the beach yesterday."

"Really." She brightened up even more. "Not many people really know him well, how fortunate you met him."

"I suppose so," I replied, "but I didn't get to know him well, seems kind of a mystery."

She handed me Sanji's book. It was long and thin, not more than maybe 60 pages as best as I could tell. The title was in the now familiar handwriting, *You Gotta Learn How to Relax—It's Only Life You Know,* by Sanji.

"Do you still want Dostoevsky?" she asked as she pulled out a brown paper bag to put the books in.

"Yeah, I'll take both, why not?"

She stuffed the books in a bag.

"Thanks," I said, leaving with both books carefully caressed under my arm.

"You'll really like that book," she yelled through the door, "it's a great one for the beach."

With my newfound treasures in hand, I slipped back to the hotel. My feet were begging for fresh air and my toes couldn't wait to wiggle into the deep coolness of the sand. As I walked by the motel office, Nate popped his head out and hailed me down.

"Hey, Louis! Just wanted to tell you Sanji called. Said he'd be down around noon to take you on a little tour of the area. I put a note on your door."

"Thanks, Nate," I said politely, surprised by this sudden invitation.

I grabbed the note off the front door and entered my room, tossing the book bag on the desk. The note was very simple.

I figured you might want to see a few of the sights, so I'll be over around noon. Sanji.

4

BACK IN TIME

"There is no history, only biography."
—Ralph Waldo Emerson

Waiting for Sanji to arrive, I settled in and picked up a small brochure about these beaches that I had found in my desk drawer. It contained a nice little history of the region along with a little local bragging. As it turns out Sunset Beach itself is probably the least developed of all the beaches along the southeastern coast of North Carolina. This area had become known nowadays as the "South Brunswick Islands" and included Holden Beach, Ocean Isle Beach and Sunset Beach, all barrier islands protecting the mainland from the mighty Atlantic Ocean. The island of Sunset Beach wasn't even discovered by city folks until the late 1950s and early 60s. Being separated from the mainland by the inter-coastal waterway, the only way onto the island was by ferry. In 1958 the Corps of Engineers placed a one-lane pontoon swing bridge over the inter-coastal waterway. It swings open every hour for boats. That was a great improvement and finally allowed more visitors to come and build houses on the Barrier Island. The bridge is old now, but the local people still love it.

A few years ago, the bridge was hit by a barge during a storm. The barge drifted into the abutment, and being a rather small structure, the bridge broke loose from its moorings and began floating down the inter-coastal waterway. This situation was remedied finally by a couple of tugs that pulled the bridge back in place. Ever since, the NC DOT has been talking about putting a modern concrete arch bridge over causeway but the locals are not happy. The brochure was adamantly against this idea. It would ruin the laid-back, easygoing atmosphere of Barrier Island and open it up even more to commercialism and urban sprawl. Sunset Beach is probably the most unsullied and pristine of the several barrier islands that make up the *Crystal Coast,* another nickname that tries to capture the pure and natural quality of the region. It is certainly the smallest island. But, they are all beautiful.

Tourists never heard of Holden Beach, Ocean Isle or Sunset Beach until the local Chamber of Commerce decided they were sitting on a bonanza in 1976 and thought up a name to sell them to beach goers. This was the brainstorm of Helen and Miller Pope. After building four condos on Ocean Isle Beach in the early 70s, they came to realize nobody knew about the place. Myrtle Beach is just 40 miles south and was starting to do a great tourist business. It made sense to them to capitalize on Myrtle Beach's burgeoning stardom and so they decided to market these little jewels of sand and sun. It was Helen who thought up the name of "South Brunswick Islands." She picked *South* because south is warmer than north; *Brunswick* because they are all in Brunswick County, NC and *Islands* because it was technically true and certainly sounded romantic. When they went up to Raleigh later that year to visit the office of Travel and Tourism, no one had even heard of the islands and, to everyone's surprise, Highway 179, being a small secondary road, wasn't even on the state tourism maps. With this problem remedied, it wasn't long before the tourists came and today the beach rental market is booming. Because there is so little commercial development, the beaches still have a natural beachy and out-of-the-way feeling and most everyone living there wants to keep it that way.

A knock at the door startled me as I was thinking of the wonders of these recently discovered islands. It was Sanji.

"Hey, Louis," he said with a broad smile, "good to see you again.

How are you settling in?"

"Great," I said exuberantly, "loving every minute so far."

"It'll get better every day, believe me. Did you get my note?" he inquired.

"Sure did and I'd love to see a few sights."

"Good, let's go, I want to show you around. You'll love this place so much. It's the best thing since peach pie. There are no traffic jams, lots of beach and no big city pollution. Come on, I'll drive."

As I watched Sanji get into the driver's seat of his 1989 BMW, I couldn't help but be amazed at how friendly he was. In fact, everyone had been friendly so far. But I knew there was more to the story. I seriously doubted I had stepped into a fairy tale. In any case, at the very least, I had come into the middle of a movie, a screenplay of a man's life, and an absolutely intriguing mystery.

We drove across the pontoon bridge back toward Shallotte. This was when Sanji reiterated the story of the bridge and said that he hoped they would never build a new one.

"This bridge is good enough, why do people always want to ruin the good places. They ought to leave the thing alone."

I agreed. The Atlantic Barrier Island on which Sunset Beach sat alone and isolated was too wonderful to mess with. But, in the back of my mind I knew one day they would. People always do mess up good things.

Driving on toward Shallotte, Sanji was beaming as he told me more about the history of these islands.

"This year is the 100-year anniversary of the town, the centennial. Nobody much knows about this place. Even 30 years ago this whole area was nothing but farms and fishing boats. The first major highway to be built was in the early 1930s. That was Highway 17 going north and south paralleling the coast. Most all transportation before that was by ship. Even the most basic supplies like sugar, flour, salt, it all came by boat. Most everyone lived off fishing in one way or another. What they didn't sell they ate. This area has the best fish anywhere. You can get any kind of fish you want. You can have tuna, marlin, grouper, dolphin, spot, blue, and huge flounder. The variety is endless. But the shellfish are the best. The shrimp and oysters are to die for. In fact, I believe without a doubt, it's the best seafood in the world. You've heard of Calabash haven't you, it's world famous for its seafood. It's a small town just down the road."

"Not really, I mean, I saw it on the map, that's all.

"Well if you haven't heard of it, good. It's really out of the way and off the beaten track. But a famous actor almost gave it away back in the 1950s. Most people don't know that Jimmy Durante used to come over here a long time ago and they say he loved the seafood diners the best. Don't you remember how he used to say, 'Goodnight, Mrs. Calabash, wherever you are?'"

"Yeah I remember that. Are you sure he was thinking of this Calabash down here?"

"Sure he was. He said that to Clarice Holden's mother years ago when she was a young waitress here. I mean that's the rumor anyway. It's a believable story, though—where else could it have come from?"

"Well if it's not true, it should be. Besides this area is so far off the beaten path, no wonder he said, 'Goodnight, wherever you are.'"

"Speaking of seafood, that's exactly where I'm taking you right now—to the best seafood in the world. There's a little place at the end of Shallotte Point called Dock 77 Restaurant, the best food in the world right down here in Shallotte."

Down to the narrow point we drove, winding along two-lane country roads straddled on either side by gigantic live oaks, old houses, trailers and fields. Occasionally I would see one of those old tobacco barns, half-grown over with trees and weeds, looking like a picture from some Normal Rockwell painting. Yesterday's rural America, what a simple life it must have been. I was amusing myself with that thought; in reality it must have been a hard life without modern conveniences, medicines and cars. It probably wasn't all that great in a lot of ways, but the tranquility and serenity of the countryside can't help but bring up thoughts of how good the ole' days must have been.

As we neared Shallotte Point we passed a huge tree. It must have been 20 feet in circumference. It towered over the little white cottage and the quaint yard and stretched out over the road. Sanji was quick to notice my interest.

"You see that tree there?"

"I sure do. It's huge. It's one of the biggest trees I've ever seen.

"That's called a 'live oak' tree and experts say it's more than 500 years old."

"Wow. I'm sure glad they didn't cut it down. It's a wonder of nature living along the coast like this. You'd think that a hurricane would have got it long ago."

"Well, there's even more to this tree than meets the eye. It has a name and a story behind it. They say that George Washington actually passed by here and sat under this tree. So they call it the George Washington Oak."

"You're kidding!" I thought he was making this one up. "I never knew George Washington came down this far south."

"Yep, he sure did, I'm not kidding. The people say that he not only sat under that tree to take a rest but he also left his handkerchief on a branch after he wiped his brow."

Now I was truly impressed. This place was so far out of the way that you'd think nothing ever happened here. But instead of a void of history, this area was unveiling itself piece by piece. It seemed full of surprises, rich in events that began to open up in me a deeper understanding that this was more than a beach resort. Hidden away in its recesses were secrets yet to be revealed.

"Tell me more," I said.

"The story is pretty simple. Every one knows that good ol' George liked to travel, that's why you see all those signs everywhere, 'George Washington slept here.' After he became president he still toured around quite a bit. In 1791 he apparently made a trip through here down to Charleston, South Carolina on his so-called 'Southern Tour.' He was on horseback, too. He came through Wilmington, North Carolina after a long trip through the vast wilderness of southern Virginia. He spent only one night in the Wilmington area in April. There's a funny story that he stopped for dinner at Dorsey's Tavern in Wilmington and, having noticed the swamps on his way into town, he asked the innkeeper about the condition of the local drinking water. 'Well,' the innkeeper replied, 'I don't know much about the water, never drank any as far as I can remember.' Good ol' George apparently wasn't entertained by this because he decided not to stay there that night.

"Anyway, he made his way down through Shallotte, which wasn't much more than a river crossing at the time and stayed at a house four miles south of here. The home he lodged at belonged to a William Gause Jr. Anyway, he passed right by here because, believe it or not, this is where the old dirt road used to be. This road goes much closer to the coast than today's road does. After a night at the Gause house he then rode on south to Charleston. Not many people know about his southern journey up north, but down here everyone is proud as a peacock about it."

Our car finally pulled up to the Dock 77 Restaurant & Motel, which sits at the mouth of the Shallotte River, right near the confluence with the inter-coastal waterway. It is not a big marina, really modest in size, just a restaurant and a few boat docks a little off the busy waterway of the inter-coastal. Lunch was a wonderful shrimp sandwich that melted in my mouth with a big glass of sweet tea. All the seafood is fresh, just off the boat. We would have had their famous oyster roast but you can't get fresh oysters from May through August. Sanji told me that oysters can only be harvested in months with an 'R' in its name. That leaves out May, June, July, August, the hot summer months.

Dock 77 is a family-run place where the atmosphere is friendly and everyone can catch up on the latest news and gossip. People like to talk, too. It wasn't long before we were in the middle of a discussion about the history of the area. Sanji started the whole thing when a friend of his, a big guy named Fred, showed up for lunch as well. Apparently he was a regular. Anyway, Fred was an amateur historian. He retired from the telephone company up north a few years back and moved down to the area. Tall and lanky, he was wearing jeans and a T-shirt. He looked intelligent, sharp eyes glistened behind his horn-rimmed bifocals. A mustache added a touch of class. He loved history, especially of the sea and coastal areas. He said he was working on a book.

"Hey, Fred, pull up a chair," said Sanji, "Why don't you eat with us today. And by the way, let me introduce Louis to you, he's down visiting from the D.C. area. I'd love for you to tell Louis here the history of this place. It really fascinates me."

"Well I'd love to join you and good to meet you, Louis," responded Fred politely. And I would be more than happy to tell you a little about what I know." He seemed delighted to have someone to talk to.

Sanji said that he had pretty much covered the George Washington piece but maybe Fred could start with the time when permanent settlers came.

"Hmmm," Fred began, "let's see where to start. Okay, right." He smiled broadly as he thought about where to begin. "When it comes to colonial settlers, the earliest known record of the Shallotte area was a reference by a horseback traveler who crossed the Charlotte River in 1734. He called it Charlotta, or the Little Charlotte River. In fact, it was the river crossing where the town got started.

"What was his name?" I asked.

"Sorry, I'm afraid I don't know that off hand. Everything is very sketchy back then, just not enough hard facts to go on. You see this area was virtually unexplored until much later and the early guys didn't write all that much."

"Really," I responded.

"That's right. I suppose you could say that the first white settlement to take hold in any serious way was in the 1750s. A small group of English immigrant families came down from Cape May. I imagine they were just looking for new land to spread out on. They settled somewhere between Lockwood's Folly and the Shallotte River. That's just a hop, skip and jump from here. At that time it was called the Charlotte River. The name Charlotte was in honor of the wife of King George III of England. Of course explorers and other adventurers came earlier but not much stuck. For 200 years, from 1550 onward, the Spanish, French and Portuguese moved up and down this coast looking for riches and good land. I suppose what they wanted most was gold, and you just don't find that stuff in these parts so they never settled here. Finally the English took over and sent in the first real permanent settlers.

Now rivers played an important part in the life of these early settlers. Roads were non-existent except for some Indian paths, so they had to rely on the river for everything. There's four major Rivers that run through these parts, the Lockwood's Folly River, the Cape Fear River, the Waccamaw River and the Shallotte River. They all drain the Piedmont of North Carolina and head to the ocean. Over the centuries they deposited all this great beach sand that we enjoy today. Billions and billions of flecks of rock, mostly quartz, have been floated down to the ocean and by constant rubbing were polished into nice round sand particles.

By 1801, Bishop Asbury, the first Methodist bishop passed through on his travels, setting up little mission stations all over the country. He must have been a little anal retentive because his main comment was that the locals had corrupted the name Charlotte. He noted its correct name in his journal and said that it had been "vulgarly and improperly corrupted to Shallotte (Sha-lote)." By then there were probably a few houses and shops, but not much more. But whether they were Methodists or not they didn't care what the correct pronunciation or spelling was so the name Shallotte has continued down to the present day. The first bridge was built in 1807 right where the existing bridge is today. It wasn't much, just some old timbers, but it made this place the main creek crossing so everyone began to use it. In 1837 the first post office was established and the name Shallotte was fixed forever.

No one really knows where the first settlers actually lived. There must have been several different areas where settlers first put up their humble dwellings. Around 1840, some 90 years after the white people first came, the location of the town center must have still been up for grabs because some land speculators laid out a new town down here near the point. It is really a great spot and perfect for vacation homes. They subdivided lots, built a few rudimentary homes and then the whole thing failed. Anyway, by 1889 Shallotte was firmly established right where it is today, at the bridge.

But the most romantic part of the local history is about the sea and the ships that sailed these waters. Ah yes, the sailing ship, that was the heart and soul of the folks down here for a long time."

Fred sat back in his chair and looked out to the water. While he paused to recollect his thoughts, I made a few notes on my napkin. I would want to remember these bits of history. They made the whole place come to life.

"From the very beginning," Fred continued, "ships were what made this place work. The trade route between Wilmington and Shallotte was a busy and prosperous run. It took a week round trip by schooner to complete the route back and forth. Farm products, especially tobacco, would be sent up to Wilmington by way of the Cape Fear River. In return, basic supplies would be shipped back for the families. Sugar, flour, coffee, and manufactured goods had to be shipped in. Ships like the *George Slover* and *Addie May* were regular visitors and crucial to the economy of the area. Besides farm products, Shallotte also exported turpentine, tar, wood and fish. It all worked wonderfully well. Twice a week ships would dock at Shallotte and exchange their cargo.

There was more to tell than I could have imagined. I was enthralled with the tales of ships and the fabric of history but the day was getting older and Sanji had planned a few more stops before the day was out. Sanji finally brought things to a close for the day.

"Fred, I'd like you to tell Louis about these waters and the Indians and all. But we got to go now. We are on a tour of the area today. What do you say we come back another day—say Saturday for lunch and you can pick up where you left off?"

"Sure. I'd be glad to come back Saturday." Fred pushed his glasses back up his nose. "See you then."

We left and went on to other areas of scenic beauty. The land itself was mostly flat pine-barrens or farm fields. The beauty emerged wherever the land and waters met. Whether at river, inlet or ocean, the land and water formed a realm of endless beauty. The place was alive with energy. I began to see where some of Sanji's ability to put things into perspective came from. He was surrounded by not only the beauty of nature, but by people in love with the land and water and who wanted to keep it unspoiled by the madness of the cities.

Sanji was a picture of health and tranquility. A vibrant sense of self and purpose shined from his eyes.

"Louis, it's getting late now but how would you like to come over to my place tomorrow? I have about thirty people coming in from Northern Virginia and their first night here I'm fixin' my famous chili. It'll be kind of nice to use the house for something besides a retreat. You can meet my wife Mary Kathryn, too."

"Okay, that sounds great, what time should I come?"

"About 6-ish." Sanji was very matter of fact but I could hear the expectation for a great evening in his voice. "I live up in Shallotte on the river. My house is located on North River Road just off of Highway 179. You can't miss it. It's 332 North River Road, just about a mile and a half after you turn off 179. You'll know you're about at the turnoff when you pass Flannigan's farm. That's the one with all the hogs. You'll probably smell it before you see it. So when you come down North River Road my house is on the left. There will be a bunch of cars parked in front of the place. That'll be a good landmark. Here's my number if you get lost." He whipped out a piece of paper with his name and number on it.

"Okay, I'm off to the store to pick up some supplies, see you tomorrow night!"

"All right, see you then."

I felt honored to be accepted so quickly. I was not usually very good at making friends. My introversion usually kept me at a distance from people. It was a real handicap at times. But things were definitely improving.

I glanced down at the piece of paper with the phone number. Scribed in small but flowing letters was a small saying,: *Forget the big things, life is made up of one little thing after another, Sanji.*

That night back in the room, scribbling in my notebook, I was reflecting on the day when Marie called.

"Hello, my dear," she said warmly.

"Hello, baby, miss you!"

"Me, too. Hope you're okay all by yourself. Not getting into any trouble are you?

"Not a bit. Just touring around a little, that's about it."

"Say, I got the information you wanted," she said, "so I thought I'd go ahead and call.

"Great, what did you find out?" I was waiting with baited breath.

"Well it looks like you have found a very interesting name indeed. Apparently the name Sanji is a popular name for people in Central India, but it comes from the name of a place, a very special place, the ancient city of Sanchi. The name means 'sanctuary.' In fact, it is a city in the middle of the country that dates back thousands of years. Nowadays it is pretty much abandoned but it has a lot of ruins of old buildings. They told me it was a place of learning and wisdom. Even Buddha taught there. A great university had even been built there during Roman times, which taught, well, you might say specialized in wisdom. People still revere it today as a pilgrimage site and some say that teachers still come from there, even though it has been closed for centuries."

"This is all very interesting," I said. "I am very surprised."

"Another thing," she added, "even though there are a lot of holy places in India, this one seems to be the oldest. "

"I had no idea," I said. "Can you imagine that?"

"Well gotta get back on a report I'm working on," she said briskly, "got a project to finish. Now don't you get yourself into anything weird."

"Okay, don't worry. I love you and I'll call you later." I was absorbed in thought as I hung up the phone. Sanji's name was not some fantasy nickname, it was real and it was important. My mind reeled a moment with more questions: how did that name find its way to an out-of-the-way town called Shallotte, North Carolina? How did an ex auto mechanic get a name like this from the East? I seemed to be opening a box of mysteries. Where these things would lead I had no idea.

5

the party

The next morning I awoke refreshed and excited. Over my morning coffee back at the little Beachside Diner across the street, I was perusing Sanji's little book. Yesterday I hadn't even had a chance to open it. What struck me first was the cover, an orange sunset over a tropical ocean with palm trees leaning in the breeze. That alone was enough to give me pause and instill a sense of peace. The sayings inside were interesting enough, different than anything I had seen before, really homespun type of wisdom. One saying did catch my attention as I scanned the pages.

Nothing is quite what it seems—
Keep looking!

Somehow this seemed deep, and true, kind of like a nugget of gold stuffed in a rather ordinary gum wrapper.

Suddenly a voice sounded over my left shoulder. It was the waitress peering at the page just over mine.

44

"I like page three, too, that's a good one," she offered approvingly.

"So you know Sanji?" I asked.

"Sure do, honey, probably more than anyone else here."

"Really, then maybe you could help me a little. Would you know how he got his name Sanji?"

"You came to the right person, sweetheart," she said, exploding with a smile. "I can tell you exactly how he got that name."

"I'd love to hear."

"Well when he first moved down here about six years ago he used to come in every day for coffee and a breakfast bagel—an egg, cheese and sausage on a bagel. Every day the same. He's kind of that way. Anyway, we would talk. He'd tell me how much he loved it here because of the peace and quiet and, of course, the ocean. Then one day he was talking about maybe buying a little bed and breakfast or maybe even a small hotel to run in his retirement. So we'd talk a little every morning, you know, pros and cons and all. Anyway, one day I said, you know, you don't want a hotel, it's too much work, and besides, these days you need to be an Indian or Pakistani to have a hotel—they're buying them up left and right. Now I'm not prejudice, it's just a fact. All the hotels these days are being bought by foreigners, especially up and down I-95."

"So then what happened?" I said, fearing she would trail off into a long diatribe.

"Well one day he was going to be late, so he called up to order his egg bagel, so he could just carry it out when he got here. I answered the phone and said, "Hello, Beachside Diner, Marge speaking, that's what I always say, and he said something in a funny little voice and I think a kind of Indian accent. 'This is Sanji—I want an *EGG* and *CHEESE* and *SAUSAGE* bagel to go. Then I knew it was ol' DB and I laughed my head off."

"So he was just fooling around and came up with some Indian name?"

"Right, so the next morning when he came in I started calling him Sanji and it just caught on after that."

"Did he ever write down these sayings before that?" I asked.

"I don't really know for sure, maybe, he always had a pen and would be doodling something. But it wasn't long after that I got my first napkin."

"What did it say, if you don't mind my asking?"

"Oh it was a joke—the egg bagel was taking a little too long so it said, *What's the problem, we aren't building a piano here.* And, he signed it Sanji. So I laughed and laughed."

"That was his first saying then?"

"The first we got here anyway. Then he started doing more and more and it just caught on. People loved them. Each saying was personal. He was like giving out little gifts from his heart."

"That is really remarkable," I said, as I leaned on every word she said.

"Yep—hey honey—got to run, don't want any more napkins like that." She walked briskly away to fetch some more coffee for the customers.

Walking along the soft sand I breathed in the new day. It was still morning and not too hot yet. The ocean water was chilly on my feet. Today I would walk first then settle down to the book. I used to run years ago but it had been a long time ago and I was not in any shape to do so.

In the warm afternoon sun I read Sanji's book cover to cover. It was a marvelous collection of original wisdom. The theme of the whole thing in a nutshell was about being at peace, not worrying about the problems we all have, and living in the color and motion of the present moment. I would have labeled it Zen, but it wasn't really, at least I don't think so. It was more a mixture of old time American pragmatism and John Wayne idealism. That's the thing, it was practical.

Never give up until you're really, really tired.

Hope is what you have left when you're all out of hope.

I was struck with the simplicity, which at first sight looked like a child could write it. But as I thought more deeply about each one, my mind took me through the trials of life and back again.

All afternoon the book absorbed me while the ocean waves kept up a rhythmic crashing against the shore.

After changing for the diner I took the drive back up the main two-lane highway to Shallotte. I hadn't even noticed it coming down from D.C. It was a small town with just three stop lights and, of course, a Wal-Mart, but I hadn't noticed much else. My Toyota Corolla wasn't the sportiest of cars but I pushed it up the road with the windows down. Trailers, old farm houses, weathered barns and a few dilapidated shacks dotted the rural landscape. Besides two or three small convenience stores, it looked like the old South, unmarred by modern development. Off to one side there was some clearing going on in the middle of a large wooded track. A high billboard sported Arnold Palmer's face, smiling and announcing the construction of a new world-class golf course.

The only person I saw along the highway that caught my attention was a middle-aged man with a set of headphones on his head. He seemed totally caught up in his music, bobbing along the edge of the road, half dancing, half strutting. I'm sure he took no notice of me cruising along, the breeze blowing my hair every which way. It was going to be a great evening, I just knew it.

Arriving just after six, cars were parked everywhere in the driveway and along the road, ten or twelve at least, all with Virginia tags. The house was beautifully set on a long narrow lot sloping down to the Shallotte River. It was a wonderful house, a contemporary Victorian with porch and high gabled roof line. The front drive was circular and bordered with a beautifully manicured green lawn. Trees lined either side of Sanji's house, leaving it beautifully situated on the river nearly by itself.

I parked my car and headed up onto a large front porch. It was obviously very new, wearing its first coat of paint on the woodwork. The front door was mahogany with glass panels on both sides and a large oval shaped cut glass panel in the middle. Good taste, I thought to myself. This Sanji is no slouch. As I rang the doorbell, I noticed my hand was shaking slightly. Sanji answered the door with a genial smile on his face and a glass in his hand.

"Hey, Louis, come on in. Good to see you!"

"Thanks for having me over," I said, looking closely at the glass in his hand. "Hooch?" I inquired.

"Nah. Not today. That's my beach drink. At the house it's a chilled bar drink, beer or wine. Name your poison." Sanji's manner was intense and focused but his movements easy.

"Beer," I said. As usual I came across dull and plain. Why did I say beer? I didn't even like beer all that much. I couldn't think too fast when I was nervous. The pressure of a social situation had me a bit on edge. Eventually I hoped I could calm down. The drink would help.

The party was gregarious, fun-loving and sometimes loud as old friends joked, cajoled, and teased each other. Food was plentiful and the chili was a masterpiece. Sanji moved quietly and deliberately here and there, filling drinks, jesting with each small group clustered in the large living room and on the walk-out screen porch. He struck me as someone who was in control, master of his own house, commanding by his presence. He was obviously masculine, but more than that, he seemed to have a hidden energy, a deep-seated strength underneath the surface. Like a tire on a car, he was solid and smooth on the exterior, but there was obviously an enormous pressure within that pushed against the walls. That interior strength and intensity might have been obscured from sight but it surely was there. It takes great substance to be so self-assured.

Over a plate of cheese and olives I met Mary Kathryn, Sanji's wife. She was a very pretty woman, a brunette with large brown eyes. Her hair was short but full and perfectly arranged. Her face was bright and she had a natural smile. When Sanji introduced us she was very curious about how we had met.

We're so very glad you could come tonight." She was genuine and interested in me. I could feel a deep warmth in her tone.

"Well thank you for having me over. It's awful lonely when you travel by yourself."

"Oh yes, Sanji told me you came down without your family," she said inquiringly.

"Yes, I am afraid so. I'm on a kind of personal quest you see."

"Oh sure, Sanji has been like that for years, always on some kind of quest. Well, what are you questing for?"

"I wish I knew for sure. I'm mostly trying to find some time to relax and just reflect on life. Sometimes I feel that what I'm looking for is a certain, well—peace. As soon as I think I almost have it, it evaporates in thin air. Do you know what I mean?"

"Sure, you and Sanji should get along just fine. That's exactly why we moved down here."

With that the party enclosed around us and our first meeting was over.

The small group that had joined us around the cheese plate was talking about politics. They seemed engaged in a heated debate and seemed to need an arbiter. One of them, a large man name Jeffrey, looked at me.

"Do you think, Louis, as a neutral party, that Clinton should have been impeached or what?" He smiled with a large challenging grin on his mouth.

I didn't know exactly how to answer so I stalled, which only heightened the debate. It was really all in jest of course; everyone seemed to get a rise just out of saying the most off-the-wall things and then poking fun at one another. Everyone knew it was a game.

The cast of characters assembled there was truly colorful. Some were Sanji's relatives and some were friends. One cousin, George, had seen a flying saucer and even talked to its pilot. He enjoyed fielding questions about secret caves and mother bases much to the unanimous amusement of all. Another relative, Betsy, was unemployed again but working on a great new idea for selling subscriptions to airports to supply magazines in the restroom stalls. She was busy introducing her fourth husband to everyone, but he didn't look all that interested. Then there were the grandkids, maybe a dozen in all. They were all over the place like 101 Dalmatians. Little Bobby fell off the dock into the river. Luckily Aunt Colleen was nearby and plucked him out. He was crying a little but was soon engulfed in loving arms, hugs and kisses. A couple of corporate types were discussing stocks and bonds in one corner. Too much for me, I didn't weigh in there.

What a great collection of people, I thought, no two the same. There wasn't a bland or lackluster one among them. Each person was full of an intense energy yet they were easy and fun-loving, too.

Inside, the house itself was gorgeous. Neat as a pin, everything had a place. Well appointed but not overly expensive, it was the product of a serious effort. The living room's center of attention was a large fireplace with a marble mantle. To one side was a whole wall of glass patio doors that showed a view of the river. Books lined shelves on either side of the fireplace along with porcelain figurines and shells. Paintings, original oils of seascapes and sailing ships hung on several walls, adding a touch of sophistication. It was a nice house, one you could really be comfortable in.

The chili was especially good, nice and spicy like I like it, and the dinner party was a delight as everyone moved around talking and cavorting. After dinner the dessert was served, frozen fruit slices along with an after-dinner brandy.

I was beginning to feel at ease with the whole group when, suddenly, a hand grabbed my elbow and pulled me back. It was Sanji. His forehead seemed to be beaded up with sweat. His eyes were bigger and rounder than normal. Something was up.

"Louis, come with me!" His voice was low, almost a growl. As we went down the stairs, he was still holding my elbow and talking sideways out of the corner of his mouth.

"I've got a problem, a really big problem."

"I'll be glad to do what I can to help." His urgency was apparent, but he still managed to keep that inner energy locked under pressure. Whatever his secret was, I hoped I could learn that kind of restraint for myself.

As Sanji led me through the downstairs family room toward a corner bathroom, a slight odor struck me. The door was closed.

"I can't let my guests see this, but I don't know what to do." He carefully and slowly opened the door and the smell hit me instantly. "It's shit," he said, "shit everywhere. It's coming out of the tub and the toilet. It's a major backwash! My whole drainage system must be plugged up. I've had thirty people eating chili and going to the bathroom continuously for two hours and my system must be overloaded."

"What are you gonna do?" I said.

"Hell if I know. I can't tell the guests. It'll ruin the party and just worry them. They came all this way and I don't want to mess their good time." He was serious. I could see a vein pumping in his temple; a crimson red blush was starting up his neck. Though he looked like a tiger ready to pounce, his outer control still exerted itself.

"Why not call a plumber?" I said.

"Hell, I can't do that in the middle of the party—do you know anything about plumbing?"

"Well, I know a little," I could see where this was heading, "but not much. You must have a blockage in your pipes somewhere. Finding it will take more expertise than I have."

"You're right," he said rapidly, "it must be a blockage in the pipes. I've got a septic tank just outside and a truck load of pipes under the backyard going every which way. I knew there was something not right about it from the beginning. The contractor screwed it up when he built the place and I've fixed it once. I thought it would be okay. Now look at this mess." He was fuming. The red from his neck began creeping up his face. His breathing became quick and ragged. He felt his shirt pocket as if for a pack of cigarettes. I began to wonder if he was going to totally blow.

"Just shut the door and let everyone use the bathrooms upstairs," I said, thinking this might buy us a little time.

"Hey, great idea. Then we can clean this up later." He nodded approvingly. We stuffed some towels under the door. I silently hoped they weren't Mary Kathryn's best ones. Sanji didn't seem to care.

Regaining his composure, he went back upstairs as if he had just taken me on the grand tour of his new home. As I followed, I wondered just how much time we bought with blockading the door. I could still smell the stench of sewage in my nostrils.

The rest of the evening was uneventful. I watched as Sanji roamed from group to group as if he hadn't a care in the world. No one there would have guessed that beneath that grand composure was a seething volcano of emotions looking for an outlet, a weak spot, to erupt. As the last guests were leaving with hugs, kisses and goodbyes, a faint smell was rising from the lower levels. The bowels of the earth had apparently opened, issuing forth remnants of scents as rancid as they were foul. Sanji closed the front door with one last polite wave, turned to me and Mary Kathryn and yelled out, "Son of a bitch, no one uses any of the bathrooms!" Then like a flash he darted downstairs to the scene of the crime. "Oh my God!" Echoes rang forth from the cavern below. "Oh my God!"

After our initial shock, Mary Kathryn and I both ran down to join him. There, standing in several inches of foaming sludge stood Sanji. The flood had moved from the bathroom out into the adjoining hallway and extended some ten feet onto the carpet.

The next four hours were a maelstrom of activity. Buckets, mops, plungers, expletives, and an old rusty snake for cleaning drains were applied with sweat and elbow grease. Each hour some progress could be seen. The backwater slowly but stubbornly receded into the abyss from which it had come.

Throughout the ordeal, which would have brought low an ordinary man, I watched Sanji engage methodically in the work before him. Oh, sure there were the occasional expletives—shit, damn, and I'll be a son of a bitch—but they were interspersed with steady work, plunging, studying drainage patterns and orders barked out in command cadence to Mary Kathryn and myself. It was a study in military precision.

Somewhere into the evening Sanji had arranged an alternative plan for going to the bathroom. He had placed a bucket in the garage with a brand new roll of toilet paper just next to it. "Until the problem is solved," he ordered, "use the bucket in the garage."

With this arrangement and the rest of the wet vacuuming completed, Sanji, trailing an odor of rotting potatoes, made his way toward his favorite rocker on the screen porch.

"I've gotta take a break." He nodded, motioning me up the stairs. "You want something to drink?"

"Gin and tonic," I said with a sense of vitality. I had been useful tonight in helping my new friend.

With that we ascended to the safety and serenity of the porch. Plumbing deficiencies would have to wait until tomorrow.

There was a full moon glistening on the Shallotte River and a gentle breeze stirred the waters. Country sounds of crickets, frogs and the occasional hoot of a distant owl belied the frenzy of activity and odors we just left below.

After a nightcap and a detailed flowage analysis, I made my goodbyes and departed into the ebbing night.

The trip to the bucket just before I left wasn't all that bad. The humor of the situation began to surface as Sanji bid me farewell.

"I'd rather have a tooth pulled than go through this again. I think I've lost three years of my life tonight. I can't believe a new house, custom designed and built, could have something so basic go wrong. What a night! But, I know one thing, you've gotta 'always think positive.'" That ever elusive inner strength I had seen when I first met him was in control again and Sanji looked the picture of peace.

I nodded and said, "Tomorrow we'll sort it all out, it's probably something simple."

"You're right, Louis, keep looking on the bright side, that's what I always say."

As I drove off, he was still standing in the doorway with a look of studied concentration. I could almost see the wheels turning in his head.

Pointing the car toward the beach, hands gripping the steering wheel tightly, I reflected on my first lesson in character. No matter who you are or how good you've got it, life can turn around and bite you right on the backside. But Sanji took it like a champ. After his initial shock he had leaped into action. He had been bent but not broken. This guy had character.

The only person I passed on the way back to the hotel was that fellow with the headphones. He was still walking, making his way from some place to some place, oblivious to my night's difficulties. He bobbed along to the beat of his music, blaring through the silence of the moonlit country road. The glow from the night sky reflected off the painted lines and the cool, fresh air felt good as I took in deep breaths of the pleasantly-scented country air, alive with honeysuckle and jasmine.

6

you gotta learn to relax

"You must learn to be still in the midst of activity and to be vibrantly alive in repose."
—Indira Gandhi (1917-1984)

After sleeping late, I awoke to a glorious day at the beach. Last night had been a wild experience to say the least. But it was fun and I was meeting all kinds of interesting people. This morning was the beginning of my fourth day and I was already starting to believe that this was no ordinary place.

I enjoyed a short walk on the beach before breakfast, kicking the sand beneath my toes and soaking up the wild yet soothing seascape. All the time I was anxious to get back over to Sanji's place to see what was happening. I would go this afternoon. Whatever had happened to the plumbing was a mystery—one that needed solving.

Tourists were swamping the place, so I tried to find a few out-of-the-way sections of beach. Down at the end of the island where it wasn't as crowded, I made myself at home with my beach chair and umbrella.

Even here there were people, so I began to just watch and observe. This was most instructive and even illuminating. What I first noticed was that, even though they were all on vacation for a week or two, there was a certain frantic level to all their activities, a study in constant motion. They seemed to rush to the beach, hurry to the water, quick build a sandcastle or fly a kite, or to rotate on their beach towels at regular timed intervals for maximum tanning effect. Teens would run headlong into the water with their surfboards, certain that they'd miss the best wave of the day if they didn't hurry. Dinner was a rush to the restaurant only to wait in line outside, usually grumbling about the crowd—not exactly the picture of peace. Rush and hurry up seemed to be the major order of their vacation days. No wonder people came home from vacation so tired. I developed a little theory about human vacations from this observation. The theory is that people do not go on vacation to rest or relax. No, instead, vacations seem only to be about changing scenery or locations, but the relentless pace of life goes on, with varied activities for sure, but activities *ad infinitum* none the less. And, of course, if one doesn't have to slow down, then one doesn't have to reflect too hard on the reality of one's existence. Right. So then people just prefer to carry on for the most part. Introspection seems reserved for a few obscure souls who find themselves alone in small pools of brackish water as the tide recedes.

I had hoped I wasn't becoming too dramatic as I sat and looked out at life by the sea, but I would not turn back from this time of examination. I would leave no stone unturned.

As a first order of business, I opened up Sanji's little book again. It was good, even better the second day, filled with gems of wisdom and practical advice. Many of the sayings struck me deep inside, stirring me to greater thoughts about this great and wonderful sojourn we call life. Sayings like:

> *It doesn't take a millstone to drown you,*
> *just one little rock at a time.*

How true that was. In the many affairs of life, our problems are like little rocks and one by one they drag you under. So what to do about it. Sanji says:

Rocks don't have brains, people do.

Interpreting this one was easy. People have control over their life; they have a brain, and a soul. If a person can just gather a proper perspective and use their own innate, divinely ordained power, he or she could overcome a great deal of life's burdens.

Still, beyond the sayings, I was continuing to meditate on the name Sanji and the ancient city of Sanchi. The name simply translated meant "sanctuary." How simple a concept but what on earth did that mean? I began to think of all the synonyms for sanctuary. Words like "peace," "happiness," and "serenity" kept coming to mind. A sanctuary was a place where a person had access to peace, or was it? I wasn't sure. Places come and go. What truly brings happiness and an inner sense of well-being? Was it success, a beautiful family, money, community, or good health? Or was it pieces of all these things? And then there was the question of our human condition: could we only have peace in the inside or was it possible to be at peace with all of creation, in the midst of chaos?

Oh, well, what did I know? I was just groping in the dark. But soon I believed I would begin to find out, here in Shallotte and Sunset Beach, here in a backwater of North Carolina, on the windward side of the Atlantic Ocean, with my new friend Sanji.

By late morning, I made my way back over to Sanji's. Mary Kathryn met me at the door with a good-humored smile and motioned with her head toward the backyard.

"He's been out in the yard with Pop all morning, digging. He's got piles of dirt everywhere and the whole place smells like a waste treatment plant."

"Who's Pop?"

"Oh, you didn't meet him last night, he doesn't like parties. He's almost eighty and goes to bed early. He's Sanji's stepfather, raised him up from age nine."

"Must be quite a man."

"You could say that for sure."

"Well, I came over to see if I could help some. Maybe we can make fast work of the whole thing," I responded reassuringly.

"I sure hope so," she replied. "Sanji doesn't really need this headache, not with what all we've been through already."

"No, no one needs problems like this," I replied without really thinking.

I made my way down the back stairs to the backyard. The scene that confronted me was disastrous. Sanji was up to his knees in excrement and it looked like a large gopher had gallivanted under the green turf all night. There were piles of dirt everywhere. A little pile here and a little pile there. Heaps of mud, dirt and waste neatly, but widely, distributed around the sloping lot. As I entered the demolition area, I met Pop for the first time. A gray stubble of a beard emerged from a kind, placid face, and a belly pushed ever so gracefully through his well-worn undershirt. He was standing there with mud up to his waist, brown-stained feet and calves, and drooping pants rolled up to his knees.

I spoke out with a happy greeting, "Hello there. What's going on?"

Pop just looked a minute and smiled and with a humorous lilt said, "I think he lost a dime."

I gave out a short chuckle. "Looks like you've been at it a while."

"Yep, since about seven A.M." Pop had this irresistible smile pasted on his face and his eyes beamed as if he were a kid at recess. "You must be Louis," he said.

"Yes, that's me," I said, "and you are?"

"Oh, of course, we didn't meet last night, I'm Pop. I was down in my room painting. I hate crowds and, besides, I go to bed pretty early." He was energetic despite his years, with a dry but very witty sense of humor.

"It's good to meet you," I said. "I'm sure we'll get to talk more."

My eyes traveled from the lawn to the river beyond. I was struck by the beauty of the Shallotte River in the bright noonday light. It lay in sharp contrast to the demolition area that sprawled immediately around me. The river was serene, gentle and flowed unhurried, rising and falling in gradual tidal fluctuations. The marsh grass stood erect and silent as egrets walked in slow motion on their long legs, looking patiently into the shallow water. Small waves lapped effortlessly against the wooden posts of the dock while the wind rippled ever so gently across its surface.

And here, just a matter of yards from the edge of the peaceful river bank, bordering peace itself, a man and a shovel were flailing away; a small tempest of activity, a captain and his tool of steel, Sanji looked up from his hole.

"Come on over here, Louis, and look at this. I can't believe it." He pushed the words out with a heavy breath, panting deeply. "This is worse than I thought. You see these pipes? There are three right angle bends from the house to the septic tank and to top it off part of the pipe runs up hill. How in the world is water supposed to flow *up hill?*"

I looked carefully along the pipe run, and walked along it, stepping off the right angles. It was plain enough to see, the pipes did run up grade for a short distance. "This is an amazing piece of botched up work," I said. "Who did this?"

"The contractor did, that's who. Now I don't know nothin' 'bout septic tanks, but I do know up from down and, unless he expected some sort of a miracle, water just doesn't run uphill! And then to put in three right angles is impossible. Pipes are supposed to have smooth and gentle bends. This is a catastrophe."

"What are you going to do?" I knew he had a major problem and it was more than serious.

"Right now I'm ready to conduct an experiment with Pop. Watch this. "

"Okay, Pop, go inside and let's do our experiment."

Obviously a plan had been contrived before I arrived that involved a hydraulic flow analysis. I walked over with Sanji to a trench where a hole had been cut in the top of a pipe. The pipe had already been cleared with a snake. The plan went something like this: a small piece of tissue paper would be dropped into the toilet. Pop would give one flush and Sanji would watch to see if it flowed by. Now Sanji explained all this to me with an engineer's confidence, hands on his hips and a look of boyish anticipation on his face. He knelt down and called out several times to Pop. "Okay, Pop, whenever you're ready."

Sanji bent over the opening and waited. "Louis, this is a test of that newfangled water-saving toilet. You might not know this, but a few years back the Federal Government got into the business of designing toilets. All for environmental conservation of course. You know what their big contribution was to domestic waste processing? You won't believe it. They decided to reduce the amount of water used for each flush. Now, the new toilets only allow 1.6 gallons per flush and I know darn well that's not enough water, especially with this bent up system." Pop appeared silently out the back patio door. "Did you see it?"

"Hell no! Now didn't I tell you so, Louis," as he rose off his knees. "That's it. Proof of the pudding, no toilet paper, not enough water. How in the world is a big deposit going to get pushed through right angles and up-hill with so little water behind it?"

With a few more commands from Sanji, Pop went back into the house for a second attempt. This time, two full flushes and success. Sanji leaped to his feet yelling and jumping like a junior high cheerleader. "I knew it, not enough water in those ridiculous new toilets. I knew it!"

Sanji prowled over the pipe system now with the intensity of a tiger on a hunt. He muttered, "Who in the world would build something like this?" He paced a few moments back and forth. "A brand new house, I mean brand spanking new!"

I really couldn't say anything, but to agree. The drain system was a total bungle. "Yes, it's truly unbelievable." The problem of course was that even if the pipes were fixed there remained the problem of too little water to properly flush the pipes on their long run to the tank. The new toilets couldn't be fixed because the tanks were simply too small. No, from now on this was destined to be a double-flush house.

Sanji was now staring at his pile of dirt and muttering to himself, covered in sweat and mud. Calculations and ruminations seemed to be rolling around in his head.

"Well," he said suddenly, "we can't fix it in one day, let's have some lunch, I'm starving. You hungry, Louis?"

"Sure," I said, "but I'll be glad to help this afternoon if you want."

"Let's eat first. I need to sort this thing out. Maybe over lunch I'll tell you a little about what I've been through here. This one takes the cake, though." He was fidgety and irritated, but pulling up his pants, he still exhibited a deep confidence, that sense of acceptance, satisfaction and relaxation that eluded me.

Mary Kathryn had made a wonderful plate of ham sandwiches accompanied with a relish tray overflowing with pickles, olives and artichoke hearts. Mustard, mayonnaise, lettuce, and the ever present ice tea, that wonderful staple of southern households, commanded the center of the table. Mary Katherine and I sat and chatted while we waited for Sanji and Pop to clean up. She was delightful and charming. Strong willed and very practical, she was not taken in by illusions or by fantasy. "I didn't want to come down here you know. Sanji was fed up with the city and thought this place would be perfect, but our kids were all still there so I was very reluctant to come so far away. But as you see I did come and I'm very glad I did, but it hasn't been easy I can assure you. People think life at the beach is all fun but you've still got all the same problems as anywhere else."

Sanji and Pop made it up from their showers and we sat down to eat. We enjoyed the meal intensely. Conversation was light owing to everyone's hunger. But after lunch we began to talk.

"So, tell me about this house. It looks wonderful but Mary Kathryn says that you've had many problems with it. Did you design it yourself?"

Wiping off crumbs from one corner of his mouth, Sanji began to reflect. "Louis, moving to paradise wasn't as easy as I thought. I love it here, but it hasn't been easy. While we were still living up north we had hired an architect and we worked on modifying some house plans together. Then we hired a local builder. It seemed like things were going well. We liked the house plans, but by the time we finished construction we had to do some major modifications. For example, you may have noticed we have a very large attic. Well it was supposed to actually be a third floor, mostly guest bedrooms, but we ran out of ready cash, fixing all the problems, and had to leave it an empty shell for now.

"I've heard it's not easy to build your own house, a lot of headaches."

"You got that right," he continued. "The first problem came when the builder was digging the foundation. Apparently, a spring comes out on the one side of the lot and it's a big one with lots of water. Well, from what I understand, no one knew how big this spring was and no one told us until I get a call one day up in D.C. That was in mid October. It was my real estate agent who called me, the one who sold me the lot, to ask how things were going. She knew we had hired a builder and work had begun in August, but she wondered if work was progressing fast enough. When I told her the house was scheduled to be finished in December, she told me that I had better get down there because there wasn't nothin' happening yet. There was just a pile of dirt in the middle of the lot where the house should be. Well, Pop and I got into the car the next day and off we went."

By now Sanji was leaning forward on the table, one hand clenched tightly. His eyes were glowing with a ting of anger.

"The whole trip down I kept telling Pop that she had to be wrong. Surely the architect, the builder, or someone would have called me if there was a problem."

He paused to regroup his thoughts and emotions.

"I couldn't believe it!" he spurted. "We got out of the car after an eight-hour drive, only stopped once to relieve ourselves, and all we saw was a pile of dirt. They were supposed to be almost finished by now. I had expected to see a whole house framed in. I called the contractor and asked, 'What's goin' on?' He said that they had hit an underground spring and didn't know exactly what to do. I told him that he could have at least called me. We were all set to move down here the end of December."

Sanji stopped for a moment and looked out the window at the river. A sense of calm began to slip down upon him again and he spoke softly. "I could tell you all the gory details of our negotiations, but, hey, it's done and over with. Let's just say we worked with the architect and builder every day for the next week. We met to find a solution to the problem. For a while I thought we were going to do Frank Lloyd Wright one better and have a stream right through our family room. But in the end I suggested that they put in a pipe to divert the spring back into the river. They did it and it worked. It just cost me a lot of extra money. Why they couldn't have called me earlier is beyond me. What did they think, the spring would just dry up on its own? Hey, they got the degrees, I'm just an old grease monkey."

He paused and then continued soberly. "I was happy to have that problem behind us but it hurt our time schedule terribly. We had already sold our house up north and were supposed to be out by the end of December. So we had to move into a condo down in Calabash and put our stuff in storage for three months while they finished. But, you know what, that's probably the best thing that happened because then I could be here every day to watch closely and it's a good thing, too. I found all kinds of problems that they would have just covered over until it was too late. Like I always say, 'There's a purpose for everything.'"

"Two of the biggest problems that happened," he started again, "were the concrete driveway and the porch. I came over one day after a rain and my garage was six inches deep in mud. They had sloped the driveway pavement so it flowed into the garage! I blew up, just lost it, I called everyone over and gave them hell. I mean I really lit into them. They had to tear all that concrete up and re-pour it with the pitch in the right direction. They weren't happy but they did it. That was just one problem. But, the other big problem was the porch." With this he paused and poured himself another glass of iced tea.

As Sanji had been talking I had begun thinking to myself how different all this was than I had imagined. I mean everyone dreams of getting away, retiring early, finding a nice peaceful spot and enjoying life. But, it wasn't as easy as that. Sanji's house had turned into a nightmare of mistakes. Every day or so he'd go and inspect the work, only to find aggravation. But he had come through it, the house looked great. I wondered if he was just exaggerating for effect. Maybe he just liked telling stories. Despite the trauma he had certainly carved out a great retreat on a beautiful river.

Sanji stood up from the table now and paced a little, forming a small oval shaped pattern in the carpet. "That's when I started smoking again—Oh, I've quit since, but I was only a month into giving them up and trying to relax and settle into this beautiful area when I had to start again. I told myself it would only be until the house was finished. This house took years off my life. Yes building a house, never again, *I'd rather lay out in the middle of the road and get run over by a truck than build another house.* That's it!"

Sanji's pacing took him over to the glass wall with patio doors that walk out onto what they call a "Carolina Room." It is a spacious screened porch with a vaulted ceiling and fans.

"You see this wall, how much glass it has?" There were long sliding glass doors below and windows above in the vaulted section. "Well, one day I came over to see things and I just casually leaned up against it to have a smoke. I couldn't believe it. The whole wall wobbled and shook. I mean the wall was supposed to be all ready to put the windows in and here it was shaking like balsawood. I'm telling you the slightest wind storm could have blown the whole thing in on us."

He was motioning with both arms back and forth, simulating the movement. Then, in a flash he took three big steps into the Carolina Room and threw his arms up. He stared at me with wild eyes.

"I called the head carpenter and showed him and he agreed that it wasn't right. Like it would have taken an expert to see that there was something wrong when the whole side of the house wobbles. I looked up at the framing and saw that there were no supports, no beams, no braces, no nothing to stabilize this wall. You know we get some really bad hurricanes down here. This wasn't funny. I discussed it with the head carpenter. He wasn't sure what to do so I gave him an idea. He just said that the architect had designed it so it wasn't his problem. Finally, I draw up a little plan for braces and take it to the architect and he liked it. So we ended up building my plan for bracing. Now, I'm just an old grunt of an auto mechanic, a wrench turner from way back. What I know about carpentry and architecture you could put on the head of a pin. We all have different gifts, you know. I've always been able to fix anything that moves, but I've never been able to saw a straight line. The head carpenter said that it looked like it would work so he built it and so here we are today—Sanji, the architect and master builder."

I got up and looked at the bracing Sanji had designed. It looked fine. The cross beams and braces really added a lot to the screened in porch, gave it character.

"Unbelievable," I said. "Good thing you were down here, who knows what would have happened."

"Yeah, it looks great now, but if I hadn't been checking every day I don't know what I would have had."

Mary Kathryn began clearing the dishes away and old Pop got up and said, "Looks like you missed one big problem, Sanji—remember to flush twice." With that said, he headed downstairs for his nap. As he stood at the top of the stairs he announced to everyone, "Yep, just another beautiful day in paradise." Slowly he made his way downstairs muttering, "*Another beautiful day in paradise.*"

Sanji paid no attention to all this activity. His eyes glazed with the look you get when you peer deep inside yourself and are thinking out a problem. Deeply introspective he whispered to himself, "Now all I have to do is fix this septic system. I'll have to study this awhile. Then in a flash he was up and made an announcement. "In the meantime everybody flush twice and don't flush anything but single ply toilet paper." We all nodded affirmatively.

Sanji and I stood now at the patio doors looking out through the porch to the river. It was a bright, sunny day and the clouds were puffy and white like small cotton balls floating across the sky. The only anomaly seemed to be the once beautiful yard, now laid bare with a white snake-like pipe angling its way between piles of muck.

Sanji murmured something about relaxing the rest of the day. The unflappable character that I first met on the beach returned to reassert his composure as his internal volcano receded.

"You just gotta learn to relax," he said authoritatively.

I heard once again the master speaking.

"Say, Louis, don't forget tomorrow at lunch back at Dock 77. Can't let a few little problems get in the way of a great history lesson."

7

healing waters

"Hope is a waking dream."
—Aristotle, 4th Century B.C.

Sanji and I returned to Dock 77 the next day, Saturday, around lunch to continue with the history lesson of a few days earlier. While we were waiting for his friend Fred to join us, the conversation took an unexpected and lively turn. It all started when a man on crutches came in right after us and sat down. Sanji watched him intently and then leaned over to me to whisper.

"You see that guy over there?" he said under his breath, "he's here for the water that's for sure."

"What water?" I responded.

"Why the healing water, that's what water."

"Where?" I asked.

Sanji spoke now in a very deliberate way, pronouncing each syllable distinctly. "The water in the river is healing water."

"Really? You're kidding?" I asked.

"Nope, not kidding, it's absolutely true."

We both gazed at the man, then at the water, and then back at the man.

"What do you think is wrong with him?" I asked.

"Probably some type of foot problem, maybe an infection I'm guessing," he said. "The waters are especially good at curing infections."

The waitress appeared sporting a ketchup-stained apron and a pad and pencil.

"Hi, Sanji, how ya doin'?" she asked.

"Real fine, Maddie, real fine. Tell me something before we order, would you?"

"Sure," she said.

"I've been telling my friend Louis here about these waters, how they have a healing quality. Now I know you've been around awhile and you know about these things, don't you?"

"Indeed I do," she said. "Everyone around here knows the stories. But of course most of the people who come down stop in here, so I hear lots of stories. They're amazing really."

Curious and a little skeptical, I said, "What exactly do you mean, healing waters?"

She laughed and explained. "What I mean, Louis, is really quite simple. People come and dip themselves in the river and they get healed. It's been happening for centuries, starting way back with the Indians. They came from all up and down the East Coast with rashes, sores, war wounds, and things like that. They came to soak themselves in the water for several days, and sure enough they were cured."

At a table next to us, a distinguished couple in their 60s had been listening intently. The gray-haired gentleman spoke up. "Excuse me, but I couldn't help hearing what you were saying. We're staying at the Healing Waters Apartments just up the road. We came down last week because my wife had an eye infection. The doctors couldn't seem to cure it, but look at her now. She's doing great!"

The lady piped in, "I don't itch anymore and the redness has gone away. I thank God for this. It's a miracle."

"How did you hear about this place?" I wondered out loud.

The lady went on to explain that she was desperate and becoming very depressed with the situation. So, when a friend told them about these waters, they came on down. They figured they had nothing to lose and everything to gain. The doctors had given up.

She went on to say, "I went down to the river each day and just began to splash water onto my face for several minutes at a time. Each day I noticed a little more improvement until you see me now. My eye is no longer red and itchy and my sight has improved. I am just thrilled and thankful that my friend had heard some of the stories about this place and passed them on to me. I can't wait to show my doctor."

The waitress said, "There are all kinds of stories just like theirs going way back. These waters have been known for centuries, ever since Ponce de Leon sailed to Florida more than four hundred years ago. Even the Indians down there in Florida knew about them. They told Ponce that the healing waters he was looking for were farther up north along the coast and described Shallotte Point to a 'T.' But the good ol' explorer was more interested in a fountain of youth than in healing so he never came up the river. The Indians have always known about it."

"But why does it have a healing power?" I asked.

"I can't say I know for sure," the older man interjected, "but I hear that there's a sea grass growing here that has a bread type fiber inside. When the saltwater rises up at a high tide it mixes with the fiber and forms a mold-like penicillin. It turns the water milky and that's what the people look for when they come down to soak in the water."

"That's exactly what I've heard," said Maddie, "and you can talk to any of the old timers, they know lots a stories about people who came from all over and got cured. It's something about the grass."

"That's right," said a lady in a flowered pink dress two booths down. The sea grass is called Juncus and it does release a type of penicillin. But it heals all kinds of things. Why I heard of this professor from MIT who had multiple sclerosis. When he came down, he was in a wheelchair. He stayed here a month, going into the water up to his neck every day. When he left, he was only using a walker and said that he was feeling great. He went home and was never heard from again, but I think he was cured!"

The man on crutches at the front table now chimed in, "That's right, we don't have any final proof, but all those stories don't lie. I'm here to find out if something heals in these waters. I have a foot infection and I'm going to start dipping it every day."

It looked like the whole restaurant was listening to our conversation and everyone had something to say about what they had heard or experienced. All that was needed was an ol' potbelly stove and some checkers to complete the scene.

Sanji announced to everyone that he had recently read a book called *Legends of the Outer Banks*, by Charles Whekkee (sounded like an American Indian name to me). "Charles," he said with great authority, "is a North Carolinian, a historian and writer, especially interested in the coastal areas. I love his ghost stories in these parts, but in this book he cites a lot of evidence about the healing quality of these waters from the history of the area."

Everyone leaned into these words waiting for more.

"But I don't take legends as facts so easily. I have real proof that the stories are true. These waters do carry a healing power. My pop sits on the dock every day dipping his toes in to cure his fungus. You should have seen his toenails when he got down here, they were really bad, yellow and all that. But he's seen real improvement. Now his feet look pretty good for a man his age. This is a magical place, no doubt about it."

The waitress looked at me and giggled. "See, it's really true. But, maybe you have to believe a little." With this she winked. "You have to believe in something. For me, I just believe that God made this whole place. When I moved down, I was a nervous wreck, but now I'm calm and peaceful. I've found myself here."

"So you've found the perfect place?" I asked.

"As far as I'm concerned this is the best location on the planet."

"So the Indians were onto something a long time ago," I said. "They seemed to know instinctively where the best places were, and where to find healing. Too bad Ponce de Leon didn't listen to them. Maybe he would have found that fountain of youth right here. If you never get sick, stands to reason that you wouldn't get old too fast either." Amid chuckles here and there, the conversations trailed off as people turned back to their lunch and began to discuss the events amongst themselves.

At this the front door flew open and in walked Fred.

"Hey, Fred, you're just in time," yelled Sanji.

"Sorry, I got held up a little this morning at the house. The missus had some chores that couldn't wait."

"Well we are all warmed up for you. We need some of that great history you got stuffed in your head. We're trying to tell Louis here about the history of this place. All we got to so far was the healing waters." Sanji was very engaging.

The waitress came over to take Fred's order. "Now don't start 'til I get back," she said with a smile. "We all want to hear."

Fred smiled a big grin. He seldom got this much attention. He should have been an academic, he looked every bit the part. He was on his own stage and he loved it. His gray hair was neatly combed and waves fell over the tops of his ears. He had an air of authority about him, perhaps because he was tall or perhaps because he talked with such confidence. Anyway, the waitress delivered his shrimp sandwich and everyone pulled up a chair.

"Okay, here it goes. You want to know about the history of the area and especially about the Indians, right?"

"That's right," we all said in unison.

He cleared his throat, wiped the edge of his mouth and began. "Well it all started about 10,000 years ago. That's when the first Indians began to make their great migration southward to avoid the cold of the last ice age. So down they came in a great finger-like movement across the Carolinas. Some headed more inland to the plateau and mountains and some came to the coast. Around this area we ended up with a tribe called the Cape Fear Indians. They had a Siouan dialect, which made them a distant relative of the Western plains Sioux and, being a very small tribe, they were probably an offshoot of the Waccamaw Indians farther inland. It's hard to know much about them because they were almost totally gone by 1715, either by disease, war or by evacuating and hiding inland. But that's later in the story. The point is that they virtually disappeared before historians could find out much about them. They were certainly living much like the Croatians up in

Hatteras, fishing and hunting along the shorelines and up the rivers. They left little evidence behind because the soils are so acidic that graves and other artifacts are just gone."

"So none of them are left today?" the woman in the flowered pink dress asked.

"Basically they're all gone except for the descendants of the few survivors who made their way inland and intermarried with the other local tribes. We figure there are some of these descendants still in Robeson County. But as far as the Cape Fear tribe itself, it's gone forever. Now back to the story…

"The first whites that laid eyes on the Indians were the French under the Italian explorer Giovanni da Verrazano. Good captains must have been in heavy demand because Francis I, King of France, had hired him, an Italian, to sail for the French flag. So Giovanni explored the Carolina coast in 1524 and in March wrote about the Cape Fear Indians. He took a glowing report back to the king about the possibilities of the new lands but not much else happened on the French side. He did describe the Cape Fears as very peaceful people, naked except for furs of small animals covering their private parts. They apparently liked the idea of trading and had no real fear of the white man.

"Two years later, in 1526, the Spanish came with several large ships, under the command of Lucas Vasquez de Ayllon. He had 500 settlers with him. They landed and settled for a time along the Cape Fear River. The captain named the Cape Fear River the Rio Jordan and that stuck for a long time. The Spanish kept up their explorations of the whole lower southeast coast line from Florida up to Hatteras for the next hundred years. In 1561 we know that Angel de Villafane visited the area and a year later the French Huguenots under Jean Ribaut tried to come here but went off course and ended up in Florida. Navigation wasn't what it is today, you know.

"Not much eventful happened until 1663 when the British adventurer Captain William Hilton explored the area as a possible settlement site for potential colonists. He reported hearing the local Indians saying something like, 'bonny, bonny' which must have been a corruption of the Spanish word 'bueno.' Early in the year he brought one group down from the Massachusetts Bay colony but they didn't last long. Seems those who survived went back north. Later that year, he brought over a group of English colonists from Barbados. He sealed a deal with the local chief, Wat-Coosa, on what is now called Big Island, twelve miles south of Wilmington. The Chief gave him a deed over the Cape Fear River and contiguous lands. He sealed the deal by giving the English two of his daughters. This might have lasted had the whites not had a penchant for stealing Indian children under the pretense of giving them Christian education. The chief ran them all out by 1667. Can't really blame him.

"At that time, in the year 1667, it was estimated that at least 1,000 Cape Fear Indians lived in the area from Cape Fear to Shallotte. But contact with the whites would prove fatal. Diseases like small pox began to hit with a vengeance. By 1715, just a little over 50 years later, when the Indian wars began in this area against the Yamasee, it seemed that there were only about 206 Cape Fear Indians left living in five villages. A Colonel Maurice Moore, who was heading south to fight the Yamasee, detoured in this area with his force of Tuscarora and made sure he would have no trouble with the few Cape Fears that were left. He didn't have to worry, the life of these peaceful coastal people was gone. It was not a happy time in the history of America. The survivors fled inland and the Cape Fear Indians have disappeared from history."

"That's absolutely horrible. How could that happen, and to such a peaceful people?" asked one person. We all agreed. It was horrible.

"It is a fact that history has many unkind faces," said Fred. "But it tells us a lot about human nature. Our ancestors were very violent people, especially when it came to securing their own self-interests. But then again, today we aren't so much different are we? Besides a few world wars to our credit, we do violence in so many other ways now. It's a tough world, you know.

Sanji spoke up now. "You know those Indians were living in a virtual paradise, all the fish and shell food they could eat, lots of land and trees, and the beautiful ocean and rivers to canoe on. It must have been the place to beat all places. That is until the white man came."

"It wasn't exactly all that peaceful," Fred piped in. "The Indians did start wars against one another and they could be pretty brutal at times. They were always making alliances against one another and would send out young warriors to find new wives and land. The weaker peoples always did succumb and were absorbed into the stronger groups. And, to paint an even grimmer picture, did you know that the Waccamaw Indians invented a type of torture and slow death for their enemies that rivals anything we have? It's called the 'prickly death!'"

"What was that like, or should I ask?"

"It wasn't pretty. They would take an enemy and tie him to a tree. Then they would stick him all over with long pine needles pushing them right into the skin. When the hapless victim was covered up like a porcupine, having endured excruciating pain, they would light him on fire. You know how pine needles burn, slow and hot. It wasn't something you would want to witness, I assure you."

"So even the Indians weren't the picture of peace and contentment?" I said.

"I'm afraid not, Louis. Contented maybe, but peaceful no. Even they were troubled by the same inner demons that plague us."

"But," Fred continued, "if you think the Indians were tough, you should have seen the pirates.

"You mean pirates also came around here?" the elderly lady asked in amazement.

"Came around? Why this whole area was their playground. It was their home. From Ocracoke down to Charleston, they enjoyed pretty much a free reign in the early 1700s. With all the secret coves, rivers and hideouts why no one could find them. Besides they were so mean-spirited no one wanted to anyway. The governors didn't have much of a militia in those days and almost no navy. So the pirates terrorized shipping at will in those early years of the 1700s. But even they met their end. North Carolina hung two of the most notorious pirates in 1718. Stede Bonnet and Edward Teach, also known as Blackbeard, had been real thorns in the side of the new colonies. After they were hung, it spelled an end to the reign of terror. But before 1718, this whole place was a pirate's utopia. I wouldn't be surprised if Blackbeard didn't have descendants all over the place around here."

With that said, Fred got up, wiped his glasses, and said he had to run.

"Hate to spoil a good party but I gotta go. The wife is expecting me back with some supplies."

"Thanks so much," I said. "Gosh, it's just amazing what history there is in all these little places." Everyone at the tables chimed in with their appreciation.

Out he went on his domestic errands.

With all that to mull over in our minds, we finished off our sweet tea. I had been mesmerized by the introduction to the past history and people of this area. This part of the seacoast was awash in history, both good and bad. Much of the history seemed to consist of groups of people just trying to find a good place to live. First the Indians, then the explorers, then the settlers, then the pirates, then colonization by new Americans and, finally, in our own day, a new group of freshly gray-haired baby boomer retirees looking for a piece of paradise. All of them in pursuit of happiness and peace. Just like me really.

But there seemed to be even deeper things than I had imagined going on here. There was a sense of intense and profound mystery around events in the region. Why, for instance, had the pirates been so attracted to this area? And, why had this region been so isolated for so long, as beautiful as it was?

I then thought about the healing waters and how people still came after centuries to find healing here. In fact, these people were right here in this restaurant.

Something about this place screamed out hope. The waters, the sea, the sky, the freshness of the land, all conveyed a sense of ultimate hope. No matter how much people had hurt each other here, no matter how much human nature had waxed good and evil in these pine forests and on these sands, one could still sense hope. The healing waters still flowed.

As we left, and made our way to the door, we shook hands and greeted everyone with a friendship that I had never experienced before.

Everyone knew Sanji and he shook all their hands warmly with both of his. Our time had been truly spent in a community of people, all seeking, all like me.

"Louis, I'll pick you up for breakfast tomorrow at nine A.M.—I've got the best breakfast joint in the universe to show you."

"Sure," I said, "why not?"

I felt we had only begun our journey. My journal was slowly filling up with ideas, hopes and plans. Learning to relax didn't seem so foreign anymore. I was starting to get the hang of enjoying life.

8

NEIGHBORS AND ALIENS

*"The Art of living is more like wrestling than dancing.
The main thing is to stand firm
and be ready for an unforeseen attack."*
—Marcus Aurelius

On Sunday, right on schedule, Sanji picked me for breakfast at a local eatery called Big Nell's Pit Stop. It is halfway between Ocean Isle and Sunset Beach on Highway 179. Among the locals this place is famous not only for the food, but the colorful collection of just plain, homegrown Americana. It's not your usual mom and pop place. Big Nell and Al, her husband, both ride Harleys and there's auto racing paraphernalia all over the place. There's a big autographed racing tire from a Richard Petty Formula Racer greeting you at the door. The floor is a checkered black and white tile and the curtains are the colors of the white, red and yellow flags at a race. I had no idea, but racing is a big thing in rural America's countryside. An entire subculture has grown up around fast cars and bikes. Like movie stars, the top racers are treated like royalty.

At Nell's everyone is as friendly as they can be. No one puts on any airs here. That's not to say some couldn't. Anybody who is anybody drops in for breakfast and lunch. Doctors, lawyers, fishermen, business owners, blue collar, white collar, no collar, you name it, this is the gathering place.

Now, some people come down this way for the seafood, Calabash-style, deep-fried and fresh as the sun is hot. But breakfast this morning was not seafood. It was good ol' fashioned eggs, grits soaked in butter and cheese, a healthy portion of sausage patties on the side and anything else off the fry pan that wasn't good for you. The menu itself was a long list of these Southern favorites, mixed whichever way you like. There was something for every taste: Big Nell's waffle with pecans and strawberries and vanilla ice cream; two eggs, tar-heel ham and grits; breakfast biscuits with gravy and liver pudding (or scrapple if you prefer) and dozens of other Southern favorites. One item really caught my eye: Brunswick stew (roadside kill in season).

Sanji waved as he came through the glass door. Everyone knew him. The waitresses smiled and blew him a kiss. He saw me and strode over to the table.

"My favorite is the chicken gizzards and fries, it always hits the spot," he said as he sat down. "In fact, if you throw a fried egg on the side it's as good for breakfast as for lunch, don't matter. But I usually just have them for lunch. For breakfast it's always the same: bagel, egg and sausage."

The waitress, a tall thin brunette in her fifties set a coffee cup down and poured out the hot brew. The air filled with the aroma of fresh ground coffee beans. The scent of coffee mixed with the loud conversations swirling all around us created a sense of a down home family get-together. The patrons were coming to life in fine style. The waitresses barked orders at the cooks and the cooks sallied back with their usual retorts.

"What dah ya think I am, yo mama?" One cook yelled. They all laughed.

Sanji soaked it all in, enjoying every syllable. He just looked at me and said, "This is the real McCoy, it doesn't get any better than this."

A large party of six had been sitting at a table behind us; a tray larger than a trash can lid went flying by on three fingers. Flap jacks, eggs, grits and hot sauce. This was an eat'n place and people meant to eat!

Sanji and I exchanged our thoughts on the last few days. I told him I had been reading his little book. Sanji nodded politely as I spoke of my reflections. He responded occasionally, agreeing that people don't really want to slow down and take a deep look at their lives.

"People like the book okay but I doubt that they take it very seriously."

Then he quickly said he had fixed the septic system yesterday afternoon and everything was now flowing beautifully. But, he went on, his days had apparently been a bit more edgy than mine had been. He wanted to reveal something that had been bothering him. Sanji fixed an intense gaze on me.

"Louis, I don't know if you've noticed that there are new houses going up all over this place, everywhere you look. When I started coming down here it was still country and a laid back seashore. But now we've got new stuff going in almost every week: houses, stores, businesses. It's going to ruin this area, I tell you."

"You can't stop progress," I said. "When people like a place they just start moving there. It's a lot like Florida. I hear that 900 people move to Florida every day. It won't be long before the place is overrun with Wal-Marts. "

"That's what I'm afraid is going to happen here, Louis. It's a terrible shame. This area is one of the last pristine beaches on the East Coast. I don't know what I'll do if they ruin it."

"From the looks of it, they have a long way to go. There's plenty of open space left." I was trying my best to be encouraging but he was right. Maybe in a few years this place would be just another tourist trap.

"Louis, I'm not just talking about the future here. I'm talking about right now. I want you to come over to the house after breakfast to see what's happening. It's about the new house they're building next door to me. Something awful funny is goin' on over there."

"What do you mean?"

"I don't know exactly. This guy is building a new house, but it's going to be really close to mine and, besides, it's not like any house I've ever seen."

"What kind of house is it?"

"It's like a brick fortress, long and narrow. It must have 20 rooms with little tiny windows. This guy is either some kind of eccentric, or he's in one of those religious cults. Then again, for all I know he may even be an alien. The house actually looks like a compound or a shelter.

"Good heavens, you can't be serious, you mean it's not a regular residential house?"

"Absolutely not! Something's not right. I think the guy is up to something. For all I know it's a base for conducting alien abductions or something."

I stared at him in disbelief. Surely he couldn't be serious. Maybe he was just joking. With a growing level of distress, I replied, "Aw, come on, you can't mean that. It's just a different kind of a house, surely."

The waitress appeared with her order pad and pencil. "Okay, what will it be, Sanji, and who's your friend?"

"Good morning, Emma, this is Louis, down from Washington D.C. I'll have the usual."

"How about your friend?"

"I'll have Big Nell's waffles and eggs."

"How'd ya want your eggs?"

"Over easy," I said.

Off she went in a sudden blur, moving deftly between tables and around a small cluster of people looking for a place to sit. She miraculously avoided a collision with another waitress laden down with five breakfast plates stacked on a tray.

Sanji leaned forward. "Come over after breakfast and I'll show you what I'm talking about. This has me a little more than concerned. I can't imagine what on earth the guy is building right next to me but we're going to find out."

Sanji dropped me off at the hotel after breakfast so I could get my car, and I followed him over after washing up.

When I arrived, Sanji was standing in the yard, peering at the new house through the trees. He was pacing up and down like a restless lion.

"Good. You're here, Louis. Let's go on over. No one's there right now."

The construction crew had not arrived yet. We went off through the woods and around the construction debris. Sanji had been right, this was no ordinary house. The garage was a massive two-story structure. At least three cars could park comfortably inside. There was an overhead room, which could accommodate a large group for a meeting. Toward the rear there was a sprawling, almost industrial kitchen. The main floor of the house consisted of a series of rooms on one side like motel suites. Opposite this row of rooms was a long living room. What was most strange of all was the fact that there were only small, narrow windows high up on the walls, no large view of the water and no porch or deck. My immediate thought was, why would someone build a big house on the water and not have any windows to be able to enjoy looking at it?

I started to get a little nervous. "This isn't normal at all," I said. My palms were getting sweaty and I felt like we should get out of there as fast as we could. A strange sense of foreboding folded like a shadow across my body.

"You ain't seen nothing yet," Sanji said. "Come on, Louis, let me show you the rest." He guided me downstairs to a large ground level room, which had to be 80 feet long and 30 feet wide.

"This must be the storage and staging area," he said nervously. "I can't believe it. This is a weird house. Something really screwy is going on here."

By this time I had enough. "Let's get out of here, I'd hate to be here when someone came."

"Don't worry, Louis, they don't come around much. That's part of the problem. If they did, I could maybe talk with them and find out what was going on. Not only is the house a mystery, the owners are, too."

"Let's go anyway. I've seen enough."

We escaped quietly through the tree line separating the two houses.

After settling down to some cold iced tea on the back deck, we talked a little, but mostly we sat gazing at the river. The tide was coming in and it was beautiful to watch the slow submersion of the tall grasses under the rising water. The fish were jumping to catch afternoon insects and the herons stood patiently gazing on the gradually disappearing sandbars. It was warm and humid but a gentle breeze blew across our faces, caressing us like angel's wings, bringing relief. Sanji was reminiscing how wonderful it was to live on the river. It was like paradise. Every now and then he'd repeat the house motto that had been coined by Pop: *just another beautiful day in paradise.*

I was becoming a believer myself very quickly. It was so much like a paradise. The beauty of the entire area was inebriating.

The faint smell of smoke was an unexpected intrusion into the placidity of the scene. We both looked at each other with distant curiosity, but in a minute it was I that sounded the alarm.

"What's that smell, Sanji?" I said.

He sat straight up in his chair and began to sniff the air more deeply like a hound dog on a scent. Apparently without our knowing, the alien house had been occupied by a construction crew after we left. A pile of debris and vegetation had been set on fire for disposal and left to burn unattended.

This would not really have concerned us except for the size of the flames that appeared near the shed at the edge of Sanji's lot. It didn't register at first, but suddenly Sanji took a fast double take in the middle of a sentence. "Holy God Almighty," he blurted out. "It's a fire!" He jumped to his feet in a flash, jerked one way then another and then yelled at me. "It's a fire! It's going to burn down my shed!"

In less than a minute, we were downstairs staring at a woodland fire between his property and the alien's. The flames were six to eight feet high, covering the woods between the houses. Sanji yelled out, "Louis, find some more hose," as he grabbed up his garden hose and shot directly into the woods. I searched in the garage and found a hundred-foot hose hanging on a wall that I lifted off and then I ran out. All I could see was smoke. Pulling a handkerchief from my pocket I covered my nose and peered into the conflagration. In a few seconds, I heard Sanji screaming. "Connect the hoses, I need more line, Louis—fast!" The thickness of the smoke and underbrush hid him from sight, but I obeyed his command. Screwing together the last connection, I yelled back, "It's ready."

For some minutes I stood looking, trying to find Sanji, but I couldn't see much through the haze. Then I thought, I've got to call the fire department, and I ran upstairs for the phone. A quick 911 and they said they were on their way. Downstairs Sanji was nowhere to be seen. Between the smoke, fire and heavy undergrowth, I couldn't tell if he was alive or dead. I decided, now emboldened with success on the hose and phone call, to follow the garden hose into the woods. Hand over hand I entered the woods. Smoke swirled around me as if in a tunnel. Sweating and holding back my cough, I was at a loss to know how far to go. It didn't seem life threatening, yet I felt as if my life was in deepest jeopardy. Just when I couldn't go any farther, a face appeared through the palmettos.

"Let's get out of here, Louis, it's out of control." Sanji, blackened and wheezing, looked like a fireman escaping from a collapsing building. Holding on to each other we ran through the remaining trees to the safety of his lawn.

When we reached the garage, the sounds of sirens filled the air. What a welcome sound to hear. Two fire trucks pulled up simultaneously, radios blaring and horns going full tilt. We threw ourselves onto the concrete driveway and just waited in relief.

When we saw puffs of steam beginning to rise in what was once a primeval thicket, we knew everything was going to be all right. We looked at each other with relief and jubilation. I was congratulating Sanji when he leapt up like a shell from a shotgun.

"Where are you going?" I yelled.

"Up to the street," he yelled back as he bolted off.

I arrived at the street just as he was finishing a round of thanks to the firemen.

A large white Cadillac with the owner of the house was pulling up behind the fire engine. As he got out of the car Sanji walked up and confronted the man. A brief flurry of insults were hurled back and forth.

"What do you think you're doing!" Sanji yelled. "Your workmen almost burned down my house!" He was right in the guy's face.

The exchange heated up until two firemen had to go over and break things up. I was stunned as I watched. Sanji had totally unwound on this guy. The next thing I knew the firemen had Sanji in an arm lock and were dragging him away from his neighbor.

I yelled out, "Don't hurt him, he doesn't mean any harm."

"Don't worry, we're just separating them. It seems like he has had just a little too much excitement today."

I couldn't blame him for being angry or for unraveling like he did. I went over to my friend and together we headed toward the house. Mary Kathryn was waiting by the front door for us.

Sanji was silent as he entered the house. Mary Kathryn took him by the arm and led him inside.

"I'm sure he'll be fine tomorrow," she said. "He just needs to rest a little."

Standing somewhat stunned, still blackened with smoke, in middle of the front doorway, I watched Sanji being led away by his faithful wife. Norman Rockwell couldn't have painted a more loving scene. What I was looking at, the tender affection, could only remind me of how important family was.

What unimaginable luck Sanji was having. Who could blame him for erupting when his own home, his own place of sanctuary was under threat of being burnt to the ground. The neighbor's construction crew had been extremely careless and the man deserved a good talking to. It's a shame that even here in what seemed like a perfect paradise one can't control who lives 50 feet from him. No, not even in paradise can a person manage to control events just next door. Alien home base or not, Sanji's property had taken a beating. In what was once a wonderful piece of riverside woodland, there now stood a cement fortress. I just shook my head as I headed back out the door.

9

the wisdom of pop

"The man who has no inner life is a slave to his surroundings."
—Henri Frederic Ameil

Sanji showed up the next morning at the hotel with his suitcase and checked in for the night. He said he had to get out of the house for a day to let things settle in his mind. I don't think I was all that surprised but he did seem a bit unwound.

After he settled in, we headed for the beach. He had his chair, an umbrella and the cooler—an obvious sign that the hooch was on tap.

The sky was beautiful that afternoon. The seabirds were soaring, lifting themselves effortlessly on the swirling winds at the ocean's edge. Long lines of pelicans, like soldiers on an eternal march, glided back and forth across the shoreline, following their leader in a gangly procession. Occasionally one of these unwieldy birds—half dinosaur, half eagle—would dive straight down into the water and come up with a fish slowly disappearing down his gullet. The sun was bright and the sand hot under our feet as we plodded on.

"Over here, Louis, this is my favorite spot."

He motioned toward a piece of beach just near the dune line. "Less traffic up there." Struggling with folding chairs, an umbrella, assorted bags of beach stuff and a cooler, which we had extruded from the car's trunk, we made our way to the place he had pointed out.

"I feel the right energy here. It's perfect for thinking things out."

By this time I was glad to unload my burden anywhere onto the sand. If there was energy there, so much the better. In only a few minutes we were totally established on our beachhead, everything in its right place.

"I can't function unless everything is organized. I mean some people can just throw their stuff all over, but not me. I like order, neatness, I can't stand a mess." With this, Sanji brushed off the sand from the sole of his left foot.

"Sand's not dirt you know," Sanji said knowingly, "it's just rocks all ground up. It's taken millions of years for good ol' mother nature to make this stuff. It's another miracle of the creation, really."

We were finally settled in now. So, we began to do what it is you are supposed to do on the beach. We looked at the endless ocean and the sand and the people. And I began to think. I began to think about life. What did it all mean anyway? I also noticed how wonderfully easy it is to think and meditate on the beach. The wind and the waves make a harmonious noise together and the sand is like a big blotter that soaks up all the miscellaneous distractions. It really is quite marvelous. As I was thinking, I realized that I had not yet asked Sanji directly about his name. I knew how he started to be called Sanji but I wondered how he came up with such a significant name.

"Say, I was wondering, Sanji, how did you get your name anyway?"

"I can't say I know for sure, Louis. It was kinda a joke I pulled on a local waitress. But I suppose it was something in my subconscious. You see up in D.C. I had people from all over the world come in to get their cars fixed. And there were a couple of people from India, diplomats as far as I knew. We'd get to talking a little and I came to find out about this place in India that was a perfect city. They said it didn't exist anymore but that at one time long ago it was a place of incredible peace and learning. It was called Sanchee. Well I guess I thought about that long and hard and wondered why it no longer existed. They said that in a big way the people of India still think of this place and yearn for the perfection it brought."

"Kind of like our Garden of Eden or something."

"I guess so, but a little more recent than that. So in a way I just thought about that place and about what it would be like to really know the truth of things. But the name was just a joke, I wasn't even thinking when I called up the restaurant that morning. Just kinda came out that I was 'Sanji.'"

"And then the name caught on and now you're Sanji?"

"Yep, it's as simple as that."

This was my perfect opportunity. "But how does that explain your wise sayings and all of that. I mean how did you get this stuff that people love so much? I don't even know what your philosophy of life is."

"My philosophy of life… Hmmmm. That's a pretty big topic don't you think, Louis?"

"I know it is but we really haven't had a chance to get into it yet. I mean I feel I'm getting to know you a little, but I really don't know what makes you tick, what code you live by?"

"You'll never know me, Louis, no one ever will. Why, hell, I don't even know myself most of the time. But to be fair I'll tell you what I can."

"Great, it'll be fun just to get to the bottom of things."

"Well okay then, let's see if I can find a good place to start." Sanji took his baseball cap off and rubbed his forehead, swabbing away a thin line of sweat.

"You see that's part of the whole problem, Louis. Where can you start? I mean this whole thing about life is crazy. There were probably two other guys sitting here 50 years ago and in another 50 years they'll be two more guys sitting here. Life in some ways seems to be an endless repetition, like the waves rolling in and the sand rolling out. Yet each repetition is not exactly the same. You see, each wave is always inherently different from the ones that came before it. And, none that follow will be quite the same. Each wave has its own strength, height, width, and its own characteristics. But what wave was the first wave? Have you ever thought of that? So to begin I think we have to first see this pattern as part of some eternal process. The point is, Louis, there is no one place to begin. One just finds oneself there in the middle of it all."

"Look, I'm just an old auto mechanic, I see things as they are. Life is simply, well, it's just there. It is what it is."

He continued. "It's a lot like when I was working on cars for my daily bread. Someone would bring in a car that was not working properly. So I'd start to look for the reason. That was pretty simple for me, I'd worked on cars for years and there's only a few parts really that go bad in a car. But then someone would ask me why the part went bad. Now that is a big question. Why? But answering it wasn't easy. The answer could be anything from bad construction to human error to just being worn out. But being worn out isn't a straight forward answer because some engineer designed the part to wear out after so many miles. Or it could be that the rubber gasket for example came from a tree in Malaysia that was near the end of its life and the rubber was not of proper consistency. Or the factory didn't have the right temperature when they forged the part and on and on and on. Who knows the real reason for things. Solomon was the wisest man who ever lived and he said it best. In the Book of Ecclesiastes he says, 'Vanity of vanities, all is vanity, a striving after the wind.' In other words, you can only find out so much. So what does he say to do about it? Just live. Solomon says just to live and enjoy one's work.

"I have found it best to follow that advice. Enjoy the moment, don't worry about trying to figure it all out. So that is what I do, I live and enjoy the moment because here we are today and then gone tomorrow."

"You think it all boils down to that?" I asked.

"I do have a little saying I use to put all this in perspective."

"Really? I'd love to hear it."

"It's really quite simple," Sanji said. "You can understand this just by looking at the endless waves of the ocean."

The sum total of our lives is here and now.

I thought for a long moment.

"So, how can you be happy if life just comes and goes and all you have is the present? Isn't there any ultimate purpose or God for you? Don't you wonder if there's a Being greater than you that made all this stuff, the earth and stars?" I picked up a handful of sand and let it slip through my fingers.

"Louis, I like you, but you just don't get *it*. Most people don't ever get *it*."

Puzzled, I said, "What is it?"

"It *is IT*. It is everything, the big enchilada." Sanji was smiling deeply and suddenly began to laugh. "It *is IT*! It is what it is, the whole pie. *It* is and when you know IT, you know the nature of things."

I felt more than a bit confused. "So you mean you can know '*IT*,' Everything? You can know why everything is the way it is?"

"That's right, now you're starting to get *It*! But you can't know it in your head, you can't figure it out, you have to feel IT, live IT in your gut."

With that overwhelming simple statement, out came the hooch. Sanji poured me a plastic glass about half full and then he took a big swig from the jar.

"Louis, let me try to explain what I mean. To do that I'm going to tell you some more about Pop. Now, he's the Grand Master! He's really *got IT*."

"All right," I said. "Maybe that will help me understand your point."

"Do you remember seeing the shed out back of the house?" Sanji asked.

"Yeah, I remember it."

"Well, when we first moved into the house Pop had that delivered and he spent the whole first year inside that shed. Hell, it can't be any bigger than eight feet by twelve feet, but he set up his trains in there and just watched them go 'round and 'round in a circle. He even installed a little refrigerator for cold beer. It was a whole year before he finally came out and started on something else. Now, that's *It*! That's concentration. Living in the moment. Hell could have frozen over for all he cared. He had created a whole world, which met his needs. He created a virtual reality in that little hut. I remember a philosopher once said that we make our life the way we want it around us, in much the same way a snail makes his shell around him. But, that's not all.

"I'd come back from fishing or messin' with the boat and there Pop would be on the back porch whittling on a stick of wood. I'd say, 'Whatdaya whittling, Pop,' and he would say, 'Nothin.' At first I couldn't believe it. There were wood shavings all around him on the ground and he was working hard on that stick. He'd just say he enjoyed whittling but really didn't want to make anything. It was just fun to make shavings. Now that's *It*.

"Better than that, he'd always go down to Wal-Mart on Tuesdays and sit in the café. He'd always order the same thing, Sprite and chips, and then just watch people go by for hours. I'd ask him, 'Pop, why do you just watch people like that?' You know what he'd say?"

"No, what?"

"He'd just look at me with an innocent grin and say, 'I don't know, I guess I just like to watch people.'

"Now, doesn't that beat all? Of course, he'd do the same thing every evening about 5:00 P.M. at the house. I'd see him heading down to the dock and I'd say, 'Where you goin', Pop?' Sure enough, every day he'd say the same thing: 'I thought I'd watch the tide.'

"So, off he'd go for several hours to watch the tide. That's *IT* with a *capital I* and a *capital T*. Pop is the most relaxed and laid back guy I know. He enjoys the moment."

"It sounds like he doesn't have a worry in the world."

"Well, that's not quite true. There are the squirrels."

"What do you mean?"

"I mean Pop tries to feed the birds in the yard every day, kinda like St. Francis or something. When we first moved into this new home, Pop decided he wanted to feed the birds so he bought a bird feeder and hung it on a Holly tree in the back yard. He also bought 25-pound bags of regular bird seed, sunflower seeds and cracked corn that he would sprinkle on the ground for the ground feeders.

"It attracted every bird in the county including cardinals, bluebirds, wrens, doves, quail, redheaded woodpeckers and a few that I can't even name. Problem is he also attracted every squirrel in the area as well. There would be six or seven on the ground and one would climb out onto the limb and sit on the feeder until all the seeds were gone. Pop was refilling the feeder twice a day. Also at night, the raccoons would knock the feeder on the ground, break it open and eat up all his seeds.

"Pop decided that the squirrels and raccoons weren't going to get the best of him so he built a stand out of copper pipe, right-angled at the top, and set it in concrete about five feet from any of the trees. He figured that they wouldn't be able to climb up that pipe or jump from the trees onto the feeder. Pop also brought it in every night; that solved the raccoon problem.

"Most of the squirrels were content with eating the seed that fell on the ground, but there was one brave one that would shinny up that pole and down the feeder, sitting there for hours until he ate up all the seeds. So Pop began a series of experiments, hanging the feeder from different heights and using different thicknesses of wire. It would take a while but that little rascal would figure out how to get down that wire to those seeds every time.

"One day he came home with a rubber snake. 'What are you going to do with that?' I asked. 'I'm going to tie it to the top of the feeder stand to scare the squirrels away.' The next day we were sitting on the veranda and watched that squirrel walk over top of that rubber snake for his daily meal. I laughed like hell. 'Looks like he outsmarted you again, Pop.'

"'I'll fix him,' he said, 'I'm going to put a shield over top the feeder.' First he tried a pie tin, then a cake pan, then a large, plastic serving platter. All to no avail. Mary Kathryn would eye him suspiciously. 'Pop, you haven't been getting into my baking pans and pie tins have you?'

"'No, I sure haven't,' Pop would reply.

"I'd just laugh.

"Another time Pop came home with a large, thin, rubber, inflatable beach ball.

"'What are you going to do with that?' I asked. 'We have plenty of beach balls around here for the grandchildren to play with.'

"'I figured that if I cut it in half it would make a perfect shield to go over top the feeder.'

"I couldn't believe my ears. 'Pop, when you cut that ball in half all of the air will escape and the ball will just crumble up.'

"'Well I never thought of that,' he said.

"Now the crumbled up ball is sitting in the corner with all the other beach stuff.

"After a while that one squirrel finally took the hint. He didn't bother walking over the snake or get around all the shields. He would make about a five-foot leap from the tree to the feeder, turn himself around and hang there with his hind feet. Then he would do a sit up and eat the seeds upside down. After about a half hour he would be so exhausted he'd just fall to the ground. An hour later he would be back at it again.

"One day I was in my bathroom and noticed a few tiny black bugs on the wall. I didn't think too much about it. If you live near the beach you get lots of bugs. The next day there were more bugs and pretty soon there were hundreds all over the house. I started investigating. I couldn't figure out where they were coming from. The next day I happened to be in the garage and noticed that there were thousands of those bugs in Pop's cracked corn. I think they were weevils.

"'Pop, come here. Look at this, you'll have to store your seeds outside. Didn't you notice all the bugs around the house?'

"'Yeah but I didn't think anything about it,' he said with a totally straight face.

"At first he stored the seeds in the trunk of his car. Then noticed raccoon paw prints all over his car the next morning. Then he tried the screened-in porch of his shed. A week later I noticed that a squirrel or raccoon had chewed a big hole in the screen and ate up all his seeds.

"'Pop, you need to put the seeds in the old trash can with a lid. That will keep them out.'

"'That's a good idea,' he said.

"Finally Pop just gave up and is content sitting on the veranda, whittling nothing, observing the tide going in and out, and watching the birds and squirrels feeding together in their little Shan-gra-la.

"Now mind you the squirrels have won. But Pop knew it and let go. Now the world is at harmony again."

"So, Pop has found a deep peace, a kind of inner tranquility where the world is just a beautiful place to watch and enjoy?"

"That's about right, but there's more to *it*. You see, Pop has let go of all striving to obtain things. He's at peace because he doesn't want any more stuff. Why, he used to keep putting new zippers in his old pants even though the back side had turned to transparent threads. He could have bought new pants and he should have, but he didn't. He doesn't need things and he doesn't need approval from you or me. He flows with the energy of the immediate present. Didn't Ecclesiastes say that 'All is vanity'? And, 'Labor is like striving after the wind?' Well, there you are, let go of striving and flow with the wind. That's *it*!"

"You do this, too? You have reached this same state of relaxation?"

"Let me put it this way, Louis, I haven't perfected the art yet but I'm close. I'm able to sustain my inner peace for long periods of time. It's not always easy because I have a lot I could worry about if I let myself. I have my house, wife, kids, and money, of course, to worry about."

"I suppose we all have something to worry about," I said. "But, it doesn't really do any good does it?"

"Nope, sure doesn't," Sanji replied. "Let's take a walk down the beach. I want to show you a little hobby of mine."

In a minute, we were casually meandering down the shore, just out of reach of the waves. Sanji had become perfectly serene and content again. Just like the fellow I first met on the beach a week ago. He had been shaken up by the various events at the house, but he was now back in old form.

"I'm a shell collector, Louis, always have been as long as I can remember. I love to find a nice shell. It gives me a real sense of accomplishment. And it's not just the beauty of the shell I enjoy—it's the sense of history—millions of years of life frozen in time in the geometric symmetry of calcium deposits. I'm talking about fossilized shells. There are all kinds of shells, each one is a work of art. Some shells are the remnants of a simple sea urchin that lived 65 million years ago in the late Cretaceous Period. Others are different forms of sea life like olives, whelks, sand dollars, tulips, murex, and scotch bonnets. You might say that's one of my quests in life, like looking for the Holy Grail. Each time I find one it's like holding an ancient time capsule. But it's not easy to find a whole one, mostly just pieces these days."

I was thinking to myself what a wonder this was, a man in his fifties who takes the time to look for seashells. I never knew anyone who could just dedicate hours every day to an activity so seemingly insignificant.

"What does it matter," I said, "if you find a certain shell? I mean finding a shell won't change anything in the world. It doesn't do any good for people or fix any problems. It doesn't do anything important."

"There you go again, Louis. You really do need to learn to relax. Why must there always be an end result? Why do you always have to 'do' something? You gotta learn to enjoy the moment for just what it is, a moment in time, a time that never was before, only exists now, and won't ever be again."

Just then, Sanji leaned over to grab a shell that a wave had just washed in and I heard a deep groan. Sanji was on his knees holding his back.

"What's the matter, Sanji?" I cried.

"It's my back, Louis. It's my back. Give me your hand." Sanji winced in pain.

I grabbed his arm and helped him slowly to his feet. He was hunched over like a broken board. One hand was holding his lower spine, the other reaching out for balance.

"I've done it again! Dadgum it! Thrown my back out."

"You've thrown a disc?" I asked.

"Yeah…uhhhhhhh…wow." He winced in pain. "Every now and then I do this. It'll be all right in a day or two. Let's head back."

Off we went, slowly and gingerly, a few steps at a time. I held his arm like an aging parent.

"It's an old injury, nothin' to worry about. This thing just slows me up a little, that's all. I'll tell you the truth, getting older is damn tough. In my younger days I used to be lean, powerful and lightning fast."

It took us quite a while to get back to the car. Sanji could only go at a snail's pace. It's amazing that a small thing in our bodies can make such a big difference in our life. Just a small disc in the back can turn us from the picture of strength into an old man in a second.

The afternoon sky was brilliant as we walked. The colors were gorgeous and the ocean waves kept rolling onto shore.

I collected Sanji's bags from the hotel and drove him home.

10

Learning the path

*"Life, we learn too late, is in the living,
in the tissue of every day and hour."*
—Stephen Leacock

It took all Tuesday for Sanji's back to straighten out, so I took advantage of the time to read, think and write in my journal. I knew I would never remember everything that was happening to me, or the many deep things I was learning, so I took pains to write down my experiences.

What I first began writing on was the idea of place, that is geographical place. Some places seemed to me to be just plain special and most places, well, just normal. I supposed that depended who you were and what you needed. Some people feel at peace in the mountains, some at the ocean and so on. But then there are extra special places, why I couldn't say, they were just extra special, filled with an unusual power or magnetism. Places like Glastonbury in England, and the legendary places of King Arthur and the Holy Grail. Or perhaps the

Serengeti in Tanzania or Mount Kilimanjaro, that lofty snow-capped peak on the equator that has captivated people for eons. Then there is Jerusalem, and a place that means peace but has been a site for war for more than 4,000 years. And, lastly, there was Shallotte with its special healing river and its beaches. These places all seemed to have some magic associated with them—not an eerie magic, but a certain kind of inner peace. Special things happen in them. Such places function as a kind of sanctuary where spirit can call to spirit. These places drew people who were looking for something out of the normal routine. They were quiet places, natural and undisturbed.

But I made a note under this entry. Things happen even in the best places—all kinds of things that disturb the peace and tranquility. One simply can't control a place. Just ask the Cape Fear Indians. History is not always kind. Even Sanchi in India was now only a memory, a ruin.

But time also heals and places can be good for a very long time. I was so glad to be in the Golden Isles and Shallotte, an area forgotten, off the beaten track, a place of sun, sand and sea. It really seemed to be a powerfully restorative place, too wonderful to get hung up on past tragedies anyway.

About noon on Wednesday, I headed over to Sanji's place. He had called to tell me his back was much improved and asked if I wanted to go for a ride on his boat. He had a fourteen-foot McKeecraft, which was perfect for fishing on the Shallotte River. Boats were not exactly my thing. I was no expert, but I longed to be outdoors on the river and this would be a great chance to experience a whole other aspect of life along the coast. I could picture myself sitting out on those peaceful waters, floating along without a care or concern. Serenity beckoned me on.

I was dressed for fishing, with my shorts, golf shirt, boat shoes and a new baseball cap. I had bought the cap special for the occasion down at a beach shop. The inscription on the cap said, *I'd Rather be Fishin'*.

When I arrived, Sanji was already down on the dock. After greeting Pop, who seemed to be munching on a peanut butter and jelly sandwich, face serene and smooth of worry, I made my way to the dock. Sanji was working next to the boat, which was suspended by wire cables in a small boat house. He was leaning over a portable generator pulling the cord with short, hard jerks. Each time he pulled, the engine whined, wheezed and croaked. Then with a great spurt, it died.

"What's up, Sanji?" I said.

Wiping the sweat from his brow, Sanji ignored me and leaned over once again to pull the chain. With a great puff of smoke and a pop, the engine failed again to start. Sanji now looked up with a locked jaw and squinty eyes and said, "This ol' thing just needs some tender lovin' care. Don't worry, Louis. I'll get it started."

I could see that Sanji was getting a little irritated as he kept pulling the cord.

"May I help?" I offered. "Maybe it just needs a new touch."

"Alright, go ahead. Maybe it does need another hand. It's been lickin' me pretty good so far."

With one pull, the generator sputtered and spit and then started off into a smooth roar.

"Good job, Louis, looks like you've got the magic touch today."

"How come you need to have a generator down here?" I couldn't quite figure out why he had to have a generator on the boat dock. I would have thought that electricity had been run down to it when it was built.

"Well, you see the purpose of a boat house is to protect and preserve the condition of your boat. The boat has to be lifted out of the water on cables to keep it in good shape. That's doubly true if you get a big storm coming through. So we have a big electric winch on top of the boathouse to lift the boat in and out. But I couldn't afford to put electric power down here when I built the dock. Those electricians charge you an arm and a leg. So, I put my own 110-volt line down here about a year ago. One hell of a job that was, digging through the yard and around the septic system to lay the line. But, as you could guess, it didn't work. It's too far and the wire wasn't large enough to carry the current. It wouldn't run the motor. So, rather than hire an electrician at those high rates, I just bought this little generator and put it on wheels. I just roll it down here when I need it."

"Seems like a lot of trouble to me," I said, still analyzing the situation.

"Sure it's a little trouble but, hey, I got time and usually it doesn't give me all this much trouble to get it started. Probably needs a new spark plug or something simple like that. I'll get to that in the next day or so."

We got the boat out and started down the river. It was a great day, not too hot, with a nice breeze that blew into our faces as we headed toward the Inter-coastal.

"This river's not as easy to navigate as it looks, Louis. It's really very shallow, especially at low tide. Did you know the tide changes the height of the river about six feet every day? But even at high tide you have to find your way around the oyster bars. Every year more silt fills the river in and the currents change the sand bars so navigating becomes a real challenge."

The ride was exhilarating. A 40-hp Evenrude motor churned the waters, pushing us forward with mind-boggling power. The wake ran out behind us in a long triangular shape, with rippling waves cresting over the smooth water.

The sense of control and mastery over the forces of nature was impressive. Man had found a way to harness fossil fuel oil deep in the ground, a substance which burns wonderfully. Then, ages ago, metals had been manufactured from different ores and other rocks and fashioned into iron, steel, brass, copper, and then these wonderfully strong elements were forged into a small box with pistons, which pumped tirelessly like a stampeding team of horses. Electricity pumped back and forth from battery to spark plugs, igniting the fuel in a controlled explosion hundreds of times a minute. The things humans could do were truly amazing.

"What are you thinking, Louis?" Sanji asked.

"I'm contemplating how smart human beings are to make all this stuff out of rocks. Like this engine on the boat. It's nothing but rocks. Can you imagine that?"

"What in the world are you talking about, Louis?"

"Aw forget it, just thinking that's all."

For a minute or two I leaned back, reclining my head to warm my face in the bright sun. The boat was gliding across the water. And all things were good.

Suddenly the boat lurched as we scraped something on the bottom. Within a blink of an eye we came to an abrupt stop. I was thrown forward and stopped just short of putting my head through the windshield. The boat slid across a strand of sand and oyster shells and came to a bumpy slithering halt.

"What in the world?" I moaned as I pushed myself back to an upright position.

"Well, *shit on a stick*," Sanji yelled. "Where in the hell did this oyster bar come from? I've never seen it before!" With that he stomped the bottom of the boat two or three times and slammed his hands down on the steering wheel. Suddenly he leaped to his feet. Standing up now with both hands on his hips he stomped his right foot methodically on the floor of the boat a few more times. "This isn't supposed to be here. I mean it. This just isn't supposed to be here. What in God's name has happened here!"

"Are we stuck?" I asked. Looking around I saw the sand and shells just inches beneath the water. The boat was sitting squarely on an oyster bar.

"We're not going to sink are we?" I was fast becoming alarmed as it dawned on me that we were in a serious predicament.

Sanji looked at me with a mischievous grin, "Don't worry, Louis, it's only an oyster bar, let's just get out and push. I think we can pop right off this thing. I've done it before."

We stepped out of the boat into a brown muck filled with oyster shells and sand up to our thighs. After about a ten minutes of pushing, through mud and shells, we had only managed to gain a few feet. Pushing had only made the boat settle in deeper. We were too far aground to get out of this one very easily. The brown mud seemed like some kind of a quicksand or something and I was getting more anxious by the minute.

"Hey, Sanji! This isn't working. The boat isn't going to sink down into the sand, is it?"

"It won't sink, Louis. It's hard about three feet down. I've been on these bars before. But, one thing is for sure, pushing is not working, we're going to have to wait for the tide to come in to lift us off. Let's get back in the boat and wait. There's nothing else we can do."

Back in the boat, soaking wet and covered in mud up to our waists, we were quite a sight to behold.

"I don't guess we'll be fishing for a while," I said, trying to be humorous.

"No, but you can grab a few oysters if you want. Only trouble is, I didn't bring my special sauce." We both laughed, but Sanji didn't look all that happy.

"Sorry, Louis. Looks like our day isn't going to be what I'd hoped for. All I can say is, *shit on a stick.*" There was that phrase again. He exaggerated each syllable with great emphasis as he slowly uttered the words one more time.

"That's an unusual phrase, Sanji." I realized I had never heard that one before.

"Sorry about that, Louis. I'm trying to curtail my cussing. I only say that when I'm really angry.

"Where'd you pick that one up?" I inquired.

"I made that one up myself, like most of the things I say. I hate to mindlessly use other people's sayings."

"Okay, I'm ready to hear this one," I said.

"If you insist. And since we're stuck here for a while I'll tell you how I got this one. Many years ago I was deer hunting in the mountains of Virginia when suddenly I felt nature calling. I picked out what looked like a good spot. There were a few sticks lying around, which is not unusual, you know, just twigs and broken branches lying on the floor of the forest. The temperature was around twenty degrees and the wind was really blowing hard. I was in a bit of a hurry because my buns were literally freezing off. So as soon as I had finished my business, I moved to one side to pull up my drawers and inadvertently stepped on one of those sticks. I couldn't believe it. That damn stick flew up and flung crap all over me, all over my frozen buttocks. Needless to say I was mad as hell. I cussed and carried on for a few minutes and cleaned myself up as best I could with leaves and stuff. All I could say for about ten minutes was 'shit on a stick,' over and over again."

I smiled. "That's a pretty funny story, Sanji. I wish I'd been there to have seen that. You know, a bird up in a nearby tree!"

"Sure it's funny now. It's given a great phrase for a situation just like this. Besides if you could see yourself now, Louis, you look just like shit on a stick."

"Oh thanks a lot, and you look like a double."

We both laughed one of those hardy, healthy laughs, the kind that only comes along once in a blue moon.

"Well, what do you say we open the cooler and have some iced tea? You know this river can get the best of you sometimes. You merely have to go with the flow. You just simply can't fight it."

Sanji took a long swig of his iced tea and leaned back in his captain's chair. "Did I tell you about my last fishing trip?"

"No, I don't believe you have." I should have known by now that there was always a story.

"Yeah well, it was early June. Shallotte Point Volunteer Fire Department has its big flounder tournament. I'd spent a whole week getting the boat ready. I tuned and oiled the engine, stocked up on supplies and fishin' gear and cleaned the boat inside and out. I mean I was ready. My son-in-law, TJ, came down from Virginia for the big day on Friday. We loaded up at seven in the morning so we could get down to the starting point by eight A.M. to register. We start the engine and get out about 50 yards from the dock and the motor dies. It just stops dead."

"You're kidding," I said.

"Nope. It died sure as I'm sittin' here."

"That must have been terrible after all the work you'd done." I was trying to be understanding.

"Terrible? That's an understatement. It was a disaster. All the contestants had to report in by 8:00 down at the point if they wanted to fish in the tournament. And, there we were, floating in the water within sight of my own dock. We practically took the engine apart to find the trouble. It took about a half hour before we found the problem. One little rubber washer was split on the fuel line leading into the engine. Air was mixing in with the gas and stalling it.

I was determined not to let one little bitty washer kill this tournament for me so we rowed back to the dock and I jumped into the car, drove down to Wal-Mart to pick up a new one. Well, to make a long story short, we finally fixed the problem and made it to the tournament to check in about nine-thirty A.M. They let us fish but it was too late to catch much and I knew that. I was in a sour mood all day. That washer, one little piece of rubber, messed up a whole weekend of enjoyment. Do you know what we caught that day?"

"I can't imagine," I said, trying to be empathetic.

"We caught one lousy flounder about eleven inches long, hardly enough for one fillet."

"So, I guess the whole day was a total loss?" I was fishing for a little insight. Sanji couldn't possibly let that incident defeat him and wreck his serenity.

"No, Louis, it wasn't a total loss. I learned a valuable lesson that day."

Here *it* comes, I thought, another saying. "Yeah. What was that?"

"Look down in that box under your feet."

I reached down and unlocked the box. There were all sorts of washers, nuts, screws and electrical tape inside.

"You see all those spare parts?" he said matter-of-factly. "That's what I learned. It was to always keep a few washers and assorted hardware on the boat for emergencies. Yep. That's what I learned. Pretty simple, huh?"

"Yep, pretty simple."

"So I have a little saying I always use nowadays: *If you got spare parts, every day is a good day!*"

Having expected a somewhat deeper reflection on life, or perhaps a more significant proverb or a saying, I was a bit deflated.

"Well you sure are prepared now," I said with little enthusiasm.

"Yes. Prepared for everything, but this dang fangled oyster bar."

I mused over our exchange for a few minutes, looking out at the water. In a certain way, he was absolutely right. There was a very deep wisdom here. Perhaps the simplicity of the response was where the truth lie. The simple, unadulterated, lesson that one must account for all the small things in life is a powerful truism. People must be prepared for life by accounting for all the little things that can happen. You must be prepared and shouldn't overlook even tiny things like an extra washer. I began wondering if I had brought any tools in my car for emergencies. Heck, I don't think I had even brought a flashlight. So, it's the little things in life, just the little things. I would write this down tonight.

"We gonna be here a while?" I asked. The early afternoon sun was getting hotter as we sat without shade in the stern of the little boat, stuck like a fly in peanut butter.

"I figure about three more hours. You better break out the hooch, my nerves are itching."

With that said, we both took a few hits off the old jar. That wonderful elixir helped us tolerate the heat of the day.

Our time on the oyster bar was not so bad. We watched the tide come in inch by inch, rising with the strong current. The rising water slapped and caressed the boat like a giant serpent coiling around us, ever tightening its grip.

It's amazing what you can see when you have time, and we had plenty of that. I noticed the hundreds of forms of life everywhere, in the water, sky, trees and the marsh grass. The water was filled with little things I never noticed before. There was plankton, small swimming things the size of a grain of sand, small fish, worms, and assorted larger fish. An eel swam by at one point, sliding its way across the sandy bottom. All kinds of birds flew overhead. You had your seagulls of course but also a kingfisher, herons, even robins and cardinals flew across the river from shore to shore. I was astounded at the earth so teaming with life. There was such diversity of forms and functions, but all with one purpose—eating. Each species spent their day searching for food. I imagined that maybe eighty percent of their time was for this very purpose, always looking and sometimes fighting for the next meal. But unlike humans they seemed to accomplish their task with a certain contentment. Each day these creatures would wake up and do the same thing over and over again. They were in one sense struggling against the world in which they lived but they did not seem to fight it. They flowed from one moment to the next in a routine that seemed devoid of worry or anxiety. Granted they didn't have the complications we do, they don't have to concern themselves with tilling the soil, planting or harvesting what they eat or with accumulating the means of exchange that we call money. In matters of relationships, these creatures don't have complex human emotions to deal with nor do they struggle with what we call "fulfillment." Perhaps this simplicity is what Sanji was aiming for.

Sanji had written out a few more sayings during the time. One he shared with me.

"Louis, I got another one here that can be used whenever you get caught in a jam. When things just go against you and there is nothing you can do about it."

"Okay, what is it?"

"The wind blew, and the shit flew."

I nodded approvingly and said, "Great, I'll remember that."

He went back to writing. He was not in the happiest of moods.

For myself, I was glad for the time on the oyster bar, it taught me to be still, to look carefully and to see the difference between what was real and what was only a maybe. I'm sure that catching fish would have been fine, too, but look what I would have missed.

Just as Sanji had predicted, the high tide slowly lifted us up off of the oyster bar and we were able to continue on our way no worse for the wear. Sanji made a mental note of this new sandbar for future reference as he circled the boat around it to head back upstream to the house.

When we arrived back at the dock, Sanji seemed quite piqued. He wanted this to be a day of relaxation for me and in his mind it turned out just the opposite. He had become agitated at yet another unfortunate incident while I had actually enjoyed the time. I noticed that I was much more relaxed and content. Perhaps we had stumbled on a little secret about the healing quality of time, especially time on this river. Nothing like getting stuck somewhere to force you to be present to what surrounds you.

11
a flunky job

*"By the time a person has achieved years adequate
for choosing a direction,
the die is cast and the moment has long since passed
that determined the future."*
—Zelda Fitzgerald, Save me the Waltz, 1932

With the boat safely tied up and raised in its upper position, we sat down on the edge of the dock for a few minutes. The river was peaceful in the lengthening light of the late afternoon sun. In a quiet moment of reflection, I was aware that I was happy to be back ashore again but the trip had been so very helpful. My time on the river had slowed me up once again. Although I had been ready for a fishing trip, we had ended up marooned on a sand bar. But in that time, I was able to see the incredible life all around me and to even enjoy just being there. I had found a contentment in the stillness and in doing nothing. Now we sat on the dock dangling our feet in the rising waters.

As the early evening approached, the river came even more to life. Fish jumped and splashed in the shadowy light. We watched in simple awe as these water-bound, sleek and powerfully built ocean Spot leapt from the water with the grace of a ballerina only to fall back to the liquid mass with a splash and a gurgle. Why they jump I don't know, but whatever the reason, it is good to be there to cheer them on in their resplendent acts of exuberance.

The sun had not yet set in the western sky. It was hanging in the balance just over the tree tops when the stillness of the river was shattered. Gun shots rang out from somewhere up the river. One shot after another shattered the hush of the early evening.

Bang…Vroom…Bang…Vroom…Bang…Vroom…

Echoes resounded throughout the bayou for three or four seconds each.

"What in the world is going on?" I turned and asked. "Who is that out there shooting?"

"That, my friend, is one of my neighbors a few houses up river. He's got a teenage boy," Sanji replied. He was not pleased. I could tell by the way he bowed his head between his shoulders and shook it slowly side to side.

"Yeah, that's the boy all right."

"What in all of heaven is he shooting at?"

Bang—Vroom…

"Beats me. He just goes out and shoots for fun. Maybe he's shooting at oysters. I don't know."

"How long has that been going on?" Clearly this was intolerable in such a lovely place.

"I would say about a year. Seems he got a gun for his birthday or something and he just goes out now and then, shooting into the water."

"That's just not right," I said in a huff.

"No it isn't, but in a way I know what he's doing. In my younger days, I used to do a lot of hunting. Of course you have to do a little target shooting and such. But it seems certain guys just need to let off steam. We would call those guys blasters. They would just blast all the time. If something wasn't moving they would blast at rocks, logs, pine cones, at anything, moving or not."

Bang—Vroom…

"Can't you get that stopped? There must be some laws or something."

"You'd think so, but not down here. There's not a thing I can do about it. I've already tried."

"You filed a complaint?"

"No," he said. And then his cheek gave one of those twitches and his eye lids twittered a little. "You can't just go and call the police on your neighbors. Besides, everyone shoots down here. But I will tell you what I did do.

"I went down to the house one day a while back. I was going to have a nice conversation, you know, ask them nicely to stop shooting all the time. Well, I knock on the door and this big fellow with a torn T-shirt and a 52-inch waist and with biceps to match answers. I no more than got a few words out when the behemoth pushes me off his front porch. He was ready to haul off and hit me when I backed off up the driveway. Last thing I heard were words I don't care to repeat. I mean to tell you this guy just went ballistic at the mere mention of a complaint."

"Sounds like a giant redneck to me." I knew that might sound insulting, but that's what I visualized, a giant hulking redneck with an out-of-control son.

"You may be right, Louis, but we don't use that word around here. Could get you into deep trouble. An awful lot of people from this area work in the sun, and they mostly all drive pickup trucks and drink a little, so we're awful careful about who we call rednecks if we use that expression at all."

"Well I used to work a lot of construction up north in my younger days, especially summers during college and I'll never forget this one guy. He was lead carpenter on a job and just as gritty and country as you can get. One day he said, 'Hey, college (that's what they called us summer guys who went to college), you know what?'

"'No, what?'

"'I know I'm a redneck and that suits me just fine. At least I don't have an identity crisis. I drink, cuss, smoke, whistle at the women, and work all day in the hot sun. But at least I know who I am! What about that, college?' He'd tell me that about every three days just to rib me."

"Sounds like he was onto something," Sanji replied.

"I'll never forget that guy 'cause then I go back to college and everyone in those days was having an identity crisis. You know, stuff like 'who am I,' 'where did I come from,' 'where am I going.' All kind of stupid questions like that. Looking back on the whole thing it was kind of pathetic. Here we were getting first class advanced education and we didn't even know who we were. Unbelievable! And this redneck carpenter knows exactly who he is."

"Yeah ain't that just the way it is."

"Sure, but, I didn't mean to get into all that," I said. "What did you do after your encounter with this neighbor?"

"I called the police, but nothing ever came of it. Old family, you know. They've been in the Shallotte area for generations."

"So this kid can just disturb everyone on the river whenever he darn well pleases?"

"That's about right, Louis." Sanji was not smiling at this point. He was wearing a sad countenance, a sort of despondency was creeping all around him.

"That just destroys all the peace and quiet around here, doesn't it?"

"Yep, sure does."

"Looks like paradise has a few hitches in it," I responded.

"I have to tell you something, Louis," he said softly. "I know all this life looks pretty great to you, and it is in its own way. But it's not perfect. It seems that just when you have things the way you want them something happens. It is as if you can't hold the universe still for more than a moment before something changes. And things always change. So change is the only thing you can count on. It is the only thing that is constant—change.

With that said, I could see Sanji struggling for more words but they did not come. Only his fingers moved as they rubbed one another in a repetitive motion, half massage and half nervous reaction.

"I can see you have something else on your mind," I inquired hesitantly.

After some quiet reflection Sanji responded, "You know, middle-age is a hell of a thing, Louis. Just when you are old enough to know how things work in life, what pitfalls to avoid, how to achieve what you really want, it's too late to do much about it. It's a great mystery really. We stumble through life and then when we understand it we're almost too old to enjoy it. I love the little saying I heard once: *middle age is the time when a man is always thinking that in a week or two he will feel as good as ever.*

"Louis, you're just about there. You are about ten years younger than me. But at my age, 57 to be exact, life is taking an unexpected turn."

We sat in silence on the dock. It was getting dark now and the birds had begun to make their way to their nightly sanctuaries.

"If you don't mind my asking, what's happening?"

Sanji rubbed his chin nervously, feeling his now day-old stubble with the edge of his fingers.

"To put it in a nutshell, Louis, necessity is causing me to make some changes I hadn't planned on. It's all about money really. It seems that for a fact, *my money has been acting a little funny lately.*"

"Oh that's cute. What does that mean?"

"That means that every time I open my wallet, the money seems to be gone. It is evaporating like magic. It's acting funny, man!"

"Sounds like my wallet. Come to think of it, my money is always acting a little funny. That's what I'll tell Marie next time I see her. Hey, honey, my money's been acting funny lately."

"Seriously, though, Louis, there's a change I'm making. You know I haven't worked since I came down here. It's been one hell of a good ride. A real privilege. So now I have to pay the piper; I have to do something about my money."

"Hmmm, what is that?"

"I'm going to have to get a job."

"A job!"

"Yeah, a job."

"But I thought you were retired?"

"Long story but the truth is my money has really been acting a little funny. In fact it is getting really low. Paradise ain't free you know and I don't qualify for Social Security yet so I've been living off a little savings I had. Mary Kathryn's been working but down here you can't earn that much so I need to supplement my income. It's as simple as that."

"What would you do?" I asked, thinking that he'd just go back to his trade as a car mechanic. "You gonna do cars again?"

"No. No. No more cars and no more wrenches. I've decided to try something totally different. I'm going to try and find a part time, no brain job. I didn't come down here to put myself under all that pressure again. I'm looking for a nothin' job, no thinking and no responsibilities."

"What kind of job is that? Digging ditches?"

"No. I believe I have the perfect idea for a nothing job. What I want is a nice, easy, indoor job, air conditioning and no dirt or grease. I'm going down tomorrow and apply as a stock boy at the local supermarket."

I was stunned. Nothing could make less sense. How could a man so skilled, so knowledgeable, so full of possibilities, think about stocking shelves at a grocery store. None of this made any sense. Shocked into silence by this thought, the image of a mature, successful man stocking groceries on shelves, I found myself rocking back and forth on my hands, staring out into the water.

"What about your book? Didn't you make some money on it?"

"No, hardly anything. I had to self-publish the book and the locals like it but no big time contract I'm afraid. I'm just about to break even on the cost of the publishing. Louis, to tell you the truth, I'm goin' to have to shuffle up some money."

I sat in silence for a moment.

"I know what you're thinking, Louis. I know it sounds kinda crazy, but I've thought about it a lot. All I have to do is show up every day and someone else can tell me what to do. You know, put this here, take that thing over there, put this stuff on these shelves. Without question, it would be an orderly, non-eventful and non-stress job. It's a sure tooting flunky job."

"But, you can't be serious?"

"Oh yes! I am serious. Now don't get me wrong. This job is not the perfect job and it is not the job I would take if I really had a choice, but it will do for now."

"You mean you really would like to do something else?"

"Of course I would," he said with a flourish.

"So, what would you take instead? I mean what do you really want to do?"

"Now isn't that the BIG question. What would I really like to do? I can tell you at least half of an answer. What I'd really like to do is own my own little shell shop down close to the ocean. I can visualize it perfectly. There would be shells, collectable art, miscellaneous beach memorabilia and maybe precious coins."

"Gosh, that's a lot of variety. Where would you get all that stuff?"

"Right from my storage locker. I've already got a bunch of it now."

"You do?" I was amazed.

"Sure. I've been collecting for years. In my storage locker I have maybe 50-60 original oil paintings, lots of oceans and ships. Did you see my Louis Sylvia in the house?"

"Yeah, the one in the living room, the whaling ship. It's magnificent."

"Right. There is no one better than Sylvia for whaling ships. He's much more famous in New England than here, but people still can't resist his work anywhere."

I was really surprised by Sanji's knowledge of painting. Intrigued even more now, I asked about his other stuff. "What else do you collect?"

"Porcelain figurines for one. There are a few displayed on the bookshelves by the fireplace. Have you noticed them?"

"You mean those figures of women in different ball gowns and dance costumes?"

"That's them. You know what those are worth?"

"Nope."

"Try $1,000 to $1,500 each."

"Good heavens! I had no idea." What was working in the back of my mind was the incredible contrast between my expectations and reality. Here's an expert auto mechanic who not only wrote a book of wisdom but who is also a connoisseur and collector of fine arts, paintings, porcelain figurines and who knows what else he collects. The biggest question was where did he get the expertise for these things? I felt like a total idiot, I didn't know squat about such things. But I was in for even more of a surprise.

"Do you collect anything else?" I knew there must be more to the story.

"Sure do. I have a very fine collection of hand-carved duck decoys. Some of which are now considered very valuable. I used to pick up a couple every year when we went down to Ocean City, Maryland. Back then they weren't that pricey. I could never buy them at today's prices."

"I can't believe this. You mean you have all this collectible stuff? My gosh, it sounds like you really do have enough for a store of your own. A good store, too."

"Then there's the coin collection as well. I'd love to deal in limited coins, especially gold."

"You mean you know all about coins, too? That's a very specialized field I've heard. What do they call that?"

"They call coin experts Numismatists?" he said without hesitation, "Anyway, let's just say that I can hold my own. When a good deal comes around I can pretty well get the best price."

"I'm almost afraid to ask. What else you got?"

"I just started collecting Beanie Babies a year ago. I've got a couple hundred, I guess, even some of the more valuable, retired ones. Everything I have, Louis, I got pretty cheap and now I could sell all the stuff I got and do okay in retirement."

For a few minutes, we just sat in silence. An overwhelming sense of awe crept over me. Here was a guy who had made all the right moves in life. He had an uncanny knack for selecting valuable collectibles and now these bits and pieces of stuff seemed to have turned to gold. The inside of his house was layered in a veritable fortune in collectibles. All bought at low prices before the boom in values. But, I didn't understand why he wouldn't open up his shop at the ocean, an ideal job. Maybe he didn't really want to give the collections up. Maybe some hidden deep desire was to keep them.

"Sanji." I broke the silence. "Why don't you open the shop?"

He looked at me with his face steeled. "Have you ever ran a shop, Louis?"

"No. Never have."

"Then you can't know that a shop chains you to the counter every day. If you can't hire help, and I couldn't, then I'd be stuck from now on inside four walls with a glass door to look out. Now, that's not living, not really, at least not for me."

"But, why couldn't you hire some help?"

"Money, Louis! And it takes a few years to build a business. So I'd be stuck for a couple of years at least until the business took hold and I could hire someone to sit in the shop."

"But that is still your number one choice? To own a shop that is?"

"Yeah, if I could stand it. Maybe later."

"So, instead you're really going to become a stock boy? That's incredible!"

"Yep, that's my next path to relaxation and enjoyment in life. No responsibility, no decisions, no customer satisfaction, just put the cans on the shelf."

"Besides that, Louis, I want to get rid of all this stuff. I'm ready just to unload all of it and simplify my life. Heck, I'd be living in a simple little trailer right now if I could convince the wife. Mary Kathryn won't hear anything of it, though. She loves the stuff we have, all of it. It's like pulling teeth to get rid of anything."

Just then another volley of shots rang out.

Bang, Vroom...Bang, Vroom...Bang, Vroom...

The echoes bounced across the water in a dying crescendo of booms. In the silence that followed, we heard Mary Kathryn yelling from the back porch.

"DB! DB! Can you hear me? I need some help."

Obviously, she did not use the name Sanji very much. Perhaps she was too close to him to appreciate his wisdom. This seemed natural, how could she have the same appreciation of the sparks of wisdom that he conveyed to others?

"DB, I just got back from the store and I need some help unloading something heavy from the car."

Sanji looked at me and smiled. "See, what did I tell you? The more I try to get rid of things, the more she brings in."

We both chuckled.

That night back at the hotel, I was bothered. The day had been full of surprises and the last one was Sanji's announcement of a job prospect. I decided to call Marie and see how things were at home. But before I could dial, the phone rang. It was Marie.

"Hi, Louis. How are you?" she asked.

"I'm okay, how about you?"

"I'm fine. I...I miss you a lot, you know."

"I know, and I sure miss you, too."

She was curious how I was making out with my quest for peace and relaxation. She probed, "Are you getting what you went for?"

This was hard to answer because I wasn't quite sure what I went for. And besides, what I was discovering was not easy to explain. I would give an honest answer, however. Honesty is always the best policy.

"Marie," I said, "I may be temporarily more confused than when I left. So much has happened in such a short time. But I feel I'm in the middle of a great discovery about life. This place down here is special. I'm on to something. I have a feeling that what I'm looking for is just around the corner.

"Sounds good to me." She let go very easily. "But I might tell you that I've been talking to our Indian friends a little more about this SANJI stuff. They have let me in on a few tidbits that might prove of interest to you at some point?"

"Yeah, like what," I spouted.

"Like that sanctuary is not a place, not a physical place anyway in Hindu philosophy. The city Sanchi means sanctuary but only in a mythical way. True sanctuary is in your soul. It's in you."

"So this place Sanchi in India doesn't have any special power?"

"None whatsoever. It was even destroyed by Mongol invaders centuries ago. There are still ruins, columns and small stone huts called stupas, but no one lives there. It's only a memory now, a mythical place."

"That's very interesting. I will keep it in mind." I was stalling while I absorbed this new information. "But, ah, well, I'd still like to find a nice place to retire one day, or a place to move to out of the city. Some places are better than others."

"I'm sure you're right, dear, anyway just thought you'd like a little more on this name."

"I do, and I appreciate it very much. It helps." I didn't exactly know how at that point but it seemed like a good thing to say.

"Good night, love," she said.

"Good night, Marie."

Even if the city of Sanchi hadn't existed for centuries I didn't really care. The IDEA was alive. There were still places like sanctuaries that you can find. They exist, I know, good places to be and live and think. I knew that Shallotte was one of them.

12

the reluctant disciple

"Disguise our bondage as we will,
Tis woman, woman, rules us still."
—Thomas Moore
Poetical Works, 1872

The next day was Thursday—shopping day, at least for Mary Kathryn, who had announced in advance that she was going to Myrtle Beach with or without us. She had important items she was planning to pick up and there was, of course, the flea market with all those tempting trinkets at bargain prices. Neither Sanji or I were all that interested but, in his own words, "It's one of those little sacrifices I have to make. Remember these words, Louis, *'If mama ain't happy, ain't nobody happy.'* They're not my words but they are true just the same."

Mary Kathryn wasn't really that hard to keep happy. She had certain needs and, if they were met, then she was happy. Being an attractive woman, she required certain accouterments to sustain a level of elegance. Her closet held a fine assortment of designer clothes, along with dozens of shoes, belts, scarves, purses, and a good number of hats for various occasions. Owing to her employment as an executive for a Wilmington-based medical firm, her closet also sported a strong selection of business suits and matching brief cases. As a finishing touch there was the inevitable jewelry case, five feet tall, with doors opening on the sides with some twenty drawers, at least.

Now Mary Kathryn was not pretentious or gaudy in any way. She simply liked to look her best, a trait not uncommon among women of taste. Sanji didn't mind either. He would often tell me how he couldn't stand women who let themselves go.

"Women should keep themselves attractive," he would say. Women in his mind were important to the world of men, but they should take care of themselves and dress in a stylish fashion. High heels were especially important for the shape of the legs.

We loaded ourselves into Mary Kathryn's lovely 1995 BMW sedan. It was a great car and perfectly clean. After a brief debate and with a flurry of activity, it was decided that Sanji would drive. He always drove actually but then again the scene was a ritual of sorts.

"Alright, you drive," said Mary Kathryn, "just as long as you don't speed and don't kill us."

"Have I killed you yet," was Sanji's standard reply. "And don't worry about my driving. I'm the best driver in the whole area."

"Sure you are, but if I didn't help you out you would've hit a whole lot of things by now," Mary Kathryn prickled.

"Okay, let's go and just relax. Everything's under control." Sanji slipped into the driver's seat.

The trip to Myrtle Beach was usually about a half hour down Highway 17. The entire area is a tourist Mecca. Why, I'm not sure. It looks like one huge strip mall with hundreds of restaurants, beach supply shops and flashing neon signs. The traffic starts to thicken up in North Myrtle Beach and doesn't let up for twenty miles. Golf courses and resort plantations consume much of the inland side of the area while the beautiful beaches, luxury condos and hotels line the coast.

Today the trip was very smooth on the way down, but Sanji did drive fast. Fast enough in fact so that Mary Kathryn had to tell him to slow up once in a while.

"Slow up, DB, or you'll kill us all," she hollered.

These outbursts were usually totally ignored by Sanji, as if they were a waft of smoke being sucked out through a crack in the window.

Sometimes Sanji would slow up a bit and say, "*You just crank me up.*"

Once he turned to me and said, "Louis, as soon as she gets up in the morning, she just cranks me up."

Traffic was fairly light. I watched Sanji as he drove, we both did. He was highly focused and serious. The road seemed more like a challenge to overcome than a strip of pavement. Any obstacle, whether it be a slow moving car or a light, was to be beaten down under the weight of his heavy foot. Shifting gears on a five speed, Sanji was sharp and deliberate, like a race driver making every movement count. And speed was important. Every minute on the road was a challenge, an obstacle course, but not one of casual enjoyment.

Mary Kathryn had a patter, she was happy to tell me all about the places we passed on the road. Each had a meaning and a place in their collective memory.

There was the place where they hold the Blue Crab Festival each year. Not only was the seafood great, especially the crab cake sandwiches, but the crafts were out of this world. Then there was the place on the inter-coastal to watch the boat parade, and another place to see the fireworks on the Fourth of July. She knew most every store and she knew the owners as well, all by first name. She was an avid shopper. But as she said more than once on the way, she never bought retail, only special bargains. Then again, there were always special bargains to be had in a place like this.

We arrived at the flea market before we knew it. Mary Kathryn leaped out and said, "Okay, I'll meet you back here in one hour." And she disappeared into the thronging mass of people and peddlers. Sanji didn't seem phased.

Not being big fans of the sweating mob of bargain hunters, Sanji and

I sought refuge in a small snack shop toward the back edge of the stands. Our walk between narrow stalls revealed a catalogue of junk, cheap imitation everything from tools to watches.

The American flea market is a cross between a middle-eastern bazaar and a Wal-Mart. You can find everything you never knew you needed. Air-brushed license plates, hand-cut wooden letters for your mailbox, bags of surplus army kitchen cookery, paperback novels no one ever read, or would want to, and a host of devices for your home, all spread out on tables in an appealing fashion. I was particularly fascinated with the several adults who sold baseball trading cards, especially since I had given them up myself when about twelve. What interested me was whether or not these guys had jobs or if selling cards to each other was the sum total of their professional career.

Food at these markets could be classified as neo-microwave: partly soybean and partly plastic. The hot dogs glistening in the rotisserie looked more like a new building product than a food source. But a line had formed in front of us and three young teens ordered a pair each, like it was the treat of a lifetime. I supposed that when covered in mustard, ketchup, and relish, you couldn't taste the actual food material anyway.

I ordered a cup of coffee. So did Sanji.

"So you come here often?" I asked.

"Yeah, about once a month. I've seen everything a dozen times. Nothing ever changes." Sanji was stirring the cream into his coffee.

"So, what does Mary Kathryn find each time?" I was curious about her enthusiasm.

"I don't know if I can really tell you what she finds. It's all junk as far as I can tell. But she always finds something. Last month she spent $100 on stuff for the house. Like we really needed something else. She's got stuff everywhere, stuck into all the corners."

"Maybe she just has fun shopping," I said.

"Sure, but I'm trying to lighten the load. We don't need all that stuff. I keep trying to talk her into less, instead she just gets more."

"It looks like, to me anyway, that Mary Kathryn doesn't really share your vision of the world."

"I'll say. She's like a lot of women. They get their security by having

119

a nice house with lots of pretty stuff sitting around. I'd just as soon sell everything and go live in a trailer."

"I suppose she's not hot on the idea."

"No. She won't hear anything about it. But I keep trying."

"I guess it's like they say: a prophet is without honor in his own home."

We sat for a few minutes just watching the swarming crowd, sipping our coffee. The day itself was pleasant enough even if the chore of waiting for the shopping to be over was less than fulfilling.

When we arrived at the entrance to the market an hour later, Mary Kathryn was already there tapping her foot on the ground.

"Let's go, guys, I just need help picking up two items I found."

Just to her left were two large concrete gargoyles about three feet high each. Faces like lions, wings, and a serpent's tail, they were to be used at the entrance to the house much like the medieval cathedral builders who placed their gargoyles at the front of their gothic doorways.

"The man said they only weigh eighty pounds each so I thought you fellows could take them to the car." Mary Kathryn was matter-of-fact.

"Well how did you get them here?" asked Sanji, motioning toward the solid stone monoliths.

"Errr—he had a sort of cart. I think he called it a dolly." Mary Kathryn's innocence was disarming.

"So now I'm supposed to lift them by hand to the trunk of the car?" Sanji was annoyed but playful.

"If you can't, I'll go back and get the guy with the cart."

"No, no, no. Louis and I can do it just fine." Sanji's manhood had been called into question and, when cornered, a man will rise to any occasion.

The next stop was Furniture World, a huge warehouse with an even bigger assortment of top quality discount or repossessed items. What Mary Kathryn thought she needed was a new couch. Whether she really did or not, I do not know. Sanji was adamant that she didn't need one. But that didn't deter Mary Kathryn. Her interior decorating fetish and her discriminating tastes had already determined the need. So a couch it would be.

It wasn't long before the store clerks were placing a new couch on top of the car's roof for the ride home. Firmly tied with ropes, the last knot in place, Sanji patiently slipped into the driver's seat. He was not paying much attention to the loading and binding operations, he just stood, arms folded, staring out into the distance. Now he was silent as we began our drive out of the store parking lot.

Lunch was now called for. We headed out for whatever looked good.

"What would you like for lunch today, my little turtle dove?" Sanji was trying extra hard to be kind and helpful on this most important day.

"How about some Mexican?" Mary Kathryn didn't hesitate. "Yep I haven't had Mexican for a while."

"So be it then."

A few blocks down highway 17 in North Myrtle Beach we saw the sign: Margarita's. Sanji made a quick left into the parking lot but it was too late to see the hump in the parking entrance. The front bumper splash guard scraped and tore out from under the wheel well. *Thump, scrape, pop!*

"Damn it. Damn it." No other words seemed to come out of Sanji's mouth.

Mary Kathryn on the other hand was not speechless. "You do that every time. I tell you to be careful and you just have to drive too fast. That's the third time you've torn off the bumper!"

"Don't worry about it, just relax. I've told you before that's not the bumper, it's just the splash guard," Sanji said methodically.

As Sanji was picking up the twisted piece of rubber, that used to be a splash guard, off the driveway, Mary Kathryn took careful pains to explain the deficiencies of Sanji's driving. But I wasn't listening. My mind had drifted into thoughts of marriage. My own marriage, other marriages, newlyweds, those who have stayed together a lifetime. What was it exactly that caused people to love each other through the years? And what caused people to begin becoming negative? This was a hard question for me. My own marriage was the same story as almost all the ones I had seen. It started out great and life-giving but at some point it was easy not to be nice. So many marriages could be beautiful and life-giving if people wouldn't allow themselves to slip, ever so slightly, into the abyss of darkness, where the light of positive thought doesn't shine. Sanji had so much to offer, so much wisdom and humor, but Mary Kathryn was not always able to see it. Years of living too close to someone seems to illuminate their flaws to the neglect of the wonder that once captivated each partner. I vowed that I would change in my own marriage when I got back to Washington, D.C. Perhaps when I return home, I could rediscover the wonder. Yes of course I would. I began to visualize the positive and exquisite qualities that attracted me to Marie. I was already missing her and my heart was a little empty without her.

I snapped back to attention when Sanji got back in the car.

"Sorry, my little turtle dove," he said affectionately.

Fortunately, Sanji and Mary Kathryn both had the patience of Job, so after 30 years, they had learned a dance, their own special kind of waltz, and so the dance went on. Deep down their love was unbreakable.

The ride home began to deteriorate almost as soon as it began. Traffic was thick, snarled like a lone steel snake, clogging all lanes of the highway back north. Apparently a cloud cover had driven all the vacationers off the beach and to the stores. We were in the midst of a long wait.

Sanji appeared to be a little uneasy. His faced had tightened up and his mouth became rather drawn.

"If it was up to me, I'd sell everything I have. The house, all my stuff, I'd just let it go. Who needs all these things to be happy? All I need is a cabin in the mountains, or a trailer, I don't care. I'd get rid of all this stuff in a minute!"

"Well you are not a hermit, and you don't live by yourself!" Mary Kathryn retorted. "I'm not going to live in an old trailer."

"Yes, I know, dear."

"Besides," she said, "where would all our kids and friends stay when they come to visit us at the beach?"

"Good point," Sanji replied. "It is fun to have everyone come down to visit us."

The rest of the ride home was tough. The traffic had begun to make us all grumpy. By the time we reached the house it was 7:00 P.M. We arrived in what looked like Jeb Clampett's hillbilly wagon. The couch on top, the concrete gargoyles in the trunk, packages in the back seat. It had been a real shopping adventure.

But I had learned a lot about Mary Kathryn. Even though she did not partake of the wisdom that Sanji so easily conveyed in other settings, she was a woman of great judgment and good spirit. She had this unflappable way about her. Nothing dimmed her outlook that tomorrow would be better than today. And, if tomorrow did come, who knows, perhaps a stop at some little store would be waiting like a little surprise from heaven.

13

a bust

"Measurement of life should be proportioned rather to the intensity of the experience than to its actual length."
—Thomas Hardy

Yesterday's shopping trip to Myrtle Beach was not exactly fun—an adventure perhaps, but more of a trial of patience and a test of wills. As for my part, I hadn't minded the traffic so much, or lugging the couch and gargoyles, but instinctively I knew Sanji was coming under increasing pressure. He seemed a bit more irritable, even aloof.

Few people really understood him. Mary Kathryn, for all her love, seemed to overlook the deep flowing river inside him. His children, friends and family, endearing and loving as they were, could not know how much he longed for that illusive place of tranquility in the world. On the surface he still had great composure, but he was starting his new job and, even though he believed becoming a stock boy was a non-pressure job, he seemed to know that there lay ahead uncertainties that would try him severely.

On the way to breakfast I stopped by the front desk at my hotel. The manager Nate and I had become used to our regular albeit brief conversations through the past days. We had talked about the weather, life, and Sanji. He seemed rather lonely on the whole and still caught up in grief. He kept a copy of Sanji's book right on the top of his desk where he could reference some cheerful quotes during the day. Today Nate asked me how my time was going at the beach. I told him all was well and that I was finding more than I had bargained for.

"Now if you ask me, this whole area is good for thinking," he said.

"I can certainly agree with that."

"How's Sanji these days?" he asked.

"Pretty well as far as I can tell, but I'm a little concerned, it looks like he's taking a job."

"Really, you don't say. Well how about that! Where's he goin' to work?"

"Down at the IGA."

"At the IGA," he sputtered in disbelief. He looked at me blankly for a moment and then added, "I guess I shouldn't be too surprised, I suppose he'll be in charge as smart as he is."

"Nope, he's going to stock shelves, I hardly believe it myself."

"Well don't that just beat all. That'll be something for sure. Probably be messages on cans of soup and stuff like that before long."

"That I don't know, but it's a shame really. He has so much potential, he could do so many things. Says he just wants a no-brain job."

"Now that does sound like stress!"

"I'm going to see him later in the day. I'll let you know how he's doing."

"Great, say hello for me. I haven't seen him for a while. You have a good day now you hear?"

After busying myself with little but a beach walk, I dropped by the store to see him early in the afternoon. The IGA Food store on Highway 41 toward Ocean Isle Beach was not an impressive structure. A simple cinderblock warehouse, it nevertheless provided sustenance to countless thousands of beach-goers every year.

When I entered through the glass doors, a cool breeze hit me. Ah, air conditioning, what a welcome relief I thought to myself. It was clean, bright, and full of food. Moving up and down the aisles I couldn't help but notice how neat all the shelves were. Cans perfectly stacked, cereal boxes all squared up with one another, and the display rack of tuna looked too neat to take a can from its ornamental circular arrangement.

"Louis," a voice cried out from behind a cart of potato chips that was headed up the aisle behind me. "It's me, Sanji."

"Sanji," I said, startled. "How are you doing, I mean how is the new job?"

"I've been stacking and piling shit all morning. It's just what I thought it would be—a real no-brainer." Sanji was smiling, even jovial. His eyes sparkled like a kid with a new bike.

"You really like stacking stuff on shelves?" I asked.

"Louis, it's not just stacking, it's art. Have you noticed the aisles? They are masterpieces of placement. Every can and box is symmetrically placed, striking a perfect balance. You could put a level down the row and see how straight the lines of sight are."

"Sure, they're great looking, but people are going to mess them all up just the same."

"You gotta learn how to relax, Louis, live a little. Don't worry what's going to happen a few minutes from now. That's the problem with people, they're so afraid of what might happen that they never do anything in life."

Sanji was right of course. The shelves were a piece of art and he was as relaxed as I had seen him for a while.

"Louis, it's a good day. Last night I got word that my son and his family will be down from Washington, D.C. around dinner. First thing we are going to do is hit the card shop around five-thirty. He's got two boys and they love baseball cards, we go first thing every time they come down. It's a whole other world watching those boys find a new card. Do you want to come along?"

"You bet. Wouldn't miss it for the world."

I should have known better. Sanji had assured me that this small excursion to a downtown Shallotte card shop would be short and sweet—then home for dinner. Something was slowly dawning on me—few things in life turn out the way we anticipate they will. I had a funny feeling that this would be no exception.

Danny, his wife Cindy, and their two sons, Danny Jr. and Steven, were a wonderful family. Danny had fallen into his father's footsteps; he was an auto mechanic, too, and made a ton of money being the fastest man on the line. The boys were nine and eleven, full of life and the vigor of youth, and so excited about baseball that I knew America's favorite sport was safe for one more generation. The card shop was utopia and they loved it as much as Grandma and Grandpa. Sanji and I followed Danny's pickup to the shop. It was at five-thirty P.M. sharp.

Smitty's Card Shop was situated on a corner along Main Street, in what might be called downtown. Of course everything was on Main Street, it was that kind of town, a perfect gem of American pioneering history in the rural south, still living its last years before the strip mall invasion.

At first sight, Smitty's looked no larger than a small garage but it was packed full of all sorts of things. While the kids looked at the baseball cards Sanji and I decided to look over the CDs. What he was wanting to find was some relaxation music to give to me. He himself didn't need any music to help him meditate, he preferred silence. But then again he was advanced, and I was still a novice in these matters.

"You need some music, Louis," he said with a concerned and hushed tone in his voice. "Once you try some relaxation music you wouldn't believe how much it can change your whole attitude."

The store wasn't crowded, in fact we were the only ones there, which was fortunate because it wasn't very big. It was maybe the size of most dining rooms. From floor to ceiling there were stacks of everything: baseball cards, CDs, assorted new age paraphernalia, beads, and incense. For a moment, I was transported back to the late sixties. My mind began winding back the clock, remembering when these stores were on every corner in college towns and I wondered what ever happened to all the shops, and of course, what happened to all the hippies? Did they just disappear? Did they all become bankers and soccer moms?

"Look at this," Sanji blurted out.

"What?" I asked. He was holding a stone with a hole through the middle.

He whispered softly so as not to be overheard. "It's a roach clip. You know, for marijuana. It holds a joint."

"Well it doesn't surprise me."

"Maybe not but this stuff didn't used to be in here, it's new, and it's not a good sign," he said, fumbling with the innocuous little stone.

As we continued looking around, there was more that came to light. A bong and a waterpipe sat on a shelf next to a lava lamp. Posters of The Grateful Dead and The Rolling Stones hung on the walls.

"This place has taken a turn for the worse," said Sanji, "and I don't like it a bit. Not good for kids, you know."

The front door opened suddenly and we both looked up at the sound of a small bell dangling from the door handle. A large-muscled motorcycle guy walked through the door and took a look around. We both looked down. It is not wise to stare at motorcycle guys. He was sporting tattoos under his leather vest, and his jeans had the standard grease marks. His wallet was clipped to his belt with a chain. To top off the outfit, a red bandana encompassed his massive head.

This guy then goes over to greet Smitty and we overheard something that we wish we hadn't. Smitty whispers, "I have your stuff, I'll be with you in a moment as soon as I take care of these people."

Dropping the roach clip, Sanji motioned to me with his eyes and a subdued, barely audible grunt, "Let's go."

"Sure, the sooner the better," I replied.

With the boys in hand, we moved for the door just as two sheriff's deputies pushed it open. Brushing right by us with guns drawn, they went straight for the counter and for Smitty. By this time the motorcycle guy had also drawn a gun—all pointing at Smitty.

All of us stood paralyzed. Even the two boys were perfectly still with gaping mouths. Smitty was apparently equally shocked. He stood frozen with eyes darting to and fro. There would be no escape today.

At first, none of us knew what we were in the middle of—a stick up, a revenge shooting, or a drug bust, everything was happening so fast. But as the seconds passed it became obvious that the motorcycle getup had been a cover for a sting operation—he was a cop.

We didn't get the baseball cards and we didn't get the CDs with that relaxing music. In fact, my heart seemed to be beating a bit irregular in the midst of this fracas.

Handcuffed and guarded, Smitty was led outside by one sheriff and the undercover cop. The other deputy walked over to see us.

"Hope we didn't scare you all," he said politely. "We've been waiting for this opportunity for months."

"Oh no. It didn't bother me any," said Sanji, "but I hope my grandsons are okay. I mean the guns might have scared them a little."

"So these are your grandsons, huh?" said the officer.

"That's right and this is my son, Danny. They're just here visiting from The D.C. area."

"You fellows okay?" asked the officer to the two kids, Danny Jr. and Steven.

"You bet," they both said in unison. "That was really neat to see those guns and the arrest," added Steven.

"That was the best," replied Danny Jr.

"Okay, you all can go home but I'd like to ask your granddad and his friend to come down with me to give us a little information," said the officer as he raised his hand in our direction.

"To the station, to give information?" said Sanji somewhat startled.

"That's right, I need your help in getting as much as possible on any suspicious activities you may have encountered in here."

"But we hardly know the guy," Sanji protested.

"Maybe, but you're a local guy and you might know more than you think you do."

"Well sure, I may be local but I don't know anything about this guy Smitty."

Sanji seemed to be getting a bit worked up and I was a bit put out myself.

I protested even more. "Now I don't think I can add anything to your investigation, I'm just here for a few weeks."

"Is that right?" said the policeman, now losing his patience. "Now exactly where are you from?"

"Northern Virginia, near Washington, D.C.

"Well what do you know? I hope you're not too big to come on down and fill out a report for me, are you?"

Obviously, this conversation was going downhill fast. Sanji then made a peace offer.

"Okay, okay we'll go down, but I'm telling you we don't know anything."

"Well just consider it a patriotic duty then."

We drove to the station house behind the squad car. On the way I was saying to myself over and over, "I can't believe it." A simple little trip to the store turned into an armed arrest and then a junket to the police station. What in the world was this all about? I wasn't asking for much in life, just a little relaxation. But sometimes the harder you try the worse it is.

"Sanji," I said, "how in the world do you figure? A little trip to the store and then all this?"

"I have a little saying to cover this, Louis. *As bad as thing are, they can still get worse.* Yep, that's the way it is and always has been. *As bad as things are, they can still get worse.*"

"Well that does seem to cover it. I'll remember that one."

When we arrived at the police station they took Sanji to another room by himself to discuss something while I waited in the police lounge filling out a report. After some extensive questioning by the police sergeant, we were out and back on the road. We didn't know much but we did get to find out a thing or two. Apparently, good old Smitty had been dealing in drugs. The store was a great front and after the undercover sting operation, they finally got him red handed dealing under the counter. I never did find out what they had talked about in there because Sanji didn't say a thing to me when he came out. All I knew was that the look on his face was dreadful and we drove home in silence. As we approached Sanji's house, he began to whisper to himself.

"I'm gonna always think positive, be happy, and don't worry about nothing," was all he said. Repeating this phrase again, I joined in; it was a mantra of course, words to bring life. Together we kept saying: "I'm gonna always think positive, be happy, and don't worry about nothing."

Soon we were back at his house and the kids and Danny were glad to see us. They came running out of the house to greet us. "Come here, Granddad," they yelled from the porch. "There's helicopters all over the place just down river! Can you see them?"

In the distance, just over the river bank downstream, making wide circular flights over the whole area, were two police helicopters. The propeller blades whipped the air overhead, sending down a dull rumbling sound across the water.

Standing in the backyard, I could overhear Sanji muttering to himself.

"I'm gonna be happy…" As I said goodbye and thanks for the eventful day, I noticed a small twitch in his left cheek, which I had not noticed before.

14

Gentle Breezes

" Who has seen the wind? Neither you nor I;
But when the trees bow down their heads,
the wind is passing by. "
—Christina Rossetti, "Who has seen the wind?" 1872

Tropical storms are not rare in the low-lying tidewater of North Carolina. In fact, they are part of the hurricane cycle that tends to plague the coastline of the mid-eastern seaboard. As the hot winds blow off the continent of Africa, they tend to develop circular wind patterns as they drift over the warm ocean waters during mid-summer. By July, energized even more by the high velocity winds of the Jet Stream, these circulating winds can become strong vortexes, functioning like giant vacuum cleaners, suctioning up moisture from the sea and sending it skyward. This high energy mass of wind and moisture thus begin their oceanic travel toward the Americas. Only the upper level winds and oceans can steer them now as they sail west.

Given the recent history it shouldn't have been a surprise that a storm was brewing in the Atlantic except it was only mid-June, not technically hurricane season. The radio and television carried warnings not to take this one too lightly. The storm was not an official hurricane, it was only a tropical storm, but it did have wind and rain. And, it had a name, Ben. The forecasters had given Ben about twelve hours before its effects began to be felt along the coast. That was early this morning and it was now getting toward evening.

Shallotte and its beaches along the South Brunswick Islands have been spared many direct hits during this century. Hatteras Island farther north along the Outer Banks is the most likely victim to the fury of hurricanes.

Nate had been happy to tell me this little history in one of our talks. It was so intriguing that I had paid another visit to *Beach Books and More* to find some more information. Hurricanes seem to be rather popular especially among writers, and about twenty volumes lined one of the shelves. I picked a newly published volume called *Hurricane on the Atlantic*. It was fast reading and packed with pictures of disaster scenes back into the late eighteen hundreds. But I was interested in the more recent history.

The first major hurricane to strike this section of coastline since 1908 was Hurricane Hazel in 1954. It was a serious storm but in the succeeding thirty years, not much happened along the southeastern coast of North Carolina. There were a couple of near misses like Diana in 1984, which did drift offshore for two days doing some damage, mostly in rainfall and flooding, but it was a relatively very small storm. Hugo threatened the coast in 1989 but ended up veering off to the south where it hit Charleston. All this good fortune ran out in 1996, however, when two very serious hurricanes would hit in the same year. Both would strike Shallotte dead on. Bertha was the first in July of 1996. It came ashore packing winds of 105 mph and caused tremendous damage along the coastline, washing away homes, piers, docks, and trees. In North Topsail Beach alone, 120 homes were destroyed. But that damage had hardly even been assessed before Hurricane Fran hit on Labor Day weekend. It was a category-two storm but seemed much stronger than even Hazel back in 1954, having a storm surge twelve feet high. Losses from boats alone topped 50 million dollars. Fran not only hit once but turned out to sea, then reversed itself coming back to shore and doing even more damage. A number of people lost their lives in this storm and damage was in the hundreds of millions of dollars.

What I realized was that that was the first full year that Sanji had been in Shallotte. He had moved down late in 1995 and his house had been finished just in time for residence in the summer of 1996. It was the year he had completed his house and his first summer in residence. It must have been a rude welcome indeed having two hurricanes his first summer. After a calm summer in 1997, it seemed things would be back to normal. But 1998 was not so obliging. Bonnie blew ashore August 3rd with 115 mph winds, a full category-three hurricane. Before it had finished it had blacked out 250,000 homes and extracted a toll of 50 million dollars in damages.

Having arrived for dinner at Sanji's, I was happy to relate that I had heard on the radio that morning that we were only facing a storm.

"What do you think it?" I asked.

"You don't want to ask," said Mary Kathryn. "No storm is a good storm."

"That's right," said Pop, "we don't like storms down here in paradise."

"Louis," said Sanji, "I hope you're not afraid of a little foul weather, it could get quite nasty the next couple of days."

"But they said it was only a tropical storm, the winds aren't even very high," I protested.

"Sure, only a storm, but one with a name!" cried Sanji. "What kind of name is Ben anyway, sounds like a fat little teddy bear. Let's all go down to the dock and take a look at the clouds."

We made our way down to the dock and the clouds looked very menacing indeed. Black swirls blotted the sky and the wind had turned into a stiff breeze from the ocean.

"Storms around here are not like up in D.C!" said Sanji. "They pack one hell of a wallop. You never know what they will do. Could be serious problems. This whole place has turned into hurricane alley since we've been here. Three major hurricanes in three years. Now this storm and who knows what's next."

Pop chimed in, "It's all due to global warming you know. It's changing the weather patterns. Nothing has been normal in the past few years."

Sanji had now composed himself and emerged from a deep thought. "I'll tell you one thing, even if we get another big one, there really is nothing to be concerned about. All this is only money and money can be replaced. You can't have all your security tied up in things because sooner or later they are going to be taken away from you."

"You're right," I responded. "Too many people have all their hopes wrapped up in the material things they own. Then they fear all their life that they may lose it. It's a surefire way not to have any inner peace." I was understanding more than I thought about life. This hurricane was even my teacher. An act of nature is not our enemy, it simply is a part of the cycle of weather on a planet traveling through space.

"So," I said, "if you lost everything you would be fine, I mean, you wouldn't care?"

Sanji looked at me with sweat beaming off his brow. "I've worked a lot of years for what I have, I'm not saying I want to lose it all in a storm. I'm going to do what I can to protect it. But if it goes then it goes."

Then winds began to stiffen as we mounted the river bank back to the house. A heavy humidity seemed to thicken all around us and drops of rain splattered haphazardly against our faces.

The grandfather clock struck seven. Mary Kathryn had suggested we have a frozen pizza for dinner since it was so late. As the pizza was heating, the winds began to pick up, howling against the side of the house. Rain was now flying sideways splattering the windows with a heavy patter. It was going to be a long night. The latest weather forecast put the storm dead on Shallotte. Sanji began pacing now, all through the house, checking every door and window, monitoring the rising tide and checking supplies.

He had put in a full store of storm supplies in the garage. Shelves on one wall were lined with potable water, canned food, batteries, flashlights, and several sizes of first aid kits.

"You can never be too prepared," he said as he passed from one room to another making various assessments.

As we sat down at the table, everything seemed secure. With the first bit of pizza still on our tongues the lights flickered and then dimmed. We all stopped and looked around. Safe for the moment, we thought. Then suddenly, as we prepared for our second bite, and hoped for a peaceful meal, POW! Darkness enveloped us.

"Darn it, sounds like a transformer just went out," exclaimed Sanji. Candles had been prepared ahead of time so in a few moments we were illuminated by the soft glow of three big ones on the dining room table. The light was very sufficient and provided a wonderful atmosphere. I imagined a time when candles were all that people had. Not so bad really. The light was different than the type produced by electric bulbs: warmer, more natural, less intrusive to the soul. Maybe this evening wouldn't be so bad after all.

When the rain and winds started really picking up it was eleven o'clock. I had decided to spend the night in the guest room rather than risk being on the beach. Gusts of wind seemed to rock the house on its foundations. The rain was steady now pounding the glass. The large patio doors bowed from time to time under increasingly violent winds.

No one noticed at first, but some leaks had begun to manifest themselves sometime around midnight. No one was sleeping of course, who could under these circumstances? The first one we noticed was in the entrance hallway. From the twenty-foot ceiling, a chandelier was suspended on a lone cord. Water was dripping down the wire and onto the floor. Pop noticed the wet floor when he got up from the couch to go to the bathroom. The next leak was in the living room. A large wet spot appeared at the top of the cathedral ceiling and drips of water, ever so slow at first, began to dampen the carpet. A bucket placed strategically in both spots seemed to solve the immediate problem. But Sanji had become very agitated. Staring at the ceiling, he was trying to figure out how these leaks could appear in a new house. He began pacing and scratching his head.

The leak in the kitchen was the final straw. The wind had aimed its forces straight at the north side of the house. Water was gushing in throughout the kitchen vent and dripping down the counter. This was more than Sanji could bear. He fumed over the shoddy construction, the lazy workmen, the incompetent architects, and every other building trade he could think of.

"I'm going out," he announced.

"For what?" asked Mary Kathryn.

"I've got to fix that leak in the kitchen. I need to caulk up the edge of that exhaust vent or we'll be flooded for sure."

"You can't go out in this storm!" she protested.

"I've got to go out, don't you see this mess, it'll ruin our whole house."

"It's a tropical storm, are you crazy?" she replied.

"My mind's made up, I'm going out to caulk it up right now."

Now the vent was a good twenty feet above the ground since the yard sloped downward toward the river on a steep slope. How he was going to caulk in the lightning, rain and wind was beyond me. We all sat there dumbfounded.

In a few minutes, we heard the rustle of a ladder against the kitchen window. The wind had abated a little but the rain was still heavy. We all went into the kitchen to look. The vent was just a little left of the window so we couldn't see Sanji so well in the dark. We mostly stood in the kitchen for the next few minutes, half praying and half hoping that nothing would happen to him.

"He's always been like this," said Mary Kathryn, "impulsive and easy to upset. If any little thing goes wrong with the house or car or boat or anything else, he goes off. He'll fix it himself before he'll wait on a repairman. I don't know what drives him this way. Everything has to be perfect or he can't settle down."

"He was that way growing up, too," said Pop. "He always had to have things done just the right way, his way, or he wasn't happy. When he was a teenager it was the same. All his cars had to be perfect or he wasn't satisfied. He'd spend days and weeks fixing them up, the body, the engine, the interior, until they look absolutely exquisite—wouldn't let anyone else drive them either."

"Well he's moved from cars to houses these days," said Mary Kathryn. "He can't even hardly go to bed if there is something that needs to be fixed. You remember the septic problem. I don't think he slept for three days."

"But," I interposed cautiously, "he certainly takes his responsibility seriously. And he does have a certain quality of peace even in the midst of turmoil. Don't you see it? He's really very different than the vast majority of people I've met."

"He's different all right," Pop and Mary Kathryn chimed in together.

The conversation paused as the top of the ladder shuffled against the vinyl siding near the window. We all looked through the glass into the darkness, wondering and hoping that Sanji would be alright. Water was still coming in through the vent but it wasn't quite as hard as before.

Suddenly, right before our very eyes, Sanji appeared in the window clutching the top rung of the ladder. But the thing is that he was moving, sideways and down on the ladder—that is, the ladder was moving with him on it. His eyes were wide open and his mouth seemed to be trying to say something as he slid by the window. He was falling—scraping along the wet siding of the house—going down with the ladder like a captain with his ship. In a brief millisecond, he was gone.

Metal crashing against the ground is a distinguishable sound. Aluminum ladders are particularly loud as the pieces of metal vibrate and bang against one another. Even though the ground was wet we could still hear the commotion through the kitchen window where we had all been frozen in time. *CRASH—BANG—RATTLE!* Echoes rang for several seconds until we composed ourselves.

"Oh my God!" yelled Mary Kathryn, "he fell."

"Oh no!" yelled Pop.

"Let's hope he's not hurt," I responded quickly.

Running down as quickly as we could we reached the scene of the accident. Sanji was picking himself off the ground where he had been covered in mud.

"Are you okay?!" I screamed.

No answer.

We arrived in the rain and wind to put our hands around him and help him back into the house. He was shaken and limping but seemed to be in one piece.

Wrapped in a warm blanket with a hot cup of tea in one hand, he described what happened. It was hard to listen without wincing but it hadn't been quite as bad as it looked. The fall was not so sudden as it appeared to us through our window. The ladder slowly began slipping, inch by inch, along the wet siding just as he had finished caulking. The slant of the ground had contributed to this but so had the wet soil, which just finally gave way under the weight of the ladder. By the time he had passed by the window, he had picked up speed and was on his way down some twenty feet. He was trying to say, "Help," but of course we couldn't have done anything. So he plummeted, all the time thinking and calculating whether the wet ground would be soft enough to buffer his fall. Like a parachute jumper, he planned to leap off the ladder just before it hit and roll. And that is exactly what he did.

His leg and hip were bruised pretty good on the side he came down on and his arm was wrenched a little. But other than that he was okay.

"Thank God," said Mary Kathryn, "that's all we need is a funeral along with this storm."

That night the storm wailed, the walls vibrated, but the windows all held and the buckets filled.

The next day the winds died down and the rain let up by early afternoon. Besides a few downed trees, the power outage, and a few missing shingles most of the houses faired very well. The weather station reported that the storm had hit at low tide thereby reducing much potential damage.

As we surveyed the house from the yard, Sanji limped along beside me to the kitchen side to see how the repairs looked. We discovered large brown streaks all the way down from the vent on the side of the house, staining the light yellow vinyl siding.

"What happened?" I exclaimed in amazement.

"I suppose that's the caulk. What a mess," said Sanji. "What a damn mess."

"I thought caulk was white," I replied.

"Yeah it is if you use white."

"You mean you didn't use white caulk?"

"No, I didn't have any left, so I used brown."

"You're kidding, not brown?" I asked.

"Yep, and what a mess, what a mess. I sure hope I can wash that off."

"I'm sure you can but it may take a while, that looks to be about twenty feet of deep stain."

"Yeah," said Sanji, "just look at that mess, *the wind blew and the shit flew*. That's all I have to say, *the wind blew and the shit flew*."

As Sanji limped over to get his hose, he seemed to have a few additional worry lines on his tired face. I stood looking at the river, flowing more peacefully again. And a soft summer breeze blew across my face, caressing me like a long-lost lover.

15

Letters from afar

"Life can only be understood backward,
but it must be lived forward."
—Soren Kierkegaard, *Either/Or a Fragment of Life*, 1843

The next morning I packed, very reluctantly, to go home. My two weeks had whizzed by so fast it was hard to believe my solo vacation was over and I was headed back to the city. My good-byes had been brief but heartfelt and warm. Sanji was busy with a scrub brush and a hose on the side of his house, Mary Kathryn had gone to work and Pop was playing with some popsicle sticks on the back porch.

On the way through Wilmington, I remembered The Blue Lagoon Bar and my little feathered friend Bob. Taking a short detour before lunch, I stopped in to say hello. Teddy was just opening the place up when I arrived and he greeted me with typical, gracious, southern hospitality.

"Hey good to see you again, man. Will you be having some lunch today?" Teddy asked.

"No, not yet, just stopped in to say hi and see how Bob was doing."

"Oh he's the same as ever, moody and cantankerous."

"Is that right," I said glancing over at his cage.

He seemed glad to see me and he gave me a flap of his wings.

"Hello, Bob, my little friend. How are you fairing today?"

"Well shiver me timbers," Bob said gleefully.

"Sure, why not, shiver your timbers, too."

"Want another beer?" he chirped happily.

"No, not this early, Bob. Just came in to see you for a minute."

Bob looked at me with those beady little eyes and he seemed to be trying to tell me something. He looked awful sitting alone in the cage all by himself.

"You know what?" I said, glancing over at Teddy. "Bob really needs a friend, I think he's lonely."

Teddy came back with a quick reply. "At $500 a crack, I don't think he'll get one any time soon."

"That much, wow. These little guys fetch that much of a price, huh?"

"Yep, especially if they can talk. He'll just have to settle for the patrons that come by here. Heck he knows lots of people."

I turned back to Bob and spent a minute telling him I knew his problem. Then I hit the road back north.

My arrival back in Washington coincided with Tuesday night rush hour, but I was amazed at my reaction to the delays on the Beltway. I seemed more interested in just enjoying the people on the road with me, a sensation I don't ever remember having before. The Washington humidity was its usual stifling best, but even that didn't seem to matter. I was home and in good shape mentally.

Marie was happy to see me and most anxious to hear about my time alone at the shore. Our first evening, we went out for a celebration dinner at a local steak place called Weston's over in Annandale. We always celebrate with steak, it seems such a powerful symbol of success and promotes a feeling of satisfaction. Besides, one can sense that they have received something significant in exchange for the big bucks it takes for a culinary outing these days.

"So what did you do for two weeks all by yourself?" she asked over our first glass of wine.

I thought deeply for a moment, trying to condense the vast experiences and thoughts I had been through, and took a sip of my Cabernet Sauvignon. "It may be hard for me to relate all of it, I mean so much happened."

"Well just start at the beginning," she said, urging me on with a look of deep interest on her face.

"Okay, let me start at the beginning," I responded after taking another long drag of wine. "The very first day I arrived, I was walking on the beach. I was absolutely thrilled to be out of this mess for a few weeks. I was walking along just enjoying everything—the sky, the ocean, the birds—the whole thing. It was a very nice day and the beach wasn't too crowded. Well, next thing I know I see this guy who's sitting on a beach chair just as laid back as could be. Well, as I'm looking at him, he gets swatted in the head by a frisbee, then the kids who threw it run over to get it and he gets sand kicked up in his face as they turn to run away. To make a long story short this guy didn't get angry or irritated or anything and I was amazed at that. So I felt like I should get to meet this guy, so I did. I just walked up and said hello. Next thing, we start having this incredible conversation. As it turns out his name is Sanji, errrr—DB, no I mean Sanji."

"Well which is it, Sanji or DB?" she inquired.

"Sanji," I said quickly. "That's the name everyone uses."

"So Sanji is his nickname?"

"It's not really a nickname, I would say it's more of a title."

"So that's why you called me a couple of weeks ago. You met this guy and you wanted to know the meaning of his name?"

"Yes, that's right, and you came through. That name is loaded with meaning. Do you remember what you found out? It means sanctuary."

"So what's the deal, is he from India or something?" she asked pointedly.

"No, he's an American, just like you and me. People just call him Sanji. It's because he has this—wisdom. I mean he's like a wise man.

He knows all about life and how to live it. It's kind of hard to describe but he knows why people are unhappy and he sees the truth about life."

She looked at me with big round eyes, not even blinking. "You mean you met some kind of guru?"

"Well not exactly. He's just a retired car mechanic, that's all. He doesn't have meetings or anything like that. He's just a regular guy who knows stuff."

"You're not getting weird on me, are you?"

"No, of course not. I'm trying to tell you I met someone who helped me. Look at me. You know how burnt out I was when I left. How I just needed to get away and relax. Well, I did, I did relax. But the only reason I could was because I met someone who showed me how. I could have never figured it out on my own." At this point I had to allay any fears she might have of me becoming mixed up in some strange cult. "But don't worry, Marie, I'm not following a guru or any weirdo. In fact, I'm not following anybody. I just have a new friend, that's all. No big deal."

Marie stared at me for a minute with her blazing brown eyes.

"So this Sanji helped you? How was that?"

"He taught me about life, about what's really important. He showed be what it means to be truly relaxed and at peace in every circumstance. I learned that you don't have to be tied up with material things to be happy. He taught me to observe everything around me, to be at harmony with the world."

"Sounds like a guru to me. You can find them all over the place, even in Washington," she said sarcastically, taking a sip from her wine glass.

"It's not the same. He's not a real guru, I mean he's not like that. He's a very normal and common kind of guy. He used to be an auto mechanic up here in D.C. And, besides, he wasn't looking for me. I found him. He doesn't want any money either like all those quacks you find up here or in California. He didn't want anything, he just made me a part of his family."

Marie was not looking all that pleased. A frown had crept across her face and she looked down into her meal, playing with her fork.

"Look," I said, "this doesn't mean anything really. I'm still the same guy you married, I haven't turned wacko, but I feel just a little bit wiser. I feel like I'm making some progress on the inside of me."

After a few moments of silence, she looked at me and smiled. "It's okay with me whatever you do. I still love you. Just don't get too spaced out on me, all right?"

"Don't worry, I'm not the wacky kind." I smiled. Marie had always had the ability to let me have some personal room to grow. We didn't always agree on everything but she had the confidence to allow me my own space. I loved that about her.

"I'd love for you to meet him and his wife Mary Kathryn and Pop sometime. You would really like them," I said.

"I'm sure I would. But work comes first and I don't think I'll be getting out of Washington much this summer. By the way, you have a pile of messages on your desk, some of them look pretty important."

I took a long look into my glass and began mumbling, "I'm gonna think positive, be happy and don't worry about nothin'. Yep, that's what I'm gonna do. Yep, be happy…"

That night I penned a letter to Sanji.

Dear Sanji,

I have arrived home fully refreshed from my vacation. Marie is fine and I'm ready to dive into work tomorrow. Thank you for your friendship and all the good times. I have learned a lot about myself and about life and I owe that to you.

Please greet Mary Kathryn and Pop for me, miss them already.

I'm making plans to come back for a couple of weeks at the end of August. Will let you know for sure.

Sincerely,
Louis

The weeks of summer moved slowly by, dragging like heavy weights around my ankles. The heat in the city was oppressive as usual.

The job hadn't changed while I was away, lots of problems, congressmen calling, work delays and on and on. I looked forward so much to my return to the sea with the soft wind blowing across my face in that paradise on the southern shores of North Carolina. A place of generous tranquility and peace. To help me in difficult moments, I placed Sanji's little book right on my desk next to a small postcard of Sunset Beach. This little altar to my sanity and an occasional letter from Sanji kept me in touch with a better reality.

Dear Louis,

Hope this note finds you well. I haven't much time to write with the new job and all. But things down here are pretty much the same. Bet the traffic is still a mess up there, right? Anyway, I wanted to let you know that I've been promoted. I am now the new grocery order manager. They fired the last one; good thing, too, and management wanted me to give it a try. I told them I didn't have any experience in the grocery business but they didn't care. So, here I am, just a flunky stock boy, Now in charge of ordering all the food for the store. I have to order all this stuff on this new computer ordering system. I'll have to use a few of my brain cells. Yeah! This ought to be a real experience.
Well so long for now, do keep in touch,

Sincerely,
Sanji

I couldn't believe it. Sanji was now taking on some big-time duties. He just started a month ago putting groceries on the shelves. Well, didn't that just beat all. Of course he would probably have more responsibility now, and probably longer hours, not to mention a few more headaches, but maybe he was ready to handle it.

A few weeks later on a Sunday night I decided to call and find out what was happening. Mary Kathryn answered the phone.

"Hi, Mary Kathryn," I said, thrilled to hear her voice.

"Oh hi, Louis," she replied in a rather worried tone.

"Are you okay?" I asked. I could sense something was wrong.

"Yes, but Sanji's not so good. I'm afraid he's on the downstairs couch with his foot in an ice bag."

"What happened?" I asked.

"It's a long story but he's been up on the roof fixing those loose shingles. Bill McBride came down to help him this weekend and they've been up there for two days. Then this afternoon it started to sprinkle and the roof got a little slippery and he fell. Thank God he caught himself. But the bad news is he pulled his Achilles tendon really bad."

"I'm so sorry to hear that, real sorry. I wonder why he didn't hire someone to do that kind of work. It's awful dangerous."

"Oh he tried. But no one would ever come. They would promise to show up for estimates, but then never come. He got so upset he just said he would do it himself. His good friend Bill is a great handyman. He said he'd be glad to come down and help. Sanji is always talking about how Bill can do anything. He even has a saying about him: 'he's a jack of all trades and a master of them all.' Well, they got the job done alright and now Sanji is laid up on the couch. I only hope he didn't injure himself too badly."

"Me, too," I said, "I hope it's only a strain."

"We'll let you know, Louis, but right now I don't think he can talk."

"That's fine. Just tell him hello for me. I'll call back in a few days to see how he's doing."

I couldn't stop thinking all night about Sanji. He must really have been in pain to not have been able to talk on the phone. The Achilles tendon is a very delicate part of the body. It takes a long time to heal. During my football days, we occasionally had someone pull that vital tendon and sometimes it took six months to heal correctly. I couldn't sleep well at all.

In a couple of days, I called again. This time Sanji answered the phone. "Hey, Sanji, this is Louis."

"Hello, Louis, how in the world are you?" he said in his normal warm way.

"I'm rather well I suppose but I was worried about you. Mary Kathryn told me the other night about your accident."

"Oh, yeah, I bunged up my foot alright. But I'm able to limp around a little now."

"Have you been to the doctor?" I asked hesitatingly.

"No, no, of course not. I don't believe in them anyway. All they do is take your money. No, this will heal on its own."

"But they may be able to help you prevent further injury," I said, trying to be helpful.

"Nahhhh, I'll just let it go for now. Anyway, I got the roof fixed, no more waterfalls in the house, those crazy builders. Do you know what I found? The ridge vents were installed improperly along the peaks of the roof, I suppose to let air out or something. But didn't anyone ever think that if air comes out, water can go in? The wind just blows the rain right up into the roof during any kind of storm at all. Well they're gone now, no more slots." He was sounding as normal and confident as ever.

"You're right, Sanji. Whoever designed that kind of ventilation didn't understand about wind. Now I hope the house is finally rainproof."

"Me, too," he said defiantly. "Just let one more hurricane head this way."

During these weeks Marie and I were growing closer. I was more open with her about my feelings and I was not anxious or afraid to be real. I was confident in a new way, convinced that life was a good adventure and that it was okay no matter what problems a person has. In fact, I was feeling much at peace about life. Even my work wasn't getting on my nerves. I took every day in stride, little things just rolled off my shoulders.

In early August, I got another letter from Sanji. I had been working hard at my job and wishing every minute I was back on the beach living a more measured pace of life. It was hard to believe what I read.

Dear Louis,

You won't believe what just happened at the store. I am now the assistant manager of the whole place. When they made me grocery ordering manager, I did my best to do a good job. Learned everything there was to know about produce, computer ordering, etc. Well they needed a new assistant manager when the old one left and they went for me. So I said okay. I may need my head examined because this means a lot more work, more hours, but also more pay.

I'll let you know more when you come back down.

Sincerely,
Sanji

Sanji was now in management. This didn't make a whole lot of sense to me. How could he do it? He had a perfect life going, no headaches, no hassles, just living and enjoying life. Of course he needed a little extra cash but to get involved in management of a food store, that was more than just a little job—that was a vocation. Something wasn't right, but I couldn't put my finger on it.

16

pirates and brigands

"If you're on the merry-go-round, you have to go around."
—Kent Thompson

The day was bright and beautiful when I arrived back in Shallotte. It had been a long two months in the city. The drive had been rather monotonous but not uneventful. A speeding ticket on I-95 didn't dampen my spirits, however. I was ready for Shallotte and the beaches at all costs. I wanted to re-immerse myself into this world where nothing mattered but the simple things, a world of peaceful reflection and tranquility. It was the place that held out the promise for me again but it was also an attitude, a state of mind. But I still had much to learn. Watching Sanji was like watching someone who was at the pinnacle of his career, except this career wasn't business or sports, it was life. He had captured the ability to enjoy all the small moments each passing hour brings.

While I had driven down the interstate, I had imagined what it was I wanted most in life. Material things and success could never bring me peace, I knew that. But I wanted to know more and I knew Sanji still had unlocked secrets to discover that might suggest how I could be lifted from the treadmill I was on. I wanted to know if there was truly a way for me to find that same inner peace that he had.

Before I checked back in at the Continental down at the beach, I stopped by Sanji's to see how everyone was. Mary Kathryn was at work so no one answered the door. I walked around back to find Sanji and Pop hard at work on the dock. Sanji was chest high in the water under the boat house and Pop was up on the pier. There seemed to be a bit of a disturbance when I stepped out to meet them. Sanji was waving his hands furiously in the air. Pop was just looking around and pointing at the water. Words were being exchanged.

"What do you mean it's right over there, Pop?" Sanji bellowed out. "I'm standing in three feet of mud here!"

Pop was quick to reply. "It's just right there, reach your hand down and just grab it."

"Reach down? In three feet of mud? Ah come on, Pop! That was a $300 wrench. It was a special tool! You've got to hand these tools to me, not throw them!" Sanji was very upset. His mechanic's tools were too expensive to replace. They were bought over years of work, mostly on time payments and were worth a lot of money.

When they both looked up and saw me coming they blurted out in a dutiful unison, "Hi, Louis!" Then they turned and glared back at each other.

"Hello, gentlemen. Looks like you've had a bit of bad luck." I shook my head from side to side as to let them know of my deep sympathy.

"Yeah. You can say that again. Just lost one of my most expensive tools right here in the mud." Sanji looked around him as if with x-ray eyes into the water as small ripples gently lapped against his chest high waders.

"Can I help?" I asked, knowing that I couldn't possibly do anything to remedy the situation.

"Sure," Sanji yelled back, "you can throw Pop in here with me." He laughed as he wiped his brow and hung his hand over the boat lift that was dangling just in front of him.

Pop chuckled a little, too, and so did I. This was better. I sure didn't want to see a commotion just as I was settling back into the area for a few weeks. I was curious by this time what the problem was, though.

"What are you fixing down there anyway?" I asked.

Sanji jumped quickly to reply, "Seems that the boat lift was not welded properly at the factory so they sent me a new one to put on. They didn't exactly volunteer the information, mind you, I discovered it myself. I was looking one day at the metal joints and I knew they weren't welded correctly. They just didn't seem right. I was sure that my boat would just drop into the water one day and float away. To make a long story short the lift company finally agreed with me and sent me these new I-beams. But then I had to put them on. Nobody around here to do this kind of work."

"Looks like a big job," I said, trying to find some words to help. "It's hell owning property. The more stuff you got, the more to fix. That's the problem with owning stuff."

This was the truth and it struck me with new severity. It was true, stuff breaks. It was a matter of looking at the bigger picture. All physical things break down at some point. It's the law of entropy. All things tend to disorder. Whatever complex stuff we find in the universe, whether natural stars or manmade machines, they always break down into less complex forms, and so forth. The universe is always working against more complex formations. For the human being, this presents quite a maintenance problem. We put mechanical things together and then they start to run down and break. At some point everything will need to be repaired. That's just it. No way around it.

I was just finishing this deep reflection when my concentration was broken. A loud sound pounded us from just overhead. It was a helicopter, flying straight overhead at a very fast speed. *Pata pata pata pata pata...vrooooom!* It was just like the day I left two months ago. The copter flew almost directly over us as it rushed down the river, covering us all with a wet spray.

"Oh shit, not again," Sanji blurted out, wiping a bit of water from his cheek.

Pop and I just stared from the dock as the craft proceeded to circle a clump of woods just down river from us. In a flash it was back out over the water making double loops around the shoreline. Then, as fast as it came, it disappeared down the waterway.

"Haven't seen one of those for a few weeks now," Pop said with his mouth half gaping open.

Sanji joined in, "Well doesn't that just beat all. They must be looking for something."

"Has to be the police," I said. "Who else but the police or military would fly like that? That was a search operation for sure, and in a 'black' helicopter to boot."

I didn't know this insight would so upset Sanji. His reaction caught me by surprise.

"What?" Sanji yelled from the water below. "You said it was the police? Did you see any markings?"

"No, not exactly. It had no markings, that's the point. That's the clue. In covert operations it's what's known as a black operation. NO markings, no publicity, tightest security possible. Totally undercover."

"Now how do you know all that, Louis?" Pop pushed in.

"It's not really much of a secret. These operations happen all the time in D.C. Lately there's been special news stories about them on TV.

"But that doesn't mean a thing," responded Pop.

"Well I'll bet you a hundred to one that something big is breaking just down there where the copter was. They don't fly these things for small potatoes," I replied in return.

"Yeah maybe so," Sanji barked back. "Let me get out of here, I'm done for the day in this muck."

Sanji slugged his way slowly out of the oozing mud one foot at a time up to the river bank. He looked like he was in one of my dreams where you can't run very fast. Like slow motion or something when I'm running from some bugaboo. With great effort he pulled one leg at a time out of the mud and climbed out onto the grass. He looked like a mud-pie, dripping from chest to ankles.

"Did you bring any clams out with you?" I asked, trying to add a little lightness to the situation."

"Real funny, Louis." Sanji didn't appear too amused. It had become obvious that he was disturbed about something and it seemed more to do with the helicopter than the lost wrench.

"Let me get out of these waders. I've got something important to tell you." Sanji was off in a mud-caked swagger to the house.

After a few moments, Sanji emerged from his bedroom dressed in his usual outfit: shorts and a golf shirt. His face was quite unusual, however, one I had not seen before. A large frown blotted his eyes and forehead and his lips were pursed, tightened along a very thin line.

"Louis and Pop, sit down please. There's more to this story that you need to know." Sanji was business-like and to the point. "I think I know what that helicopter was looking for and I think I know exactly where they're looking."

"You do? You know what they are looking for? This sounds serious." I was beginning to be perplexed. What exactly did Sanji know?

"I don't know how serious but I can tell you that a lot has been happening around these parts. Too much for my taste." Sanji leaned forward in his seat to lend greater emphasis on this information. "Do you remember that shop where we got caught in the middle of that drug bust?

"Sure, how could I forget it?" I said affirmatively.

"That was apparently only the tip of the iceberg. You see there's been a rumor going around here that there's been some drug trafficking along the river. Apparently small boats are coming up river under cover of darkness and unloading drugs right down here at Old Slough Bottom Road. At the end of the road there's a natural little inlet that comes up into the woods, perfect for small boats to slip in and out unseen. That helicopter you saw today probably was the police. I put an anonymous call in a few nights ago."

"You did?" I said stunned. "What did you tell them?"

"I told them that I had been down the road on a previous night, just kind of looking around because of all the rumors, and that I came across two small boats unloading something." He sat back in his seat and put his hand under his chin to think a moment. "But I didn't tell them who I was. And, I didn't tell them I had been seen."

"What? Seen! You actually drove back in there and they saw you?" I was flabbergasted. No more words came to my lips.

"Yes, I was seen. I had no idea anything was really going on. I was just curious about all the talk. Anyway I pulled in with my lights off about ten P.M. two nights ago and sure enough I had the shock of my life. I was starring in the face of about six men standing at the edge of the inlet under the trees. I froze for a moment and we just looked at each other. Then I got my wits about me and slammed the car into reverse. I never backed up quicker in my life, and with no lights on either. But I think they might have seen my face through the windshield. It was a pretty bright moon. They might have seen my car, too. Anyway they probably got enough of me to track me down if they wanted. Yesterday in the store it seemed like everyone was giving me the evil eye. Someone knows who I am for sure. That copter might just might be the mob for all I know." Sanji's brow tightened up, causing deep creases to appear in his forehead.

I sat looking straight at Sanji with disbelief mixed with fear. Pop and Sanji just looked back at me hardly blinking. We all sat there in silence for a moment. You could cut the air with a knife. This was all incredible. It was like a story you read about in a novel and one that doesn't end well: "Innocent civilian gunned down by mob." Sanji put his head down and was looking at the floor.

I spoke first. "Sanji, do you really think they saw you or are you just thinking it was possible?"

"No, Louis, it's more than possible. I'm sure they saw me. It was just too clear a night."

Pop finally broke his cautious silence and chimed in, "You know your tire tracks are still out there. The police might be looking for your tires as well. A BMW is pretty rare in these parts." Pop stopped and looked at each of us in turn. Sanji had now turned a shade of red I had not seen on a human being before.

This was big, really big.

Outside the sound of the helicopter had returned. This time it seemed much closer.

I'm not sure which one of us moved first. But in a split second we were all on our feet peering out the porch windows. The copter had circled around the house several times and was hovering just above the dock. In another instant it was gone, scooting just above the top of the water toward town.

"I can't take this!" Sanji said as he moved toward the kitchen. "Something is not right. Somebody is watching me, what should I do?"

"Darn if I know," I said. "We don't even know who the copter belongs to. I think you ought to call the police and find out what's happening."

"Call the police, you got to be crazy! I don't want to get involved, they may see my tire tracks and decide I'm part of the problem like Pop said." Sanji's eyes were widening as big as saucers.

"Well you could just ride this out and hopefully they'll all go away."

"That's the very problem," Sanji exploded. "If that is not the police in that copter then it's someone else, and if it's someone else they ain't looking for criminals, they're looking for me. And the fact that they are here means they found me!"

I nodded my head to indicate my fundamental agreement with his assessment.

"Hell, I'm going out to the front porch for a puff," Sanji said in a frump and made his way to the door.

Pop said, "Yeah, he started smoking again a few weeks after you left early this summer."

While Sanji had two or three smokes pacing back and forth on the front porch, Pop and I sat in the living room looking around and thinking. I was staring into space, wondering about the whole scenario. Who could it be? Maybe it was the police like I thought; after all, Sanji did call them. But maybe Sanji's fears were well founded, maybe it was a criminal underground searching for him. We couldn't know just then, we simply didn't have enough evidence either way. It was clear we would need to wait and find out.

With the helicopter gone, its humming only a memory, the afternoon began slipping away and all was quiet. The song birds began settling serenely into their nests once again. The sun was on its daily descent over the trees on the far side of the river.

The day had now been restored to some semblance of tranquility. All was now quiet but all was not well.

17

Church of Blessed Assurance

"Christianity might be a good thing if anyone ever tried it."
—George Bernard Shaw

Sanji had not mentioned ever having gone to church thus far in our times together so I supposed he had never gone, at least not for years. I certainly hadn't been for a long time. I suppose that is why I was caught totally off guard when he suggested we go on Sunday. Church for me was one of those mysterious institutions where at different times in my life it has been very important and at other times it has been totally irrelevant. I had no idea when I had planned to go back again but tomorrow morning certainly hadn't been in my game plan.

Shallotte sported a number of churches from every flavor in the Christian spectrum. There was, of course, First Methodist and First

Baptist, which held the prominent locations along Main Street. As one scouted up and down from these prestigious bulwarks of southern-style, middle-class religious associations, one could also find the ever present Episcopal church, St. James the Fisherman, as well as several smaller Baptist churches that, at some point in time, decided First Baptist wasn't conservative enough for them.

Along the several highways to the beach, sprouting up like lone outposts of dispensational truth were the independents: Assemblies of God, Gospel Lighthouses, Bible Baptist, and so forth. These churches liked their messages intoned with a bit more passion than was acceptable downtown and their singing needed a bit more of a contemporary edge not to mention some bodily inflection. Some were especially fond of ecstatic utterances and "prophecies" which, if one was properly attuned, would provide direct access to the mind of God.

This is an admirable collection of religious peoples and buildings. Much good work has come from them over the years. Their future looked bright as each Sunday families made their way through their doors.

The Church that Sanji chose was not one of these standard varieties. I should have guessed that he would be as different in his choice of churches as he was in everything else. He was not an institutional man, that was clear. Apparently he was looking for neither a nod from polite society nor an experience of modest religious duty. He wanted more, much more than the normal and quite modest esoteric dish being served up and down Main Street. After his experiences of late, he was looking for something deep. I didn't know exactly what he was hoping to find but whatever it was I was eager to find out. Something had begun churning in his mind since the helicopter had appeared.

Sanji picked me up at the hotel at eighty-thirty A.M. sharp. I hopped in and off we went at a rather leisurely pace. Mary Kathryn and Pop didn't come this morning. Mary Kathryn didn't like experimental churches and Pop, well, he hadn't seen the inside of a church since 1930.

"Louis, I have found just the right place to go to church this morning."

"I'm sure you have. I can't wait to find out what you have in mind."

"Me either. I just have a hunch that I need to go to a certain place I've been hearing about. The whole town is talking about this one little church and I want to see what it's all about."

"What kind of talk?" I asked.

Sanji grew quiet. He stared ahead into space, his eyes fixed on the road ahead. He answered slowly. "There's talk of a church that is having a very unusual revival. People from the established churches don't like it. That's exactly why I'm interested."

"What kind of revival?" I asked with intensified interest.

"How do I know? I've never even been to a revival—have no idea what it is. But I do know one thing, something big is happening and I'm going to see it first hand. When people talk there has got to be a reason."

"Aren't you afraid that you'll get into something you wish you hadn't?"

"Like what? What should I be afraid of? I think that this kind of rumoring is exactly what happened when Jesus walked the earth. People talked and said all kinds of stuff about him. All it meant was that something was really happening, there was a movement. Don't you see? When that happens people who don't want the status quo threatened begin to talk. They criticize. So, fine, that's my cue that something serious is happening."

I was beginning to understand now that Sanji was interested in more than I could have thought. He was open minded in spiritual matters. He didn't relegate certain people or phenomenon to dismissive categories like kooks or frauds. He wanted to penetrate to the truth of all things. Even Christianity, as problematic as it often presented itself, was not out of bounds.

My curiosity became almost unbearable. "So you think Jesus was a true prophet or even the Son of God?"

Silence again tightened the air in the car. "Most people don't understand Jesus. That's pretty evident from history. The Jesus many preachers preach never existed, they say whatever they want, most of them. Jesus cannot be made to say whatever you want him to say. He was perfectly clear in his teachings."

"It sounds like you know a lot about this whole Christianity thing. I didn't know—"

Sanji interrupted. "You didn't know because you are not watching or looking carefully enough. You can't see what your prejudices or biases don't allow you to see. This is the way it is with most people. They make assumptions on far too little information."

"I'm sorry, I didn't mean to suggest you shouldn't know about Christianity, it's just that—"

"It's just that you did suppose that in your own mind. Do you see what I mean? In your mind you actually did make that supposition. But, now you may know that actually I do know about Jesus, the real Jesus that is."

We were heading right down a dirt road outside of town when Sanji made a sudden right into what looked like the driveway of some kind of warehouse building. It was a long, narrow structure, concrete block walls and a shallow, shingled roof. There were no windows on the side we parked but there were cars, and plenty of them. I counted at least 45 cars stuffed into that little gravel parking lot. I had a funny feeling that this was going to be one of those experiences I would write about one day. People were heading to the front door of the West End Community Fellowship in droves. There was an electricity in the air.

As we approached the front doors, which were two plate glass window doors like you would find on the front of an old five-and-dime, Sanji turned to me and smiled. I believe we are in for a real ride so hold on to your seatbelt, Louis."

A small man with a muscular build and a strong handshake greeted us at the door. "Welcome to the meeting this morning, gentlemen. Please come on in and make yourselves right at home. We love visitors here!"

We made our way to a narrow auditorium with metal folding chairs extending all the way from a low stage in front to the back door. Music was already filling the space. A live band was warming up on the stage and people were milling around in front of the group. Some were singing quietly, others were holding their arms in the air, waving them gently as to a host of heaven. We found two seats in the middle and sat down.

I couldn't help but reflect over my whole life and churches I have known. Having been raised Catholic, I had tried a number of avenues of Christian faith. There was the Campus Crusade people in college. They were persistent if not so sensitive in their constant evangelizing. I had believed at that delicate time, though. It was a good conversion really, it's just that it didn't stick. College fraternity life beckoned me back to the world. Then there was the Episcopal church after marriage. Perfect for society but a little lacking in passion or exactness in doctrine. Anyway, I could see clearly that I had never been in any church that was so committed to the singular worship of God that they actually made people on the outside mad. But what fueled people's anger? Was it out of hate or envy or disdain, or what? Maybe this would be the experience I needed. Yes, I decided to be open to whatever unfolded.

The band was now winding down its warm-up and a calm settled down on the gathered throng. The impromptu pre-service worshipers at the front now began kneeling down around the stage and others moved toward the seats in front. Suddenly the saxophone player hit a high, winding set of notes that almost sounded like a bugle charge. The drummer hit the snare and symbols and with a smashing sound the whole band came alive. The lead singer bellowed out, slowly but with the passion of a soul singer:

> *"He's got fire in His eyes and a sword in his hand,*
> *And He's riding on a white horse, across this land,*
> *He's calling out to you and me,*
> *Will you ride with me?*
> *Will you ride with me?"*

In the flash of a moment everyone was on their feet, hands in the air and singing with the gusto of a crowd at an Irish Pub. The saxophone wailed with the music, lifting it as if on wings, and the electric bass kept a strong beat pounding through the animated crowd.

Sanji seemed quite caught up in the music. He was gazing at the band and then the people, and his body was moving ever so slightly to the beat. Even as I watched, almost mesmerized, I, too, was being caught up in a wave of praise. I felt as if the floor of the room was gradually falling away from our feet and that the whole building was being lifted up into a new dimension. The band played on, song after song, and the words were all projected onto an overhead screen so we could sing along.

At first I didn't even hear him talking and then in the back of my mind I heard a voice speaking. Without realizing it my eyes had been closed so I opened them to find the saxophone player now holding the microphone in his hands. He was saying something about God being present in the sanctuary, that the place was being filled with the Spirit of God. He wanted us to "take hold of God" to "press into His Glory." Not really knowing what he meant, I was content to look straight ahead and just "feel" the sense of the holy.

It wasn't much longer until the sax player made his way down front. He left his instrument on the stage. With microphone in hand, he started to address the congregation. Many were pulling themselves off their knees, others off the floor, and some sat with their heads looking straight up to heaven. I soon found out that this fellow was the pastor. He was short with wavy brown hair. He was muscular and tan, about forty-ish. He began to preach but not like anything I had ever heard before.

"You all out there know me pretty well. I call things like they are. I don't make up nothin' and I don't pretend. If God wasn't here I'd tell you, and if He is here then I'd tell you that. Too many people just lie to themselves. They play church. They come in all stressed out, not believing anything and then they leave the same way. Most churches don't want anything to happen that changes people because they don't want anything to change. Amen?"

"Amen," came the loud response from the crowd.

"And let me tell you something else," he began again as he started to walk down the aisle. "You and me are sinners just like everyone else. There ain't no difference. We are all rotten until we get right with God.

Everyone's out after number one. If you don't believe it, just think about it a minute." He paused and looked the whole crowd up and down.

Sanji was squirming a little in his seat. I don't know what he was thinking but whatever it was, something was getting to him.

The preacher continued. "You all know me. I was a real tough and bad kinda guy. A real rambler. Drinking, smoking and fighting. That's what I lived for. I didn't give a flip about God. A lot of you were the same way. In fact, most of this congregation is nothin' but a bunch of bandits, thieves and rouges. That's right, that's who we are. I ain't proud of it, but I know one thing, we never went for anything that wasn't real. And, brother, I'm going to tell you now, this Jesus is real. He can turn you upside down in a heartbeat."

I glanced over at Sanji just in time to see a small bead of a tear trickle down his face. A quick wipe and it was gone.

"Jesus doesn't want you to be perfect first before he accepts you. He wants you to come in whatever condition you're in today. Today is the day to let Jesus into your heart. Are you ready?!!"

The service was over before I knew it. I must have drifted off in my own thoughts. So many things crossed my mind. I had some resistance to these kinds of things, that much I realized. I didn't want this kind of religion. It seemed old fashioned, even manipulative, yet somehow, deep within, I was touched. Loving hands from an unseen place enfolded me in love. I was acceptable to God, even if I wasn't perfect. God was stretching out a depth of love I had long ago forgotten even existed. Whatever it was I felt, it was real.

After hugs, embraces, and innumerable handshakes, we were out the door. Sanji was silent, but there was a glow on his face, a peace like a deep, flowing river. In the car he looked at me and smiled. "Louis, I need a cigarette after all that. That was the real thing."

18

a small crumb from god

*"The vanity of human life is like a river, constantly passing away,
and yet constantly coming on."*
—Alexander Pope

As we left the church parking lot, I felt a great peace within. This church was really different and my soul was revived. Sometimes you can read about spiritual things but sometimes you just have to jump in.

Turning out onto Main Street, I wondered how marvelous church could be when the powerful worship of God's people was set free. The other church parking lots were now empty. Just large brick buildings looming over their domain.

Sanji spoke first. "Let's get back home and have a nice breakfast, Louis. I'm sure Mary Kathryn has put some fresh coffee on."

"Great," I replied. "A couple of eggs would sure hit the spot, too."

Little by little, Sanji began glancing up into the rear view mirror. It was a subtle movement at first but soon he began staring steadily to study something behind him.

"What are you looking so hard at?" I inquired rather puzzled.

"Don't look around right now but I believe we are being followed," he said with tightened lips.

"You mean a car is actually tailing us?" I asked startled.

"That's exactly what I mean."

I was stunned. A car following us? Why? Was it a car from the church? Had someone actually decided to tail us? I couldn't believe it.

"You've got to be kidding," I said.

"Kidding I am not. There is a black sedan with two men following us. They're trying to hang back just a little but they've just turned behind us."

Sanji began to press the accelerator peddle. "We can't go home, Louis, we'll have to lose them." The accelerator peddle was now pressed to the floor.

"Where can we go?" I asked with my heart beginning to beat hard within my chest.

"We'll head to the beach and lose them on the way. If they keep up, we'll just blend into a crowd at the main pier."

The car was now moving maybe eighty mph down the highway.

"Are they still there?" I asked.

"Yep, they've sped up. That proves it, they really are following us. Must be those same helicopter people." Sanji sat stiffened like a race car driver, jaw tensed, hands locked onto the steering wheel. The trees flew by. We passed one car then another. The black sedan was still in pursuit.

"There's a small loop up here, I'll lose them there," Sanji said excitedly.

With a swift turn of the wheel, Sanji put the car nearly on two wheels as he made a hard right onto a dirt road in a thicket of trees. With sand flying up behind us, he tore through the narrow passage and into the woods. The road curved to the right and just ahead daylight and the asphalt highway appeared. Sanji slowed the car to a crawl as he watched the road.

"There they go," he said. The black sedan flew by.

In a mad dash, Sanji jetted onto the highway in the opposite direction. In a quick 30 seconds he was back onto another dirt road off to the north. "This will take us out to the beach. We've lost them now for sure."

Farmlands stretched out to the left and woods to the right. Sanji moved the car quickly down the beaten dirt road. Bumps and potholes didn't matter, he maneuvered skillfully around them or just bounced over them. In a few minutes, we were back onto a paved road and in a few more minutes we were at the beach.

"You did it," I said. "You lost them."

"Yeah but now what? Who in the world are those guys? Why in the hell are they following me? That's what I want to know." He was very serious and intense. As we pulled into the pier parking area, he lit up a cigarette and took a deep draw. I need one of these bad. Come on, Louis, let's get out onto the beach."

We walked along through the throng of sun worshipers sprawled in front of the pier and made our way toward the north where the beach was thinly populated. As we walked, I noticed that I was still shaken up, my stomach felt a bit of an ache. Sanji didn't look much better than I felt. His face was almost ashen and he fumbled with his hands in his pockets. This was a most unusual set of events. What in the world was happening? How serious was this predicament and what would come next?

"You know, Louis, ten years ago I would be ready to fight. I would just dig in and find out who this was and take care of it. *I used to be lean, mean, and fast as lightning.* But not anymore. I am a man of peace." Sanji was almost talking to himself as we walked, rehearsing his new world view.

"You may be a man of peace but those guys who are following you don't seem to be interested in peace. You don't tail someone in a car chase unless you want something pretty bad." I wasn't much help, I realized, with this statement but I was confused. How does an average guy attract such attention?

"Louis, I don't know what's going on with those guys but I know I have peace inside. I don't need to worry. What's worry goin' to get you anyway? No, that's not the way. I remember well the last time I was in a jam with the house and all the problems and I had a sign from God that kept me from despairing. I remember it like it was yesterday."

"You had a real sign from God?" I asked greatly surprised.

"You might not think so, maybe nobody else would either, but I know what I know—it was a sign alright."

"What was it?"

"Louis, as I've told you before, I've been a shell collector almost all my life. I love shells, all kinds and I know the names of them all. I've found olives, whelks, sand dollars, tulips, murex and scotch bonnets. But there is more to the story than just collecting. You see back in 1982, out on Aseteague Island, all by myself, I stumbled across a strange-looking fossilized shell that I hadn't seen before. It was partly damaged unfortunately but it peaked my curiosity so I took it back and did a little research. It turns out the shell was a hardouinia mortonis—a sea biscuit. The sea biscuit come from a sea urchin that lived during the late Cretaceous Period of geological time and went extinct about sixty-five million years ago along with the dinosaurs. Since 1982, for the last fifteen years, I've found many broken ones, but never a whole one. Can you imagine what it would take to find a whole, undamaged shell that's 65 million years old?"

Sanji continued after a long pause. "Early on a cool February morning in 1997 I was shelling along the high tide line not far from here. I had as usual come across a few broken biscuits but something inside of me started to move with anticipation. I did something that surprised me at the time: I began a little prayer to God. Do you ever do that, Louis, just throw up a little prayer to God when you need something really bad?"

"Sure I do, I mean sometimes anyway," I replied.

"Well something inside of me just reached up straight to God and I said these simple words: 'Lord, I sure would like to find a whole one.' Suddenly a large wave rushes in and deposits an absolutely perfect sea biscuit at my feet. I mean perfect in every way. I called it a 'small crumb from God.' And I said, 'Thank you, Lord.' In that one small moment I knew that I was in the presence of God and that he heard me and that he cared for me in every way. From that moment on I knew I didn't have to worry about anything. Whether it was the house being constructed over a creek, or hurricanes, or whatever, I knew then, deep inside, that everything would turn out alright. Nothing is too small or too large for God. Even throwing a shell at my feet, a crumb when you consider all the needs in the world, but he did it, he put the shell right there for me. That's how I know that I can be at peace. I can relax because God is in charge of everything."

We paused now and just looked out over the water. The sky was a deep blue and the waves were a bright luminescent green as they rolled in. It was a good day to be alive. It was a good day to be here.

"Do you believe these things, Louis? Do you believe that God did that for me?"

"Errrr, sure, Sanji, sure I do."

"I'm looking for another sign these days, Louis. A whole lot of things are happening. You've noticed a few of the problems rolling my way but you haven't seen them all; I've got big decisions to make."

I pondered this remark for a moment and then asked, "You've got bigger problems than these guys chasing you?"

"Not really bigger, but serious nonetheless. Tomorrow I have to give the store an answer as to whether I'll become manager of the whole place or not."

"Manager?!" I shouted. "You've got to be kidding. That would mean 60-hour weeks not to mention the headaches. You would do that?"

"I may not have a choice; it looks like they need me pretty bad. They had to fire the last manager, all kinds of problems. Now they need someone who knows the store and who can handle people."

We both let the silence pass as we continued our walk on the beach. I was stunned. The excitement of the day had been enough for a year. Now I was discovering that Sanji, despite every attempt to escape the claws of civilization was being snatched back into the midst of a hectic, consuming business. What would be next?

As we came back within sight of the pier it had turned into late afternoon. The sun was sitting in the western sky, still strong, but not as direct. Hesitantly we mounted the weathered, wooden steps to the pier and just at the top of the climb we stopped in our tracks. Leaning back against the opposite side of the handrail was a man whose expressionless face was steely white. He was obviously waiting for us, smoking a cigarette, patient as a snake, all decked out in a navy blue double-vested suit and satin tie. It looked like he'd stepped out of *Miami Vice*. My first thought was Mafia. It had to be. A black sedan with the motor running was waiting in the parking lot below.

"Mr. Kennedy! Mr. D.B. Kennedy," he uttered as we pulled ourselves to the top landing. "Or should I call you Sanji, too, like all the other dingbats around here?"

We both looked in stunned silence at the man.

They've found us, I thought to myself, and my first instinct was to take off running in any direction I could. Sanji was motionless, solid as a rock, and faced the man squarely as if he was ready for a fight.

"Look," the man said, "I work for a man named Mr. Macmillan, I suppose you have heard of him, haven't you? I'm supposed to deliver a message to you so here it is. Mr. Macmillan says you don't answer his letters so I'm delivering this message in person. He wants to see you tomorrow afternoon in his office. Here's his card." He reached out his hand, which sported several gold rings, and handed it to Sanji. Sanji took it and looked at it closely.

"Is this the Mr. Macmillan who's the big shot downtown?" he asked.

"Yep, that's the one. And he says you're not too polite. So he hopes you don't disappoint him tomorrow. That's four P.M. in his office. Got it?" he said abruptly.

Sanji eyed the man carefully and then he spoke. "What if I don't show up for this so-called appointment?"

"Oh you'll want to show up, that's for sure. It really is in everyone's best interest. You be there, okay?" That's all he said as he turned and walked off the pier.

The passenger door of the black sedan swung open and the tough guy got in. Then the sedan darted quickly out of the parking lot in a puff of smoke and dust.

"Bunch of assholes," Sanji muttered. "That's what they are, just a bunch of assholes."

I noticed his left cheek and lower eyelid were starting to twitch again, just like after the store bust. He felt his pocket for a cigarette.

19

storm watch

"My great mistake, the fault for which I can't forgive myself,
is that one day I ceased my obstinate pursuit
of my own individuality."
—Oscar Wilde

Late summer in these parts of North Carolina is always hot. The rains that come sometimes in the afternoon cool things off nicely and take the denseness out of the billowing heat. This Sunday afternoon we would have a rain. Out over the water, a squall had started to build up offshore, its menacing, dark thunderclouds rising like giant mountains over the seascape. A stiff breeze was starting to well up and the smell of salt sprinkled the air. The rain was headed our way. After watching the black sedan pull away, we made our way to the car.

On the way home we were mostly quiet. Sanji puffed on a cigarette and I found myself staring out the car window at the fields and stores and whatever else appeared on the roadside. My thoughts skirted from one event to another. This had been the most unusual and scary day of my life. Even now it seemed that the story had only begun to unravel and who knew what lied in store for Sanji tomorrow. This adventure was turning into a mystery but it wasn't fun or interesting or anything else but bothersome and perhaps dangerous.

"Are you going to meet this guy?" I asked.

"I think I have to, Louis, it doesn't look like they are going to let me go until I do. Do you have any idea who Mr. Macmillan is?"

"Not really," I said.

"Mr. Macmillan is a new big player in town, everyone knows him. He's from New York, he's rich, his family goes way back, and he has connections everywhere. He blew into town like a tornado about two years ago and began setting up shop. The first thing he did was buy the oldest bank building in town, he just bought it. In fact, he buys whatever he wants. There's lots of rumors that he's into everything, legal and not so legal, if you know what I mean."

"Do you think it's safe to go?"

"How do I know, Louis? There's some crazy things happening here this summer. Maybe he's part of the mob, what do I know?"

"Okay, so he's a big shot. But what in the world do they want from you? Do you think he's drug running? Is it about the store? Is it about the river? What could they want?"

Sanji straightened up in his seat. "Louis, I honestly don't know, his letters never said what he wanted, just that I was summoned to his office. I sure don't respond to stuff like that. Now it looks like he's part of something bigger than I could have imagined. What has me concerned is that they found us and they can find us again if they want to. I have to go to that meeting. Maybe I can work it all out with them and settle whatever it is that they want."

"Maybe they just want you to be quiet. You know, not talk to anyone about what you've seen."

"Maybe," Sanji concluded.

As we pulled up in front of my hotel, Sanji looked at me and said, "Louis, tomorrow is a big day. Get some rest. I'd like you to come with me to that meeting at four. Can you do that?"

"Of course I can. You need a good friend right now and I'll be there for you. But I've learned something from you about facing adversity. And I'm going to rehearse those words you always use: *Always think positive, be happy, and never worry about nothin'*."

173

The next day was Monday. Sanji went to work at the grocery store and I lounged at the beach all morning. I reread his book while concentrating on the ocean and clouds. Great stuff. It helped me focus on the important things in life.

Around noon I couldn't take the anticipation anymore so I drove down to the store. When I arrived the parking lot was full, baskets everywhere, and tourists clad in Bermuda shorts and T-shirts were making their way faithfully to stockpile all the goodies a family can consume in a week. A large stack of watermelons was being unloaded near the front door and the heat of the parking lot cooked the bottoms of my feet as I walked up to the automatic doors. I anticipated the cool of the air conditioning and it did not disappoint. Just inside the frigid air hit me with a wonderfully refreshing blast. I looked at the office area that was slightly raised above floor level and there was Sanji. He saw me and came out of the half door and stepped down to floor level.

Immediately I noticed the white rectangular badge on his shirt and the red print that said *Manager*. I couldn't believe my eyes.

"You did it," I said in amazement.

"Had to," he said back in a very businesslike voice. "Come on to the back room a minute, Louis, and I'll explain."

Before we reached the back store room, Sanji helped one elderly lady find the green beans, directed one mother with two tots in tow to the baby food, and consulted with a stock boy who was having problems with a labeling machine.

"Now then," he said in a low voice so as to not be heard. "I didn't really want this job and I won't stay very long but I had no choice this morning. The owners gave me a huge raise and full benefits plus the run of the store. They also put the old pressure on, told me there was no one else. They begged me I'm telling you, begged like children."

"But what does this mean? I thought you came down to retire, take it easy, think and all that. You know, get out of the rat race."

"Well it looks like I'm back into it for a little while. But not for long. I give it one year tops and I'm out of here. Besides, I need a few friends right now because I don't know what's coming at four o'clock."

"You may be right about needing a few friends but now you'll have little time for anything that you came down here for. Your whole life will be work again."

"We'll see. Let's just make it to four o'clock, then I'll know how the cookies will crumble."

Up to now, we hadn't talked about it but I was concerned about his, and my, safety and I realized I was having second thoughts.

"Don't you think you should call the police?"

His mouth flew open. "Call the police! This guy probably owns them! No way."

"Okay then," I said, "I'll see you about three-thirty. I'll drive you over."

"Great, see you then."

With that being said, he was off in a dash to the front of the store.

"Show yourself out, Louis, got to run. Got thirty employees to supervise and a big shipment coming in today!"

The afternoon slipped by quickly and three-thirty P.M. came soon enough. I made my way back to the store and picked up Sanji.

"Ready?" I asked.

"Yep, ready. Let's go." Sanji had kept his manager's badge on.

As we left the store, he produced a small quart jar from a bag he was carrying. "Hooch?" he said in an almost gleeful voice.

"Sure, never a better time than right now." I took a big swallow.

"You know what I say at times like these? Very simple: *Why worry about the future when yesterday has still got its teeth in your ass!*"

We drove downtown Main Street and made a right uptown. The address we had been given was an office on the second floor of the County National Bank.

We pulled in to the parking lot and made our way to the front of it. Customers were coming in and out. In we went and up the stairs to the second floor. The corridor we reached was well lit and warmly decorated. Fine carpet covered the floor, mahogany side tables with porcelain vases lined the hall.

"Looks like my kind of place," Sanji said.

Looking down the hall we saw two men in suit coats waiting at a door. They were the men from the chase, looked like organized crime if I ever saw any. One of them waved us down. Our walk was methodical, necessary, but my stomach was knotted up. This would be the answer to the questions that had been raised the last couple of days. At least it would put an end to the speculation.

The men greeted us at the door.

"Just one minute, we'll let Mr. Macmillan know you're here."

It was only maybe fifteen seconds before they returned.

"Go on in to his secretary's office, he'll see you in a few minutes."

I've seen better offices, but not by much. A gorgeous blonde sat at a cherry desk just inside. Beautiful silk drapes hung in a graceful arch over the windows. An oil painting of a mountain stream hung over the credenza on the left. Crystal water glasses sat on a silver tray along with a silver water pitcher and ice bucket.

"Mr. Macmillan will be right with you, gentlemen, please have a seat," said the blonde.

We sat down on the plush red leather waiting room chairs and waited. I couldn't understand why a powerful man like this would send a thug to deliver a message to Sanji after a car chase. Nothing was adding up in my mind. Even if he hadn't answered the letters there were other ways of contacting a person. Absolutely nothing was making any sense.

The door to the adjoining office opened suddenly and out strode a tall, fit and gray-haired gentleman with a broad smile.

"Hello, Mr. Kennedy, glad to meet you. I'm Mr. Macmillan.

"So I guessed," said Sanji highly irritated.

"And your friend?" asked Macmillan.

"Sure, this is Louis. He's a friend of mine, hope you don't mind."

"A friend of yours is a friend of mine. Come on in and let's have a talk."

Being a businessman Mr. Macmillan got right to the point.

"Mr. Kennedy, I know you don't know why you're here so let me get to the point. I'm developing the new golf course along the Shallotte River. It's going to be called Paradise Golf Plantation and it's going to be one of the very best in the South. Why, even Arnie is backing this one up. He and I have become good friends this past year. Anyway my site planners told me you live right across from the proposed thirteenth fairway and have one of the most beautiful views on the whole river. Mr. Kennedy, may I call you D.B., I'm willing to make you an offer to buy your place."

At this, Mr. Macmillan leaned back in his chair, smiling one of those broad salesman smiles, white teeth gleaming and blue eyes sparkling like a child in an amusement park. We all sat there in stunned silence for a moment.

"Mr. Macmillan," Sanji said, "I need a couple of questions answered first before I can even entertain any talk of business."

"Sure, go right ahead, we're all friends here."

"First of all, who are those thugs you sent chasing us to deliver the message about this meeting?"

But before Macmillan could get an answer out Sanji fired another question.

"And what do you know about that helicopter flying over my house?"

"You must mean my private helicopter. I use it for looking over land. We've been over the river a few times in the last two months. A few days ago when we were looking at your place and a few other places down river. I hope we didn't alarm you." Mr. Macmillan's twinkle never went out. He was a first-class salesman. "And those nice gentlemen aren't thugs, they're employees of mine, faithful ones, too, I might add."

A look of relief spread across Sanji's face. He and I now had the answers to the mystery of the copter and the chase.

"So you're not involved in drugs along the river or anything like that?"

"Hell no. What on earth are you talking about? I'm a legitimate business man."

Sanji then continued. "I thought you already had all the land you needed for the golf course, that's what the paper said anyway?"

"The paper was mostly right. There is only one thing I was lacking, that was a site for my club restaurant. You see I need a premier location, a site with a million-dollar view to put in a five-star eatery. What I need is an unparalleled view along the river next to the course, and you, Mr. Kennedy, have my view."

We sat in stony silence for a moment. My own ears couldn't believe it. The beautiful house, view, water, wildlife, sunsets, the sanctuary, everything, might just be sold here and now. The dream that Sanji had of beating the rat race, of retreating from the hubbub of the world might just disappear into another multimillionaire's pocket like so many dreams had in the past.

"Mr. Macmillan," Sanji said quite suddenly, "my place is not for sale, now or ever."

Mr. Macmillan didn't miss a beat. "I thought you might say that so let me ask you if one and a half million dollars helps you think a little clearer?

No answer.

"I'll let you in on a little secret of mine, Mr. Kennedy. I happen to know you need a little cash. Retiring isn't as cheap as it used to be. And I doubt you want to run that grocery store forever. But if I can't buy your place then I already have a contract on the place right next door to you. You know the house, the one that looks like a brick shit house. That house has the second best view on the river. Unfortunately I'm afraid that your property won't be so secluded as it is now. We will probably have anywhere from two to three hundred people a night, not to mention private parties, weddings, and all that sort of thing. The noise might just be considerable." He continued smiling as big as ever.

"But I'll stop you with zoning, a law suit; you can't do that in a residential area!" Sanji was red in the face now.

"You might be right but you seemed to have missed something. As of last Tuesday night, that area is now zoned for multi-use. I'm very sorry for your troubles."

The conversation had gotten down to business all right—hard, dirty business. There seemed nowhere to turn. Sanji was thinking....

"I'll need a couple of days to think on this," he said. Sanji got up off his seat and put his hands in his pockets. "I'll get back to you. Let's go,

Louis, I think we're done here."

With that we were out, past the secretary and the thugs, and down through the bank.

"This is where I have my bank account," Sanji said, "I guess they know everything about me."

20

a place
to think

"Whatever you may be sure of, be sure of this—
that you are dreadfully like other people."
—James Russell Lowell

A grave site was the last place that I expected to go in order to sort out the horrendous situation Sanji found himself in. But that was exactly where he wanted to go.

It was Tuesday afternoon when Sanji picked me up, the day after our infamous meeting. There were at least four hours of daylight left. He had never mentioned this place before and I was puzzled. But as we drove he explained.

"Louis, I have a little secret place I go to once in a while to think. Of course I'm always thinking about something, but this is a special place for heavy thinking. I don't imagine that anyone in the world knows about it anymore but it brings me back to basics every time I go there. You'll like it, don't worry."

We headed down a back road toward the river, under the pines that stood tall against the sky. The road was sandy but firm. Off to the left was a pull-off, a wide place in the road.

"This is where we need to park and walk a little ways. Hope you don't mind a little exercise," Sanji said.

"Fine, I can use it. It will help relieve the tension."

The walk was mostly through a woodland path, but here and there we ran into logs to climb over and a few sticker bushes. The pine forest wasn't dense but it was dark under all the pine branches. In about fifteen minutes, we were out on a small knoll overlooking the river but surrounded by trees. The ground ran down on all sides. To the north the slope ran down into a gully overgrown with small bushes and vegetation at the bottom, but on the south side there was also a gully but this one was actually a slough, a water inlet from the river. It was fairly deep looking but only continued for about thirty yards and then it ended in a grass-covered bank.

"This is the place," Sanji said, looking all around him. "This is an unbelievable place."

"It's nice, real nice," I said out of obligation more than anything else, "but what's so special about it?"

"Look over here," he said. With that, he moved toward the river a dozen yards or so and knelt down on the ground. With his hands he pushed away a few weeds and then I saw it—a gravestone, broken with age, now lying almost flat on the ground, but with very clear hand-hewn markings on it:

Mary Lowell
died 1862
aged 19
A summer flower that fled away too soon

"One of the first white settlers in these parts was the Lowell family. They came here in 1850 and settled along the river right here. Over there's the remains of an old cabin just over on the other knoll." He was pointing to just uphill from the gully. "It seems they had five kids, Mary was the eldest, probably the pride of their lives. But something happened, probably a sickness, and she died, so they buried her here on top of this little mound overlooking the water."

I didn't know what to say so I just stared down at the broken tombstone, at the etched writing, at the weeds.

"You see, Louis, the Lowells came here from somewhere, probably Virginia. They came here to start a new life, to get away from wherever they were, to leave their troubles and bad fortunes behind. No doubt John Lowell needed to open up some new opportunities to work, to make a decent living, and not waste away his strength and his youth working for someone else. I guess he got tired of making someone else money while he and his young family scrimped by on paltry laborer's wages. No, this place represented freedom, new hopes, opportunities unbounded."

Sanji continued in a heart-felt, wonderful monologue about life and freedom: "I went to the courthouse to look up the information on this family once I discovered this place. There wasn't much of course, records back then were pretty sketchy. But I found out that the father was John Lowell and his wife was Sarah. They had bought this small strip of land along, what was then, almost a virgin river, from a land speculator out of Wilmington. It didn't cost much, but probably all they had. Anyway, they moved down here right around 1850 and set up a homestead. John was described in the court documents as a 'laborer,' but here, along the banks of the Shallotte River he would be much more. He would come to start and own his own business. The business he chose was tarring ships."

Sanji continued and I grew more and more interested in the story, especially wondering where it would all lead.

"Do you see that slough or small cove just down this knoll, Louis? That is nature's perfect shipyard. Small schooners and sloops can easily slip in and out of there and they used it as a sort of dry dock. Once they were berthed in the cove, the tide would do the rest. As the tide went out the boat would find itself resting on the smooth, sandy bottom, and then all of the ship's wooden hull was exposed to the air. Once exposed, the tar men would apply the thick, gooey tar pitch between the planks. The pitch was easy to come by since they got it right here in their backyards, right out of the pine trees. Can't you just see them down there now, Louis, with buckets of pitch, working on a long, sleek sloop with tall sailing masks, coming straight up into the trees. And most of all, can't you just imagine the freedom of living in these woods, no bosses to tell you what to do, your own business, your own fortune to make or lose? Can't you just feel it in the air, the salt, the sea and the smell of the free life?"

He paused now for a moment and looked around, smiling; his eyes were closed as he listened to the breeze in the trees and the songs of the birds as they scampered about the branches. I imagined Sanji was listening to the voices of the men as they labored with the pitch, telling stories, joking, even cussing at one another as they sweated under the afternoon heat to bring a ship back to life with fresh pitch. Perhaps he even heard the sound of voices near the cabin, of girls playing in the backyard, of mama calling out the backdoor. By now even I could see the whole scene and even smell the fresh baked bread cooking on an open hearth and the fish drying in the sunlight. Yes, deep inside I could even feel the freedom, the sense of hope and the love of a family surviving together in an isolated and dreamy place. And I could almost feel my heart beat with the pride that John felt, the young laborer turned entrepreneur with five children, a beautiful wife, and a place of his own in the wilds of North Carolina tidewater country.

Sanji continued. "Many people don't know what it takes to get started, Louis, the risk, the raw courage to set out on your own. Some people want this freedom bad enough that they will do anything to get it. Others just sit back and take whatever circumstances life gives them. Isn't that funny, Louis, how people are so different? But I'm an awful lot like this John. I feel like I know him, like he and I are kindred spirits. He came here in 1850 and I came in 1996, one hundred and forty-six years later. Doesn't that just beat all?

"But that's not the end of the story of course," he continued. "Paradise has a cost, it's not free. So in 1862 that sweet little girl who was 7 years old when they arrived died. It was probably a fever from malaria or typhoid, maybe even yellow fever. They had all those here back then and no medicines to cure them. You either lived or you died.

It was in God's hands, so, she died. And then they buried her here on this knoll to overlook the river and the boats and the freedom."

Here again Sanji paused for reflection and I paused my listening to look deep into my soul for a resolution to the age-old dilemma, why do the good die, and why do some die so young? It always seemed so unfair to me yet it was the way of life. Nothing would change that. All that was left was to try and understand it and understand a God who allowed it. That was the hard part, a God who allowed it.

Sanji began again. "Louis, Mary may have died here, but four children lived and went on into life. Their son, R.F. Lowell, went on to make a lot of money from the 1880s to 1958 when he died. He made the money in land and trade. So he and the next generation of descendants, the children and grandchildren of John and Sarah, went on to inherit the dream and have their every wish fulfilled. They inherited a little piece of paradise.

"And now comes the problem," he said. "Those who have come to own all that land, that magnificent inheritance, have now succeeded in selling it off to an outside speculator, a golf course magnate, who wants to convert this paradise into a rich man's playground. Hell, Louis, I don't even play golf. What do I want with a golf course, fancy golf shirts with hand-stitched insignia's, clubhouse dinners, foursomes at 7 A.M., and on and on? I'm a simple guy with simple tastes. I don't need all that crap. Don't you see, Louis, the freedom that John and Sarah craved for and fought for is being sold out. Pretty soon all the good land will be turning into one big golf plantation and gated community and most of us will be working as servants to the new masters. It's a bad vision of the future, Louis, a real bad vision."

"But everyone doesn't see it that way, Sanji," I said. "Those who sell the land can go to new places, buy new houses on new frontiers, even bigger and better than before. There's always some place to go if you have money. Some call this progress, raising the standards. New and better houses, recreation and so on. And now more people are upper-middle class and can buy in if they want. And on top of all that, so many people like golf nowadays, they think it's a sign of a successful life. They crave it like mother's milk."

"Then you like the idea of golf communities, gated sanctuaries springing up and taking the best land in this country?"

"No, of course not. It's just that the reality is that people with the money always end up with the best land, always. It's just a matter of time before they get it, but in the end, they always do."

Suddenly, from behind us a voice spoke up and nearly scared us half to death. We were both engrossed in our conversation, watching the river through the trees, and we hadn't heard a sound. We both lurched around, startled, to find Mr. Macmillan standing about twenty feet behind us.

"Hello, gentlemen, I hope I didn't scare you."

We were both still quite taken aback and couldn't utter a word.

"That's alright," Mr. Macmillan said. I get spooked all the time myself you know. I thought I might find you here, though."

"How did you know that?" I said.

"Because I know a lot about you, Mr. Kennedy, all good mind you, of course. It's just my business to know things, it's nothing personal. Anyway, my men let me know I could find you here. They kind of like playing spy, but they never mess with anyone, they just like to keep their eyes open."

Mr. Macmillan shuffled his feet a little, pawing the ground as he thought of his next words.

"Look, if you don't mind, I would like to have just a few words with you. I pretty much figure you don't like me and I'm pretty sure you're ready to write off my offer. But when I heard you had come out here, to the spot where my great-grandfather started this whole thing, I just had to come and find out why you were so interested in this place."

Sanji, who began this little episode by being visibly angry, now softened, his jaw muscles relaxing.

"What are you talking about—your great-grandfather? You're from up in New York or something!"

"I am indeed, but there is a lot you don't know about me, Mr. Kennedy. It was an accident of history maybe, but this land belonged to my real great-grandfather who was John Lowell, the first permanent white settler in this area."

"You have got to be putting me on. What kind of game is this?"

"No game at all, Mr. Kennedy, it's fact and it's a bit of a long story. But I can make it brief."

"Go ahead," Sanji said stubbornly, "I can't wait."

Mr. Macmillan continued unperturbed.

"You see, all this time I thought I was a Macmillan but our family hid a secret all these years until I could get some research done on my own. My great-great-grandparents were from New York, a privileged family by the name of McPherson. They had two daughters, Sarah and Elizabeth. Sarah was the younger and, with great shame to the family she had a baby out of wedlock. And guess who was the father? Yes that's right—John Lowell. Only in those days you didn't keep the child, you adopted them out or gave them away. In this case, they gave little Joshua to Sarah's older sister Elizabeth who was already married, and guess to who? That's right, to a Macmillan, Guy Macmillan that is. This was all in the mid 1830s. So Joshua was not really a Macmillan, he was a Lowell and John Lowell was his father. When John and Sarah left and came down here to leave behind the black mark on them, Joshua was forgotten and was raised in the Macmillan clan just like a real son. Well all this time I thought my lineage was Macmillan, descended from Joshua Macmillan. But then I uncovered the truth, that my lineage is Lowell and my great-grandparents began a new life down here. So you see, my roots are in Shallotte, Mr. Kennedy; my kin all lived and died here. I am a part of this coastline, more than most people will ever know."

"Supposing that was all true, what do you want to talk about?" Sanji uttered in a strong but muted tone.

"I'd like to know why you come out and visit this spot, what you find in it, maybe why you come back?"

"That's pretty easy to answer, Mr. Macmillan. I come here because your great-grandfather John had the same dreams I do. He wanted a place to get away from the problems of civilization. He wanted peace, hope, a place of quietude where he could spend his days. He wanted what I want Mr. Macmillan, just to be left in peace. Can you understand that?"

"Sure can," he said forcefully, "sure can. I've spent my whole life looking for the same thing, a place where I wouldn't have to be bothered with all the crap in this world."

"With all your money you mean you couldn't find it?"

"What I mean is that you can't find a place to hide from the world, it doesn't exist. Besides even if you found it you wouldn't be happy, money can't buy happiness, or peace or tranquility, or anything that really matters. Oh, you might be able to get a secluded piece of land alright, but, happiness, no way."

"So you do know what I mean? You understand why I came to Shallotte to get out of the city. You understand why I love that house on the river, why I want to be near the ocean, why I found Shallotte perfect because it was hidden away from everything and everybody. If you understand that then why are you buying everyone out and putting in such a huge development?"

"Ah yes, there's the million-dollar question, isn't it? Why indeed would I want to ruin the way things are, spoil the natural secludedness, bring in thousands of golfers and tourists, turn the place into a place for the well to do? Right, why indeed. Well I'll tell you why, Mr. Kennedy: because if I don't, someone else will and besides all that, the people want it. We, and people like me, only build what people want. If they have the money they will spend it, whether it's on golf villas or beach front homes or religious condominiums in some damn TV Evangelists's theme park. You see, Mr. Kennedy, we build only what they buy. It's that simple."

"So you're telling me that if you didn't build this thing on the river, someone else would?"

"That's right. It's going to be built, that's for sure. Too much demand down in Myrtle Beach and not enough land left. It's spreading up here because it's the only way to go. Besides that, the seafood up here is unbeatable."

I piped in now. "So you are going ahead with the full-scale development?" No matter what the little people want you'll develop the area?"

"I'm afraid that I have to, no choice. It's me or someone else. And

I think I can do more justice to the idea than the other sharks out there."

We waited in silence for someone to speak. I looked at Sanji but his face was blank now and his eyes were staring off into space. My heart was sinking in my chest as I thought of the lost dream of a sanctuary, not only for Sanji, but for me, too. Everything I had begun to believe was possible was now slipping away. Sanji's dream had become mine, too. It was my hope that was crashing along with his. If his sanctuary slipped away mine was just behind.

Sanji spoke but his voice was now a whisper. "I still need a few days, Mr. Macmillan. I haven't made my mind up yet but I'll let you know."

"Fair enough, Mr. Kennedy, take your few days, that's the least I can do for someone with the same dream as my great-grandfather. I can wait."

With that, Mr. Macmillan turned to leave and we watched as he made his way carefully back into the trees.

21

hurricane

"There is a budding morrow in midnight."
—John Keats

We didn't have much warning. Hurricane Dennis had been in the news for a few days but was supposed to have struck much farther south except the jet stream had shifted, sending it skipping to the north. The weather report gave us about twenty-four hours before it struck the southern coast of North Carolina. All guesstimates were putting its force at near a category-three storm by the time it made landfall. That meant a very strong storm, winds in excess of a hundred miles per hour.

I had one of my usual breakfasts at the Beachside Diner across the street from my hotel. It would be my last for a few days, Nate had told me to pack up after breakfast, everyone had to go inland.

Marge was there waiting on tables as usual. The whole place was alive with a hubbub of conversation. The hurricane was now on everyone's mind.

"Will you be closing, Marge?" I asked.

"Sure we will, can't last those big ones, not here on the beach."

"I guess everyone's going to close down, and me on the last of my vacations this year. It's just not fair."

"Yeah, not much is fair in life. But you don't have it too bad, sweetie. On the north end of the beach there's a couple of houses that are already sliding into the ocean. One more big one and they'll be gone for sure. But hey, just think what Sanji says."

"What's that?"

"It's right in his book: '*Storms come and storms go in life, the only question is whether they blow you off course.*'"

"Oh yeah, that one. I thought for a minute you were going to cite another little ditty I had learned." (I of course was thinking, *the wind blew and the shit flew*)

This morning I noticed someone I hadn't seen for a while sitting on the other end of the diner all by himself. It was the guy with the headphones. He was eating and bobbing his head up and down to the music.

"Who's that, Marge?" I asked. "I used to see him walking around."

"Who you talking about, honey, there's a hundred people in here."

"The guy by himself with the headphones."

"Oh, that's Ruddy," she said. "He's been around a while."

"But he seems really, well, different," I said.

"He seems that way because he is. He used to be a securities trader up north until a year ago. But from what I understand he just gave it all up and came down here. He has a little money I guess, but he lives in a beat-up trailer just over the bridge. Seems he just wants to be left alone, doesn't talk to nobody."

"Gosh, poor guy."

"I wouldn't worry about him, Louis, he does alright."

Back at the hotel, Nate told me I had two messages, one from Marie and one from Sanji. Both sounded pretty urgent.

I called Sanji first because I might have to leave town. He was still at the store and in a near panic.

"Louis, did you hear the news?"

"Something about a hurricane," I said. "Supposed to be a big one, too."

"Plenty big alright, how about gigantic, and if the path stays as they predict it's going to head dead center to Shallotte. This is a nightmare!

190

Look, I know you need a place to stay tonight and I need some help getting the house ready, can you come over?"

"Be there in a jiffy, they are evacuating the beach anyway. Let me pack up and come over."

"Okay, but the store is packed and it's going to take a few minutes for me to get out of here. I'll be looking for you, Louis, we've got trouble coming."

"I'm on my way."

I placed a quick call to Marie. She was very concerned about the storm but I told her it was fine. I'd be staying up in Shallotte with Sanji. But I could hear concern in her voice.

Clouds were beginning to darken as I pulled into Sanji's driveway. A strange orange light pushed its way between the swelling billows of clouds. Having never been in a real hurricane, I didn't know what to expect. If what I had seen on the news was any indication I would prefer not to find out. Category-three hurricanes may not be the biggest, a five is the strongest, but they can do a lot of damage, and have the capacity to take out everything at the shore line, reducing houses to splinters. This is one adventure I hadn't bargained on after returning to finish a few weeks of vacation.

Sanji had already stockpiled the necessary building materials to prepare a house for such a storm. The last thing he wanted was to get caught at a line in the hardware store just before a hurricane. A stack of plywood greeted me in the front yard. Around back some of the windows had already been taped up with masking tape, big Xs, as if to say to the winds, no entrance here. Pop had been handling the lower windows. Tools littered the driveway to the point that it looked as if the hurricane had already struck. On top of a twenty-four-foot ladder Sanji was hard at work taping the upstairs windows. He looked like a one-armed paper hanger, clinging to the ladder with one hand, trying to run tape with the other.

"Hey I'm here," I said, "what do you want me to do?"

"Great, we haven't got much time," he said, panting. "Start grabbing stuff and put it all in the garage. Trash cans, lawn chairs, plants, whatever else you find. Everything has to go inside or the wind will blow it all away."

"Okay. I'm right on it."

Mary Kathryn, Pop, and I busied ourselves for the rest of the afternoon putting stuff away. Pop of course, being in his eighties, moved slowly but deliberately, examining each item as he carried it in. He was steady and calm, not at all upset by the imposing danger.

Mary Kathryn on the other hand was highly concerned about Sanji on the ladder. Every five minutes she would yell out, "Watch not to fall off that ladder, D.B." Besides monitoring Sanji's imminent danger, she carefully relocated her plants and yard ornaments. The radio blared in the background with the latest coordinates of the storm. It was Mary Katherine's job to update us every so often on the strength and direction of the hurricane. These reports were much appreciated but did not carry good news. The storm was steady, not increasing in strength but still heading right for us. The entire coast of North and South Carolina was under threat.

The good news was that the storm was slackening up a bit. Winds seemed to be slowing and now the forecasters were calling it a category two but still dangerous since it could intensify yet over the warm Gulf Stream waters. At least things were improving. We could definitely stay at the house and not evacuate to a shelter.

Meanwhile on the ground we had made good progress. All the furniture, plants, etc. had been moved in. Windows were taped before dark and emergency water and flashlights were all set out.

The last thing that had to be done was pulling the boat out of the water. If the storm were to rip it loose from its ropes then it would be dashed against the shoreline. If it were to hit at high tide, the damage would be many times greater than if it hit at low tide. The storm surge itself would be eight to ten feet and the tide was normally about six feet each day. Even tied tightly into the boathouse, the little fishing boat wouldn't stand a chance at high tide. The boat had to be run down to the ramp at Dock 77 and hauled out onto a trailer and brought back to the house to be put into the garage. This was a big job on top of everything else and Sanji hated it.

"Louis, this is a real pain in my ass to pull this boat out. I've had to do it four times now in four years. Here, you drive the car and trailer down to the ramp and I'll meet you there with the boat in about fifteen minutes." He handed me the car keys and out the back door he flew.

We managed to get the boat out of the river and back to the house without much of a problem. The waves in the river had only been small swells at this point so the boat ride wasn't too bad for Sanji.

We backed the boat into the two-car garage.

Around 10 P.M. the wind had kicked up with gusts of sixty-five mph. The lights went out as expected and they would remain out until late the next day. The wind howled at times, pushing, shoving, and whipping the house like a play toy. A leak appeared in the roof in the living room early in the evening, assuring us that a shingle or two had been lifted off the roof. It wasn't bad, just annoying enough with its drip, drip, drip into the bucket to irritate everyone. Pop wasn't bothered, though, he mused about Chinese water torture but nobody laughed too much.

Lightning thundered outside off and on as we sat pensively in the downstairs family room illuminated by the flickering candles. The house would be safe enough tonight, but what was not safe was the "home." So much had transpired in just a few days that all our heads were spinning like tops, bouncing off of every wall.

Perhaps it was just me, but I could perceptively feel Sanji bending under the strain. The smile was gone from his face and the hearty self-confidence was repressed under layers of worry. That evening was better than expected, however. The wind blew but not so hard. The hurricane had dropped its wind speed miraculously and suddenly to only about seventy mph. Even though the eye of the storm hit directly on Shallotte, it was so weakened that little damage had been done throughout the night. But that didn't mean we had no problems. A storm is a storm after all.

22

Golf anyone?

*"When Fortune empties her chamber pot on your head,
smile and say, 'We are going to have a summer shower.'"*
—John A. Macdonald

Within two days, all the debris had been cleared, power restored, and minor damages repaired around town. The hurricane had been a small one and everyone felt very lucky indeed. What had not been repaired was Sanji's troubles—what options did he have and was he indeed on the verge of losing paradise?

Back at the store, Sanji was under steady pressure. Customers, mainly tourists, began pouring back into town ready to finish off the Labor Day week. The store was packed, orders for goods were backed up and no extra help could be hired to insure that the store maintained its profit margin. Sanji was livid. On Tuesday, he came back to the house late. I had come over for dinner but he wasn't there when we ate. Mary Kathryn, Pop and I were worried. We were all now caught in a vicious waiting game. No solutions became evident, only frustrations. When Sanji did arrive, we had already adjourned to the porch to overlook the river at sunset. The beauty of the place came alive as we watched the birds wing over the water.

"Hello, honey," Mary Kathryn said as Sanji's head peeked through the glass patio door.

"Good evening to all," Sanji replied. Then without any further greetings or salutation, he announced, "I've quit the store. That's it. I've just quit tonight. I'm not going back."

We were all stunned for a moment but I was not surprised. It had been coming, we all knew it. Sanji had to quit.

"Do you want to talk, dear?" Mary Kathryn asked.

"Nope, I want to eat dinner and then think. There's some more news but I can't tell you yet. I've got to think about it for a while."

Off he went to the kitchen to warm himself a plate of spaghetti and garlic bread.

After Sanji had finished eating we joined him in the living room.

"Well," Pop said, "what's the news?"

Sanji's hand was shaking slightly as he lit a cigarette. "It's like this. I went to work today knowing I would quit. That was settled in my mind. No way was I going to stay in another rat race another minute, not down here, no way. But I was waiting until quitting time. Meanwhile I decided I would pursue something I hadn't thought of yet. I decided to call the U.S. Army Corps of Engineers to see whether or not any permits had been issued to put any new facilities on my property along the river."

"That was brilliant," I said with a rush of excitement.

"Sure, but what I found out was not good news. Within one hour of my call, two government guys in suits showed up at the store. Unbelievable! They didn't say they were coming. In fact, the woman on the phone just put me off and said something about getting back to me later. Well, I kinda figured that's the government for you, so I just mentioned that I would make some other inquiries and let it go at that. One hour later, these two suits show up."

Sanji was visibly shaking now. His trembling hand flipped the ashes into the ash tray.

"What did they say?" we all asked in unison.

"They told me I didn't need to worry because new permits had already been issued and all the papers were in good order. But here comes the kicker, these guys weren't from the U.S. Army Corps of

Engineers at all. I asked to see their ID and one was FBI and one was DEA—Drug Enforcement Agency. You won't believe this but these were the guys I saw on the river that night. They were working undercover on a huge drug smuggling operation in this area. They had seen me, they knew who I was and they were just waiting for me to make some move to stir things up. What they want is no trouble, no press, no headlines, no stories. They want quiet until they finish their sting. They said they didn't give a shit about the golf course and that any moves to fight it, bringing a lot of press, etc., would cause their smugglers to move their operations. These drugs are all flowing to Washington D.C. and Atlanta and thousands of lives were affected. No, they said, they couldn't allow me to make any waves right now."

I couldn't believe my ears, neither could Pop or Mary Kathryn. We all were stunned to the core.

Sanji continued. "They told me to straighten out—either learn to like golf or get the hell out of the way!"

"What did you do then?" asked Mary Kathryn.

"What could I do? I looked at them a long time, staring into their eyes, but they didn't even blink. They weren't smiling either. There wasn't going to be any negotiating today. Nope—no negotiating today, that was for sure." Sanji reached into his pocket for another cigarette and lit it carefully.

"You know," he said, "I quit smoking when I came down here, now I'm chaining again. Must be the stress."

"The government can't do this!" I shouted. "It can't stomp on people like they were pawns or serfs. This is America!"

"You're very patriotic, Louis, really you are, but this is an America with a lot of problems. It looks like I landed in the epicenter of the whole mess. How about that, all of America's crap seems to flow downhill right to my doorstep in the middle of a small town in the middle of nowhere. That just beats all!"

Just then the phone rang. *Ringgggggggg. Ringgggggggg.* Mary Kathryn stood up and walked over slowly to answer it. She picked up the receiver slowly, and we all held our breath.

"Hello," she said shakily. She listened. Then she looked at Sanji and said, "It's him, it's Mr. Macmillan. He wants to talk to you."

Sanji walked brusquely to the phone. He took the handset and spoke. "Yes, this is Mr. Kennedy. I had guessed you'd be calling by now."

Sanji began to listen and as he listened he began to pace up and down beside the dinner table. All at once he stopped moving and said in a very loud voice, "I'm not selling, you can take that to the bank, Mr. Macmillan—I'm here to stay."

I don't know how people get the strength they do but Sanji had stood his ground. He was fighting the behemoth—something much larger and more frightening than fiction.

As he walked out of the room all I heard him say was, "Golf anyone?"

23

floyd

"I believe that man will not merely endure: he will prevail. He is immortal, not because he alone among creatures has an inexhaustible voice, but because he has a soul, a spirit capable of compassion and sacrifice and endurance."
—William Faulkner

During the following few days all was quiet. I was content to rest at the hotel and I spent many hours walking the beach and thinking. Mostly I was thinking how my own life wasn't so bad after all. With the exception of a few irritations, I could honestly say the city wasn't all that horrible. My suburb was uneventful for the most part but at least predictable. It seemed as if no place on earth could provide any true Shangri-La. That was all an elusive dream, evoked in poems but not to be realized. No indeed, peace and sanctuary must be found within. So be it.

Sanji called on Tuesday.

"Hey, Louis, let's play some golf!"

"Are you kidding me," I said with deep suspicion in my gut.

"Kidding? Would I ever kid you, Louis? No, seriously, let's go."

"Alright," I responded without much enthusiasm, "when?"

"Right now."

"Okay but I'll warn you now I'm not very good."

"Hey, you haven't seen no good until you see me."

"Alright," I finally said, "I'll be ready in 20 minutes."

Fairhaven Golf Plantation was just south of town, a beautifully landscaped place in which nature had been subdued into a perfect idyllic picture of Eden itself. Small serene lakes, manicured lawns stretching in every direction, even sand traps with their glistening white sand all conspired to provide an other-worldly playground. God himself could not have done better than these architects of fun and fancy have done.

It was fun to watch Sanji play this game of golf. I've not seen a swing like his before. Of course I've never seen an ex auto mechanic play golf before. He seemed to swing the golf club like it was a baseball bat. He broke every golf convention known to the game. The fun part was watching his reaction when the ball went into the woods, which was very often. He would stare at the ball until it had been absorbed by the forest and then he would kick his right food into air and mutter some words, which would need a translator to cipher. In the end, it didn't matter since he had bought a large supply of balls at the clubhouse.

Golf is an incredible game really, so much like life. You hit the ball and then watch carefully to see what happens. If you are an amateur you pretty much watch yourself get into trouble. Then you chase the ball so you can hit it again. All the time you are trying to get to a little hole marked by a flag. Basically, when the ball finally falls into the hole you feel very good, like you have accomplished a splendid task. Actually you haven't done anything at all. After eighteen of these sessions you find yourself hot, a little tired from swinging and you go to the clubhouse for a cold beer to celebrate the fact that you are now finished. Although nothing more than a walk in the park has been performed, you and your foursome sense some great pride at having done better than last time. Often times the loser buys the beers. Isn't that just like life. The loser often has to pay. The insult of having finished last isn't enough. One more diminishment helps seal the sense of losing.

On the tenth hole, just as we were ready to tee off, a golf cart darted up to us. It was the head groundskeeper. "Just driving around to let everyone know that a new hurricane has formed up in the Gulf Stream.

They're calling it Floyd. Supposed to be a whopper. Anyway, it's still about two days off."

"Thanks," we said, and off he drove.

"That will be number five if it hits Shallotte. Five hurricanes in four years. What do you bet it will hit here, Louis?"

"It couldn't," I said quickly. "It just couldn't head this way. Not again!"

"I'll bet you ten to one it will head right here. Why not? The kind of luck I've been having here it would be just the right touch. Don't you think, Louis?"

"That's all you need is another hurricane. But, hey, look, maybe it will come to nothing."

We drove home quickly after the game without the final beer to celebrate. Immediately we turned on CNN and got the coordinates of the storm. It was still forty-eight hours off shore but was seemingly headed to Florida if its track stayed steady. Maybe it wouldn't hit after all.

That night everyone in Florida began boarding up their properties and a mad house was spreading through the deep South. We watched TV till late and the track was holding.

Early the next morning, though, things had changed. The storm, now approaching category four, was shifting to the north and would come close to Jacksonville, maybe hitting it but the jet stream was expected to keep it just off shore. By midday that projection was confirmed and the rest of the southeast coast was put on hurricane warning. By the next morning the forecasters had been proved right and, even though the hurricane was reduced somewhat in strength, it was grazing Jacksonville and heading north. Its path was now putting its landfall at the border between North and South Carolina, right at Shallotte.

This storm was massive, hundreds of miles in diameter and packing powerful winds. It would stay over Gulf Stream waters just enough to maybe strengthen it some more. This was not a storm to fool around with.

I packed up my stuff to leave the hotel and went over to Sanji's. I was sure I'd have to just evacuate and head north so I was prepared to say goodbye for now. I drove over and the house was all taped and hurricane proofed.

Sanji was outside gazing at the sky. "Looks like this is the big one, Louis. This is the big kahuna. It might just take out everything."

"Ah come on. It could still change course. It's got about 12 hours yet."

"Don't think so, ol' friend. No, tonight Mary Kathryn, Pop and me are going to the shelter. Can't take another one in the house. Too much could go wrong. No, we are heading to the shelter for sure. If you would like to stay with us we have a nice church to stay in downtown. It won't be crowded, just a few church people and friends. We're going to call it a hurricane party. Besides, we heard the roads are a terrible mess with all the evacuations. You'll just be sitting on the highway so why not stay here?"

"You're probably right. It would be just as safe to stay here as try to drive out in all that traffic."

"Great, then we'll hang out here until early evening. If the storm gets us it will be here in force beginning about eleven P.M.

The clouds began their now familiar spiral pattern early in the afternoon. Gray, dark and menacing, they began collecting like giant vultures hovering over some predestined prey. The rain started, too. A steady drizzle was interspersed with occasional, strong drenchings driven by gusts of wind. The news on TV, however, was mostly good. The storm was dropping in strength because of shear winds and was down to category 3. The problem was no one knew for sure whether it would gain or lose strength before it hit shore. Still more troubling and unbelievable was that it was projected to make landfall almost head on Shallotte. By three P.M. Sanji, Pop and Mary Kathryn had packed up and were ready to go.

"This is like some kind of movie," said Mary Kathryn. "We have prepared for hurricanes now five times in four years. And we are talking about direct hits here. It really is hard to believe." It was obvious now that the strain of all these events had even worn down her usually optimistic and positive personality. She hadn't slept well lately and the lines shown under her eyes.

As we left the house, the streets were already being inundated with water and the rain was heavy. The wind was picking up some and the clouds were now massed in the sky, blocking out all remnants of daylight. Reaching the church, we unloaded our gear and ran inside, getting a little drenched in the process. The church itself was called Morningside Methodist, a large wooden structure with a tall steeple, all painted a lovely white. It was the perfect picture of a small town American church, right out of a Rockwell painting—true Americana. Inside we were ushered to a back room, which would be our shelter for the night. I supposed it was normally used as a Sunday school room, maybe for the younger children since it was plastered with wonderful pictures and stuffed animals of the Biblical variety: camels, donkeys, a lion and assorted sheep.

People began showing up and gathering in the large fellowship room. Furnishings were sparse except for the assortment of lawn chairs that had sprung up around the room. To our great surprise, some unlikely characters showed up as well. There was Ernest, Sanji's next door neighbor who had almost burnt his house down earlier in the summer. Then there was the guy with the headphones who had been picked up by several of the women's auxiliary. He was quiet and very glad to have a place out of the rain. Next, to our surprise, were some of the people Mary Kathryn worked with, a doctor and his wife. They were happy to see each other and went off for a chat. The biggest surprise was when the doors to the fellowship hall opened to reveal a heart-stopping shock. It was Mr. Macmillan, his wife and son. The whole room went quiet for a moment until Mr. Macmillan spoke.

"Welcome," he said. "Welcome to Morningside Methodist. I'm on the board of elders and all of us here will be glad to help you with anything you need."

Sanji had lowered his face almost to his knees, hoping not to be seen. Here he was in a shelter and who would show up but his arch rival and nemesis. This night was already turning out to be more torturous than any storm. How in the world did everyone he disliked so much get invited to this shelter, exclusive at that, on the same night?

"What is this," he muttered to me under his breath, "some kind of conspiracy?"

"Don't worry about it," I said, "we'll just go to our room and ride out the storm. In the morning we'll all be leaving."

"Yeah, I suppose you're right. Let's get out of here."

We moved back to our room and prepared our beds. Pop got the cot because of his age and the rest of us slept on the floor with pieces of foam. It wasn't so bad. Before we knew it, we were all asleep and the gale was howling outside.

I don't know what happened first, whether it was the loud crashing and crunching sounds, the water under my hand, or the loud shouting at the doorway to our room. It was pitch black so I couldn't see anything. One of the voices was unmistakable. It was Sanji and the voice of another man at the door shouting. It was hard to make out the words at first with the wind outside blasting against the walls of the church. I picked my hand up off the floor and out of the water and sat up on my foam. Now it was clearer. The man was saying we would have to evacuate this section of the church.

"I'm telling you," he barked loudly, "that the steeple has fallen. It has been blown down and there's a hole in the roof in this section. You have to move to another room!"

I looked at my watch. It was two-fifteen A.M.

Sanji yelled back, "Alright, where do we go?"

"You'll have to go to the fellowship hall with the others!"

The piercing beam of a flashlight was now searching the room. Water was covering the floor and dripping down one wall in a trickle.

"Okay," said Sanji, "let's get everyone up."

By now everyone was up. Mary Kathryn was rubbing her eyes, Pop was groaning and muttering to himself, and I was pulling myself out of a sloppy mess of what was once dry bedding.

"So much for shelter," Sanji yelled out to the room, "everyone up for another evacuation?"

We gathered up what we could and made our way to the fellowship hall, which was now illuminated with a combination of candles and lanterns. People were stirring around, the coffee pot was on and the air was buzzing with conversation.

Our guide told us what happened when we entered safely in to the large room.

"We are all very lucky tonight," he said, "the steeple blew over and nearly collapsed into your wing. By the grace of God it fell into the courtyard instead. We are all very lucky tonight." I was beginning not to feel lucky anymore. We weren't even safe in a shelter, not even in a church. We had narrowly missed being crushed by a steeple of all things. A holy spire that calls people to worship, the very symbol of belief in a loving God. I supposed, however, that we were still safe by some divine providence so I began to assure myself that we had not been abandoned yet by providence.

The rest of the night we sat up in our lawn chairs, all but Pop that is, who was fast asleep again on his cot. For our part the waiting was laborious. The rain didn't seem to let up. In fact, it seemed to be increasing in intensity through the night. The transistor radio, which had been set up on the counter next to the coffee, was broadcasting continuous reports on the situation. The good news was that the storm had actually hit at level two, with the winds having reduced in velocity just before landfall. The disturbing fact was that rainfall was much more than anticipated. Fifteen inches had already fallen in the night so far and more was coming down every minute. With the ground in the area still saturated from previous rains, this was a real problem. The emergency officials were telling people to evacuate all low-lying areas.

At dawn, around six-thirty A.M., if you could call it dawn, a number of men made their way outside to look over the situation. Their report wasn't good. It was still raining heavily and the entire downtown area of Shallotte was one foot underwater. This meant that we were cut off from all the areas south from the church including Sanji's house. On hearing this news, Sanji panicked.

"We've got to go," he cried out to us. "We've got to get back to the house before the water rises any farther. If we don't someone could get all my stuff."

Without any protest, we all stuffed our overnight bags and out the door we went. It was still raining hard. The news report said it would probably rain all day and flood all the rivers and streams in the eastern seaboard. Sanji was not going to wait for this to happen.

Sanji's BMW was not so high off the ground but he swore that it was waterproof and that the engine wouldn't stall. As we entered Main Street, all we could see was water where the bridge was supposed to be. We stopped and looked and a pickup truck made it through. It wasn't too high yet.

Sanji maneuvered the car into the water slowly and we were doing very well for a bit, then suddenly, Pop, who was sitting in the front passenger seat, spoke up.

"I thought your car was waterproof," he said.

"It is, why?" said Sanji.

"Because my feet are getting wet," Pop said in a nonchalant way.

"Wet!" At that, Sanji opened the door and water gushed in. Quickly he closed the door again. "Oh shit," he said, "we're floating. Pop, get in the driver's seat and steer, we got to push the car back out the way we came in."

With that being said, Sanji jumped out and I followed. Pop climbed over into the driver's seat and we pushed the car back out. It wasn't so hard because the car was actually floating by that time. All we had to do was just push it lightly along.

Safely off the bridge and back on dry road, we stopped and surveyed the situation more carefully.

"You'll never get through," I said. "Is there any other way around?"

"Maybe, just maybe, if the other bridge isn't flooded yet."

We were standing in the rain looking at the flooded road and shops when a small four-seater pickup came splashing through on the other side of the bridge toward us. Into the flood it dashed. In a second it was in trouble. The waters were running swiftly across the top of the bridge and had caught the truck in a cross current. It smashed against the bridge railing and was pushed to the edge of the bridge where it got caught on the curb. Three teenagers inside opened the windows and began yelling for help. I had no idea what to do but Sanji had already run to the trunk of his car where he had a rope.

"Tie me to the car, Louis, I'm going in after them."

"You can't," I said, "it's too fast."

"Tie me off!" he yelled back. Then as he was tying the rope around his waist he waded into the water. It must have been fifty feet or so. I tied my end to the bumper using a half hitch.

As Sanji waded in, a crowd had gathered. It was the people from the church shelter along with a few shop keepers and finally a policeman. We all watched as Sanji pulled one teenage girl and two boys to safety. One by one he pulled them out and brought them over to the roadway at the end of the bridge. I helped pull the rope to assist Sanji as he fought the knee high water now lapping over the bridge. A couple of other guys came over to help and together we reeled Sanji and the teenagers in. When he reached dry road with the third one, the pickup, with a loud crash, tumbled off the bridge.

It was a heroic miracle. Everyone applauded. Mr. Macmillan stepped up and gave Sanji his dry rain jacket to put on. The whole scene was incredible. The kids were shaky but happy. The crowd was pleased and the policeman was shaking Sanji's hands and slapping him on the back. I'll remember the jubilation as long as I live.

24

good news
and bad

*"Let not your peace rest in the utterances of man,
for whether they put a good or bad construction on your conduct
does not make you other than you are."*
—Thomas a Kempis, writer, 1379-1471

It was Friday, September 17, the day after Floyd. Angry clouds still stirred in the sky, a ghostly reminder of the onslaught of the previous twenty-four hours. Rain pattered intermittently on the windows now, almost timidly, trailing off as the daylight grew stronger. Large pools of water submerged lawns, streets and roadway ditches. Tree limbs were thrown about the area like kindling, still sporting the final leaves of summer.

To call this a catastrophe would be too light a thought. As news reports came in later in the morning we discovered that half of North Carolina was under water. Thousands of pigs and cattle were drowned, just as many homes were flooded out in wave after wave of water that was being described as the biggest storm ever to hit the mainland of the Carolinas.

Sanji, Mary Kathryn, Pop and I sat stunned in the living room. Although it appeared Sanji's house was basically intact, structurally sound, leaks had appeared in critical areas. The wall of the fireplace from floor to ceiling was blistered where water had drained in around the roof flanges and drained down the wall. The large, beautiful antique mirror that hung above the fireplace was now on the floor in pieces, having pulled itself loose from the wet plasterboard. A number of roofing shingles had been lifted up on the south side of the roof and water had drained into the attic, pooling on the plywood floor and soaking all the insulation into a knot of fiberglass.

We toured each part of the house, saying thanks to God for the most part and soaking up drips with bath towels in various places. It could have been worse, we all said so. We knew this storm had spared Sanji of the worst. Our spirits were cheering up quite a bit until Pop came out of the lower bathroom.

"Hey, everybody, I think we have another small problem down here," he said politely.

The inspection following revealed a dim prospect. The septic was back-flowing due to the inundated septic field. The same foul smell we had experienced months earlier was back with a vengeance.

Sanji just stared blankly, one eyelid twitching erratically.

"Don't worry," I bellowed, "it will clear up as soon as the water goes down on the lawn."

Mary Kathryn moved stoically to the closed door and mechanically pulled out two buckets and headed for the garage.

Sanji and Pop both slouched into a couch and Pop cracked one of those little smiles.

"Just another day in paradise," he said, looking straight at Sanji.

Sanji mouthed the words over a few times in a soft whisper, "Yep, just another day in paradise, yep, just another..."

There are moments in life I had come to realize when everything either comes together or when everything falls apart. And while these seem to be opposite ends of the same spectrum, perhaps in some fantastic way they can sometimes be one and the same thing. If things are to truly come together in such a way that a new, more wonderful reality is found, the old reality must be broken; it must fall away, even though it may appear as a great loss. Certainly, things for Sanji and family were falling apart. Floyd was a capstone of disaster and even before the rains had fully dissipated it seemed as if it might be one calamity too many. I wasn't sure what could prepare anyone for such incredulity. Even with all of Sanji's savvy wisdom, his worldly insight had not prepared him for a succession of disappointment such as had occurred in these last few months.

We almost didn't hear the phone ring. It seemed a distant, hollow sound, meaningless and only vaguely familiar. But Mary Kathryn recognized it first when she came back from the garage.

"Hello," she said bravely.

We heard only one side of the conversation and it seemed disjointed.

"Yes, of course—Yes, we are—Yes, things seem fairly okay here…Pardon me?—Yes—Really?"

"Sanji," she yelled, "it's for you. It's Mr. Macmillan, he wants to talk to you."

Sanji blurted back, "No thanks."

"But you really must come and hear this, he's got some very good news."

"Of course he does," he said, "the whole area is underwater and he's lowering his offer on all the properties he wants. Buying wholesale now I suppose."

"I don't think so, now here take this phone." She handed him the portable receiver.

"Hello," he said bluntly.

We were all staring away as if hoping not to hear any more news of any kind today but Mary Kathryn was winking at us and nodding approvingly toward the phone.

All we heard were Sanji's words.

"Yes," Sanji said. "Good news, okay I'm ready…Well that's a very pleasant surprise. You won't be building the clubhouse next door. Why, thank you."

Sanji listened for several minutes.

"And so that's the bad news, some other developer is going to come along. Only a matter of months?"

Silence as he listened some more.

Sanji cringed. "Hero? Nonsense! News crew, Mayor? What, are you kidding me? Please no!"

Another pause.

"Well I appreciate your compliments but really it was nothing," he said politely.

By now we were all standing on our feet, mouths agape.

"Okay, I'll see you later. Goodbye." Sanji put the phone down. and slumped back onto the couch and let out a great sigh.

"Oh my, oh my. Good Lord, help me!" he said.

"What?" I cried out. "What's happening?"

"I don't know what to say first," he murmured under his breath, caught up in deep thought.

Mary Kathryn said, "Just start at the beginning, dear."

He continued in thought for a moment.

"Okay," he said hesitantly, "here it is. Mr. Macmillan will not be developing the clubhouse next door. He said that he has realized how much this place means to me and was so moved by what I did yesterday, saving those teenagers, that he thought I was too much of an asset to the community to intrude on my privacy. That was the good news part."

"And the bad news?" Pop asked.

"Macmillan said that he could hold back people a little while but it would be only a matter of time before another developer found his way in. The property along this river is just too valuable; someone else will surely come and snap up the lots next to us by offering a price no one could turn down. Then the properties would be developed into something big. He couldn't stop it forever."

"But it could be years before the lots were sold and developed," said Mary Kathryn.

"Sure it could, but people are moving down so fast from the North that the pressure is huge to get more projects built," replied Sanji.

"So what about the mayor and the news crew, what was that all about?" I asked.

"Well that's the wildest part," replied Sanji. "Macmillan said that he and the whole town were so impressed by the rescue that TV 7 wants to do a story. Seems they need some positive news to report along with all the damage reports."

"So what happens next? Do you go to the studio or what?" I asked.

"No, you won't believe this, they're all coming out here to the house."

Again we all sat for a moment in utter amazement. Sanji never wanted any publicity. He wanted peace, quiet, and just to be left alone. The whole idea of a news crew and live television appearances was not his cup of tea.

"And," he added, "they're coming today, in a couple of hours."

"A couple of hours!" screamed Mary Kathryn, "I am a mess and so is the house. No, they can't barge in like this."

"I don't think there is anything we can do about it," said Sanji. "It seems a large group is showing up and the mayor will be with them."

"A large group of who?" asked Mary Kathryn, now fully incensed.

"I don't know, Mary Kathryn," said Sanji, "I just don't know."

Now I interjected something since I saw it was going downhill fast.

"Hey, maybe this could be good news. Maybe you can make a pitch on TV to save the river. You know, make an appeal."

"That's all I need," replied Sanji, "to rile up a bunch more people, organize a 'Save the River Committee,' chair meetings, be in the news every week, not to mention the threats from developers, contractors, real estate bandits, and so on. Yep that's exactly what I need."

"Just a thought," I replied.

"*And the wind blew and the shit flew,*" Pop said. "Right, Sanji?"

"Yep, you got that right, Pop."

The twitch was starting again in Sanji's eye lid, and it was now affecting the upper side of his cheek and eyebrow.

"Mary Kathryn, please go get my patch," Sanji asked.

In a minute she had produced a black eye patch, which Sanji immediately stretched over his head and covered his left eye.

Pop said it first, "So now you're a pirate?"

"Why not," retorted Sanji. "I can't stop this twitch and I sure can't go on TV looking like a maniac."

"Yeah, a pirate gag is a whole lot more respectful looking," I said, smirking slightly.

"I'm thinking positive, Louis, remember my saying, 'Always think positive, be happy and don't worry about nothin'. Well that's exactly what I'm doing."

Sanji got up off the couch and, as he crossed the room, he said, "I'm going to hit the can, or should I say bucket." As he walked there was a noticeable limp in his right leg. "Looks like my tendon's acting up again. Well, when it rains it pours."

Sanji closed the door to the garage and disappeared. It was only a minute, maybe two, and the door bell rang.

"My God," cried Mary Kathryn, "they couldn't be here already!"

"Don't worry, let me go see, it couldn't be the news crew yet," I said.

I jumped up and headed to the front door. The glass side panels allowed me to look first before I opened. Surprise grabbed me by the throat; there was no news truck, no mayor, only two men in dark suits. I stepped back quickly and caught my breath. Who on earth is this? I thought.

Opening the door slowly I said, "Hello?"

The taller of the two men spoke first. "Mr. Kennedy at home?"

"Well maybe," trying to think quickly, "who are you?"

"That's between us and Mr. Kennedy. Is he here?" said the shorter one.

Thinking that this was official business I asked them to wait a minute. Running back downstairs, Sanji had just emerged from the garage with a look of disdain on his half-covered face.

"Sanji," I said quickly, "there are two men in suits at the door and they want to see you."

"Really?" he returned, "and I suppose the President himself is showing up just in time for the news story!"

"Hell if I know but they look like they mean business."

Sanji walked stiffly and deliberately up the stairs, calling after me, "Louis, come on up and lend me some support."

Sanji let the men into the living room and we sat around the coffee table. The gentle splatter of water drops echoed from the fireplace.

"Mr. Kennedy, we are here on government business. May we ask who your friend is?"

"This is Louis, my closest friend. He's okay. We talk about everything."

"Louis, do you live down here?"

"No," I said, "just visiting. I'm from D.C."

"Okay then, you can stay if you promise to keep this conversation a secret. Nobody knows, do you understand?"

"Yes, I do."

"Mr. Kennedy, good to see you again. I'm sure you remember us when we came to visit you in the store. Sorry about scaring you like that, just a job you know. Anyway, as you know we're from the DEA and we've been working surveillance for some time now just down the river. Well, the storm has wrecked the landing site we've been watching, the one the drug operators were using, and the calls we've monitored this morning indicate that the group is going to begin using a new drop point. And, to be frank, Mr. Kennedy, we have no idea where that is right now."

Sanji sat up straight and replied, "Fine, so what does that have to do with me?"

"That's a good question," the tall man replied, "and, well, normally we don't make this kind of request, but we need your help."

"My help? What on earth are you talking about?"

"What we are talking about," said the shorter man, "is we are going to ask you to help us out a little. We call it light surveillance."

"Light surveillance!" Sanji blurted out.

"Yes, that's right, Mr. Kennedy, surveillance. You see, you know the banks along the river pretty well, what with your exploring and all, and well you'd be perfect."

"Why's that?" I said.

"Because we have word that you're quite a hero now and our sources say that you will soon have a very high profile around Shallotte. What that means is that you'll be able to move around very freely, be invited to homes along the river and you'll be meeting all kinds of new people. Don't you see, this opens up all kind of doors for you—you're local. We at the DEA don't have a low enough profile to be snooping around a whole lot."

"You have got to be kidding," said Sanji, "I don't want anything to do with this."

"Oh don't worry, Mr. Kennedy, the government will be more than happy to pay you for your efforts. It could be very rewarding."

"And dangerous, too," Sanji said.

"I don't think so, you will never be suspected of anything. Don't you see, you are a hero here now."

Sanji looked at both of them with his one eye, his one cheek half covered by the black eye patch, twitching ever so quickly.

"Well, Mr. Kennedy," the tall man said again, "we have to leave now. The mayor is on his way and we can't be seen here. Just think it over, alright? And we'll be back in touch later."

"Sure," said Sanji, "sure. I'll give it a lot of thought." I knew he was lying.

The two men left as suddenly as they had come in a green Buick and disappeared down the road.

With the door safely shut Sanji limped back to the fireplace with his hands on his head.

"For all the love of God how can this be happening, Louis? What did I ever do to deserve this?"

I was engrossed in reflection and almost didn't hear his sentence, or his desperation. My thoughts had carried me back to India, to Sanchi, to the school, to the mystics throughout the generations who had stated so clearly in their writings that life was a strange mystery, an existence in which the human soul foundered between heaven and earth and where humans strive hard for that certain peace yet cannot obtain it. They had said that you cannot find rest in a place or even in an idea, only in the interior spirit, which has found union or unity with God. Christian mystics had said the same thing over the centuries. The world may or may not be an illusion, who knows, but it is solid and real enough, yet the world was a place of frustration and trial. Yes, certainly a trial. Sanji was finding this so true. There was no escape it seemed.

And as I watched, before my eyes the trial grew more intense. It seemed as if that peace could not even be bought for a price, by Sanji or by Mr. Macmillan or by anyone. That peace lay somewhere off or somewhere within, I wasn't sure.

"Louis, do you hear me?" Sanji barked.

"Yes, Sanji, I do, I was just thinking."

"Well were you thinking about what I should do next or just daydreaming?"

"A little of both I suppose."

"Well tell me what you think," Sanji said, groping for ideas.

Before I could answer Mary Kathryn and Pop had emerged form downstairs. Pop had something in his hands. It was a jar with ice and a yellow liquid. "Some hooch?" he said.

"How could I refuse," Sanji replied.

Mary Kathryn brought the glasses and Pop poured out the elixir. Now Mary Kathryn who doesn't usually drink proposed a toast "to paradise."

We all said in unison, "To paradise."

The grandfather clock had just struck three P.M. when we heard a commotion outside. The sound of cars, horns, and voices slowly filled the air outside the house, a great cacophony of noise of every sort. We had finished our second glass of hooch and waited in silence like a prisoner before the gallows. Life as we had hoped had all but been extinguished, a new chapter had begun.

Mary Kathryn said, "Well what are you going to say, Sanji?"

We waited in suspense.

Sanji put down his glass slowly.

"Well shit on a stick," he exclaimed, "let's go."

We all walked toward the front door which by now was clamoring to be opened.

"Let's do it," Sanji said, looking out at us from his one eye.

When he opened the door, we beheld a sight we could never have imagined even in our wildest dreams.

Hundreds of people filled the front lawn from the house to the street.

Cars were parked everywhere up and down the road. A large TV 7 van was parked in the driveway with two large satellite dishes on top. The mayor's black sedan was next to it. Balloons, banners and a kite flew in the air, unfurling the message, *We love you, Sanji*, and a large banner read, *The Hero of Shallotte*. Dogs barked and the wind still blew intermittently through the trees.

A great cheer went up as Sanji stepped out of the door. He stepped gingerly out the front stoop on his injured ankle and, as if he had been preparing for his moment for a lifetime, he waved to the crowd.

Each of us stepped out behind him to even more cheers.

Now the mayor moved forward with the TV crew close behind.

I was so amazed, so caught up in the excitement, that I had almost forgotten what had just transpired in the last twenty-four hours. Having nearly been killed in the collapse of the church steeple, nearly drowned in a flood on Main Street, and blown away by a hurricane, having my own vacation ruined, and witnessing the demise of Sanji's property under the hand of developers, all this was a faded memory now.

The camera crew switched on its lights and a large microphone boom was extended in front of the mayor as he came up the front steps.

The mayor was a rotund man of about sixty with a large head of white hair and a somewhat sunburnt face.

"Mr. Kennedy, I presume, or should I say Sanji." He reached out his hand and took Sanji's hand in his. "It gives me great pleasure to extend a warm hand of congratulations on behalf of the town of Shallotte. Mr. Kennedy, you are a hero to the people of Shallotte. The young people you saved yesterday were precious to us. One of them was my son, Thomas. For that I am forever grateful. The young lady in the car was the daughter of one of the oldest families in town, Pamela Jones, and the other young man was the star football quarterback of our high school team. Sanji, if I may, we, the whole town, give you thanks."

Applause rang out from the crowd. Now it was plain to see that the entire Shallotte High School Football team had turned out in their jerseys. The TV cameras panned in closer.

"Mr. Kennedy, you are a hero today in Shallotte, do you have any comments to make to the listening audience?"

It was then I noticed that there were actually two camera crews, one from Channel 7 local news and the other said CNN. I couldn't believe my eyes, how big could this get? This whole affair had turned out to be much more than a small town celebration. It would obviously be played on national TV.

"Mr. Kennedy," said the TV 7 reporter, "in the middle of such danger, how did you summon up the courage to jump in and save three young people from that torrential flood? Did you know how dangerous that could be for you?"

The microphone was shoved under Sanji's mouth.

He spoke—the crowd was hushed.

"I am a simple man," he said. "I'm just an old car mechanic. I turned wrenches for 35 years. I don't think I am a hero and I sure didn't mean to be one. I only did what anyone would have done."

"Sir," the CNN reporter interrupted, "you are very modest indeed. Would you like to say anything to our audience around the country?"

"The last couple of days have been the toughest of my life. But today I can see that something good has happened and for that I am very happy. So I would say one thing to everyone: never give up on people; in the end, people are all we have."

"But, sir, we have heard that you came down here to get away from people, to just find some quiet spot to retire. In other words, we heard you wanted to get away from people and all their problems."

"What I wanted to get away from is people who are hustling all the time, always trying to make a buck or take advantage of you. Yeah, sure, I wanted to find some peace and quiet, but I would never give up on people, especially when they are in need."

Now the mayor stepped forward again.

"Sanji, we would just like to let you know that Shallotte is your home now, if we can ever do anything to help you just holler, ya hear?"

"Sanji," said the TV 7 reporter, "we have heard that you are a man of wisdom in these parts, any words of wisdom for the audience?"

A hush came over the crowd.

Sanji spoke for the waiting crowd.

"People need to be more positive and not dwell on all the bad stuff that happens in life, so here is what helps me. It's one of my little sayings: *Remember to always think positive, be happy and don't worry about nothin'.*"

A great round of applause went up along with cheers and shouts.

"That's our man, Sanji is our man!" shouted the crowd.

Balloons were released into the air with an applause. Cheer upon cheer followed. The mayor lifted his hands in the air in clenched fists. "That's our man, Sanji—he's our man."

One by one the crowd pressed forward to shake his hand.

How to describe the scene I will never know. Only that it was as if out of a great obscurity, Atlas himself had come on stage. A hero had been born and Shallotte was rejoicing in its good fortune. By now the country was also partaking of this special moment thanks to the instant magic of space age communications. Millions around the world would also be witnessing this small obscure town's celebration. And, they would be discovering a new hero, too.

The camera stayed fixed as hundreds passed by to shake Sanji's hand. The mayor was smiling brightly as he took the same hands next to Sanji, sharing if not a little in the limelight.

Sanji was a sight to behold, patch over one eye, slightly graying hair brushed back, suntanned features accenting a vibrant figure, robust and strong, except for the recurring limp. But underneath I could only imagine his thoughts, his anxieties and fears. I wondered how this whole scene fit into his plan to find a peaceful paradise. In reality I knew too well this was not what he had in mind when he arrived six years ago.

As the crowd streamed by I noticed a number of people I had come to know during my time in Shallotte, and some I had only seen once or twice. There were Sanji's neighbors, all of them, moving together in the line, the alien and the massive guy whose son shoots all the time off the dock. There were the owners of Nell's with their motorcycle friends. There was Billy the preacher and some of the folks from the Church of the Blessed Assurance.

And, up on the road I could see the fellow with the headphones and cap, just standing and watching from a safe distance. He didn't speak to anyone. He watched as if the whole scene was a live performance of some Shakespearean drama—he may have had the best perspective of all.

In about an hour the whole crowd had dispersed along with the cameras and dignitaries, for there were still other matters to attend to. Many homes had been flooded and part of Main Street was still under water. This momentary and glorious interlude must now recede under the weight of other realities. The mayor's parting words were, "We'll see you later, Sanji, we have big plans for you."

25

last boat out

"The Only evidence of life is growth."
—Cardinal Newman

Back inside the house we all gathered around the fireplace, which had for all intensive purposes stopped leaking now. The mirror was still in pieces on the floor and we stepped gingerly around it as we made our way to the couches.

The phone rang and as usual Mary Kathryn jumped up to get it.

"Sanji," she said, "it's the kids. They're all at Lisa's house and they are watching you on CNN. They can't believe it."

"Just tell them hello, don't want to talk right now—got some thinking to do," Sanji replied.

Mary Kathryn nodded her head and continued in the conversation with her daughter. "Can you imagine," she said as she took the phone into the bedroom and closed the door.

We slept uneasily that evening. I stayed in the guest room at Sanji's and we all made our obligatory trips to the bucket in the garage.

Sanji was on the phone early the next morning. I didn't know who he was talking to, and he didn't volunteer any information. He made several calls.

"Louis," he finally said later in the morning, "want to go for a ride?"

We headed off for Dock 77. The road was still littered with tree limbs and the houses and trailers along the way looked like a morning after a big drunk. Tattered lawns, shingles blown everywhere, pools of water where there shouldn't be water, all witnessed to the strength of the storm.

The car took us down to the dock where it had been a hundred times before. We jumped out of the car and Sanji went inside the store.

"Wait here a minute, Louis, I'll be right back."

I waited for about ten minutes, gazing at the river and the boats. Most were okay but a few had been battered and a couple of smaller skiffs were flipped over, one still in the water and two on the shore. I suppose the boats could have been hit a lot harder, they had been well protected in this river estuary.

Sanji came out of the store with a key chain dangling from his hand.

"Okay, Louis, let's head out to Dock B."

Dock B was a long concrete dock that berthed some of the larger boats, and a few ocean yachts. Our walk took us to berth 8, and Sanji went alongside a cabin cruiser. It was older, made of wood, not fiberglass, and had a fresh white paint job that made it look crisp and worthy.

"This is it," he said, "this is the one."

"The one what?" I asked.

"Why, the one I just bought."

"You bought a boat?" I asked with great surprise.

"Why, of course, but it's not a boat, Louis, it's an ocean-going cabin cruiser. It's fifty-five feet of mahogany and spruce. It's got twin diesels and enough room underneath to sleep eight. And you ought to see the galley kitchen, it's incredible, not to mention the storage."

"But what are you going to do with it?"

Sanji paused a second.

"I'm sailing on, Louis, I'm pulling out of Shallotte. I sold the house this morning to Mr. Macmillan and I'm clearing out."

"How about Mary Kathryn and Pop?" I asked.

"They're both coming along, too, don't worry. And you know that wherever I go you and Marie are always welcome to come and visit. I mean that."

"But where are you going? How can you leave now, the whole town loves you and your house is safe for a long time." I knew things had not worked out the way Sanji had wanted, that he had less peace with all the pressures on him, but I did see hope. My heart was sinking at the thought of Sanji, Mary Kathryn and Pop leaving. It was the end of a dream, the sudden eclipse of all Sanji's hopes, and of mine. How could I ever expect to find a place like this, a special place at the ocean, where I, too, could find rest and peace? If Sanji left now what would I look for? But deep inside I knew this paradise was disappearing under bulldozers, with golf condos and restaurants and golf plantations as the new South emerged from its slumber. Where could I now hope to go?

"Louis, I'm heading out to Costa Rica. That's the place now. Tropical ocean, quiet villages, sprawling houses on ten acres of land overlooking the rain forest and the Pacific. Yep, that's the place to go these days. Still virgin territory, Louis, and you can live on half the income than up here. No taxes either."

I could see he was serious as he stepped up the ladder and boarded his new boat. Waves slapped at its aft and it rocked gently in the rolling water.

"Come on up, Louis, and take a look."

I climbed behind him up the ladder and stepped on board on freshly varnished spruce deck planks. It was lovely indeed. Sea air brushed around the deck, swirling with a soft mist of salt brine.

"I just have to check out the diesels, Louis, come on down. The man said they weren't new but in good shape."

Sanji tinkered with a few levers and knobs and then cranked up the engines. They came to life with a spurt and buckle but they turned over and began to rumble just like big diesels should.

"Good alright, very good," he said as he adjusted the carburetor. "I think they'll do just fine."

We went into the galley for an inspection. The cabinets were made of pine and had recently been refinished. Amenities flourished—a new fridge, microwave, and running water.

"Let's check out the head," Sanji said with a look of anticipation.

Sure enough the toilet flushed! It was a great day and Sanji was smiling with pride.

"No septic on this baby," he said, "no more septic."

"But how are you going to pilot this in the ocean, that can't be easy all the way down to Central America."

"I've got all that figured out. I've hired a local captain to take us down and show me the ropes on the way. By the time we get there, I should know all I need to take it anywhere else I want. And who knows, I might just sell it when I get down to Costa Rica."

I sat down in the galley. It was too much. Too big a leap for me. It's one thing to buy a beach house, it's another entirely to buy a boat and head to Central America. That took guts, brawn, and insanity, I didn't know in what order.

"I know what you're thinking, Louis," he said as he sat across from me, putting his feet up on a ledge. "You think I've finally lost it, that I'm trying to escape and find some far off Shangri-La."

"Yeah, I kinda think that. I just don't know if you can find what you're looking for. I mean, I want it, too, the perfect place, but how far can you go to find it."

"Now I need to let you in on a little secret, Louis, something that I haven't said before but I'll say now." His face got serious but with a slight smile etched at the corners of his mouth. "These past few months have taught me something new. Believe it or not, I don't really know everything. But one thing I do is *try to learn one new thing every day.* That's how I live, Louis. And I've learned a valuable lesson here in Shallotte.

"All this time I had been hoping to find a place that was perfect, peaceful, and maybe even a little Garden of Eden where I could spend my days in comfort and tranquility. And maybe I was misleading myself, and you, that once I found such a place, and perhaps I had found it here in Shallotte, I would be at harmony with myself and the universe. Now I'm sorry if I presented things that way but, hell, I'm only an old grease monkey, you know. I have to learn things the hard way, by trial and error mostly. But now I have come to realize that no matter how hard we look, places, pieces of earth will never be enough to give a person inner peace. No, Louis, the real truth is perhaps much more subtle than that."

"How's that?"

"To be quite simple, inner peace is found in the striving for peace."

"In the striving?" I asked.

"That's right, in the process, Louis, in the striving. If you think about it, you see that the human race is caught in a very precarious and impossible situation. We are stuck between two extremes, earth and heaven. That is, we are caught halfway between flesh and spirit. Inside each of us is a desire to belong to this planet, to dwell in peace and happiness, to find the right kind of place to live and enjoy. But our spirits are of heaven and they can never be at peace here. They long for something bigger, better and more perfect. Don't you see, Louis, that our inner spirit can never be at peace with just a spot on this rock hurtling around the sun. Our spirits long and strain to rise above. We are divided, Louis, half angel and half beast."

"So how do we get peace in this life?" I asked.

"Ah, yes, that's the big question isn't it? What experience has taught me is that we must find our peace in the striving. *We must rest in quest.* We must settle in our own minds that as long as we live we will ever be in the balance of the good but not perfect, of the now but not yet, of the building up and the tearing down."

"But that sounds hard to do," I said. "How can we be happy when things around us are falling apart and such a mess?

"It's by knowing that this world is a mess and then knowing that the mess is okay. And the mess is okay because God made it that way. It's in the mess that we find our happiness. Life is rugged, unrefined and you can't control it. I've sure tried in the last six years, that's for sure. And most people try to control things around them. We build perfect homes, golf courses with perfect green lawns, and all that, but they don't last. Nothing lasts long. But our spirits do. So we rest in knowing we can't control the world. My God, most of us can't even control what we eat much less what it would take to put ourselves in a perfect world. So, Louis, it is in the middle of the mess that our spirits are most at peace, as long as we recognize the reality of it all. Then by striving to make things better, we are most happy, leaning forward into the wind so to speak. Where people make their big mistake, where I made mine, was in thinking you can one day stop striving for the better, to just stop and sit in bliss. No, that'll never work."

"But I don't understand how this all fits in with Christianity or any religion for that matter?"

"That's really quite simple, Louis. Jesus himself never had any peace in his lifetime. Just look at what happened to him. They ended up killing him. But he kept on going, kept on teaching, kept on healing, and so forth. Finally he marched right into Jerusalem. There was no peace for him, except on the inside. Everyone saw how he had perfect inner peace even as the world fell apart around him. You see, he understood that the world was chaotic and he understood his mission, to keep on going even in the midst of the chaos. Don't listen to what half the preachers try to tell you, Louis, read it for yourself."

"So," I said, "it seems pretty clear that you're not going to Costa Rica because it's a better place?"

"Hell no, there are going to be problems there, too. But you see it's the going, the looking, the trying that I am now looking for."

Sanji took off his eye patch and I saw that his twitch had stopped. His face was serene and calm.

"And, Louis, keep looking for the good things in life."

As we stepped off the cabin cruiser, an old grizzled sailor was waiting for us.

"Mr. Kennedy, I suppose?"

"Yes, that's right! Captain Thomas?"

"Right, mate, at your service."

"Good, good to meet you."

"Day after tomorrow then?"

"Right, at seven A.M. then?"

"Better make it ten, tide you know."

"Okay, see you then."

"By the way, my wife saw you on TV yesterday. Says you are quite the hero. Sure you want to leave so soon?"

"Yep, we're all set."

"If you say so but sure goin' to be a lot of people missing you around here."

"That's okay, tomorrow they'll find another hero—I'm quite dispensable actually.

That night and next day Sanji, Pop and Mary Kathryn were packing clothes. I had asked about all the stuff—the furniture, paintings, collectibles—and Sanji just said he sold them with the house. He sold lock, stock and barrel to Mr. Macmillan. Got a great price, too. Mr. Macmillan promised to hold it and preserve it as long as he could. I thought that was a grand thing to do. Then he told Sanji he could have it all back if Costa Rica didn't work out. This Macmillan was turning out to be a terrific guy. Who'd have guessed since he was a big time developer—you just can't prejudge people.

Monday morning came and we headed for the boat. The plan was for me to drive them down to Dock 77 and after they left I would turn over his car to the kids and then head back north to D.C. For me it was a terrible day. I still couldn't believe how fast things had happened. My feelings sea-sawed within me. I had contemplated my long talk with Sanji, the whole peace-in-the-midst-of-struggle thing, and had come to grips with it somewhat, but what about friends who had to watch others in their struggle and striving. It wasn't easy. But I was trying to be the man.

By the time we arrived at Dock 77, a stiff wind was blowing from the northwest. It was overcast and drizzly, signaling a change in the weather from summer to fall. White caps and mildly high seas were being reported on the radio.

All was quiet. We arrived at eight A.M. to get all the stuff aboard. Pop and Mary Kathryn were happy enough, as if they had been through such transitions before. They were stoically bearing it, they were with Sanji, one in spirit, and they knew that they would always go wherever he had to go. For them it was both love and adventure, a kind of sympathy with life and fate.

Everything had been stored below deck and the clouds began to clear away around nine A.M. Captain Thomas pulled in with his duffel bag. Apparently he would sail to Costa Rica and fly back home. Sanji paid him well. He tossed his bag on deck, breathed in deeply and sighed. "It's good to get back on the water. It's where I find real peace. Just the ocean and us."

Sanji and I looked at each other and grinned.

About 9:30 A.M. two cars pulled in, and who they were I couldn't be sure. Then Mr. Macmillan stepped out of one car and the three teenagers that Sanji had saved stepped out of the other. Then a second person stepped out of Macmillan's car. It was Marge, our waitress at the Beachside Diner. She was holding a paper bag in her hand as she walked forward with the others.

Sanji turned to us and looked with a sense of anxiousness. "Thought I was going to get out of here with no more fanfare."

"We're going to miss you, Sanji," the teenagers said as they approached.

Marge, with tears in her eyes, handed Sanji the bag. "Thought you might just need a few egg, cheese and sausage bagels for your trip."

Then the three teenagers stepped forward with another gift.

"This is something from our whole class at our high school," Pamela Jones said. "We wanted to show our appreciation so we all chipped in and got you this."

My mouth dropped open when they lifted up a cloth that was covering a beautiful yellow parrot in a wrought iron cage.

Pamela lifted up the cage and handed it to Sanji.

"We wanted to give you something special," she said sheepishly and she stepped back with the two boys.

Mary Kathryn, trying to hold back her own tears, said, "They love you, Sanji, look at them, they really love you."

"I know," he said and stood there watching.

Captain Thomas yelled forward, "We shove off in five minutes, right at high tide. And by the way, it's a nice gift but we can't take it on the boat. Parrots don't do well at sea in a boat this size. Not a good idea if you want to keep him alive!"

Sanji looked at Mary Kathryn and Pop with disbelief. Then in a moment of inspiration he turned to me and said, "Louis, would you be willing to keep him for me, you know, so he can stay here?"

"Well sure I can, I'd be glad to. Anything for a friend."

"Do you mind, kids, if Louis keeps him here for me? I'm afraid he can't make the trip on the ocean with us."

"It's okay, we'd rather have him safe," the tall, lanky quarterback said.

I took the parrot in one hand and hugged everyone on deck. First I grabbed Sanji's hand then gave him a bear hug. Then I hugged Mary Kathryn and Pop and stepped down the ladder. I couldn't prolong the good-byes, it was simply too hard to bear. My own eyes had swollen with tears.

The boat slipped its ropes as the small crew ran around the deck. Diesel smoke poured forth from the exhaust ports as Captain Thomas took the throttle and inch by inch the boat moved away from the dock. I hadn't noticed before, and hadn't even asked, but a big name in large italic black and gold letters had been newly painted on the stern—*Sanchi.*

Slowly she slipped out of the berth and into the channel. The crowd cheered and so did I. The *Sanchi* was heading out to sea. Sanji winked and waved at the small group huddled together on the dock.

As the boat moved to higher throttle, I could see large puffs of diesel fumes coming from the engines. Then as the captain hit full throttle we all heard a loud crack, and a menacing after-boom and a large blue cloud floated aloft out of the water. Sanji, who was still quite visible, jumped up and down on the deck, his hands waving wildly in the air. As the cloud of blue smoke began to cover the deck I believe I caught the words over the din and blur: "*Shit on a stick! Well just shit on a stick!*"

As best I could tell one of the two diesel engines blew but Sanji was just motioning the captain on with one hand waving wildly forward. The sea cruiser stubbornly glided out to sea. As the boat disappeared, lurching and belching down the river, I wiped a tear from my eye and turned around.

I greeted each of the small assembly of well wishers and, as I was shaking hands, I noticed one other man had joined us, standing a little distance off. It was Ruddy, the man with the headphones. He was looking at me and motioning me to come over. After a few handshakes

I walked over slowly.

"I've been watching you for a while," he said with a forlorned look.

"You have? Well I've seen you around, too."

"Say I don't mean to bother you, but when I see you I'm really, ah, impressed with the way you handle things. And, to tell you the truth, if you're going to be around a few days, I sure would like to talk to you about some stuff. You know, things I've been going through. I sorta need some answers."

I was taken aback for a second, hardly over my own grief. And then I looked into his eyes, and his searching expression. Then in an instant I understood. For the first time in my life I finally understood.

It was about the striving, wasn't it? The journey to peace is where we find the peace, and we were all on that journey: Sanji, me, Pop, Mary Kathryn, Marie, everyone. And on the way, we have each other, we help each other. I would never find a special place to rest, but only in the movement of life. And in the midst of life's unfolding, we have each other and we have God and we have peace. I couldn't ever be more ready than I was right now.

"Let me introduce myself," I said. "My name is Louis, what's yours, my friend?"

"Ruddy," he said shyly.

"Good, Ruddy. Sure, I'll be around. Let me call my wife and tell her I'll be a couple more days. Then what do you say we go have some breakfast?"

As we began walking to the car I looked down at the cage and the new feathered companion in my hand.

"Say, little buddy, do I ever have a nice new home for you on the way back to D.C. It's not ritzy or anything, but you'll just love it. It's a little dive called The Blue Lagoon, and you can meet Bob…"

the
BEGINNING...

Printed in the United States
30113LVS00002B/40

9 781413 757279